Also by Ray

Buyout – A Roy Grove

For five ordinary guys and one rather extraordinary woman, the only escape from the corporate rat-race is to buy the company they're working for: take it all to a new level, save hundreds of jobs and make some serious money.

But it quickly becomes clear that nothing is as easy as it seems. The bid is quickly undercut as twisted corporate politics and personal vendettas take over.

When the buyout becomes *all or nothing* for the management buyout team, it all spins out of control: marriages fall apart, lurid secrets are discovered, life savings are spent on the stock market, illegal insider dealing becomes a matter of fact and blackmail, theft, betrayal and manipulation are the new rules of the game.

A once-in-a-life-time opportunity turns into a lurid nightmare.

BUYOUT is a gripping and compulsive page-turner about the power of money to unveil the deepest in human nature. It's also a story about chasing one extraordinary dream. At an extraordinary price.

Also by Ray Green

Payback – A Roy Groves Thriller (2)

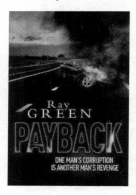

Roy Groves is Operations Director of a successful company manufacturing dashboard instruments for luxury cars.

A fatal motorway fire is traced back to a fault in the product supplied by Roy's company. Was it a tragic accident or something more sinister? As Roy and his colleagues battle to establish the cause of the fire, and save the company from bankruptcy, they discover that they have been the victims of sabotage.

Eventually, it emerges that an old enemy of Roy and the rest of the team has reappeared and is intent on destroying the company and every member of its management team. Once just a business adversary, their nemesis is now so consumed with hatred that he is on the edge of insanity; he resorts to blackmail and even murder in the pursuit of his goal.

PAYBACK is a chilling tale of how hatred can twist and corrupt the human soul.

Chinese Whispers

A Roy Groves Thriller (3)

By Ray Green

Chinese Whispers

Published in Great Britain by Mainsail Books in 2015

First Edition

ISBN 978-0-9575138-7-7

www.mainsailbooks.co.uk

Prologue
Helmand Province, Afghanistan

The Jackal armoured car ahead bounced and bucked alarmingly as it negotiated the bumpy desert track, kicking up dense clouds of sand and dust which swirled and churned in the stiff breeze. Sergeant Tim Steele, following in the second vehicle – a Coyote armoured personnel carrier – struggled either to see clearly or breathe properly, in spite of the goggles and the dust mask which he was wearing.

This was Tim's first tour in Afghanistan, and so far, after two weeks, it had proved uneventful compared to his previous two tours in Iraq, where he had been involved in some ferocious fighting. All he had done so far was take part in regular patrols like today's, during which he had not even seen, let alone engaged the enemy. These patrols were physically exhausting, though; his back was starting to protest at the pummelling it was taking and his throat felt as dry as the sand all around. Never mind, they should be back in the relative comfort of Camp Bastion within around forty-five minutes.

Then it happened. He saw the fireball erupt a split second before the ear-splitting sound of the explosion assaulted his ears; his face was blasted with a stinging volley of coarse sand carried in a fierce rush of scorching hot air. He recoiled involuntarily, clawing at his face and his goggles, trying to wipe away the sand and dirt as his vehicle came to an abrupt halt, slewing sideways on the sand as it did so. When his eyes were able to penetrate the cloud of smoke and dust, what he saw made his heart jump in his chest and his breath catch in his throat. The Jackal lay on its side, rocking back and forth a couple of times before coming to rest. There was a huge crater covering the full width of the dirt track, and a shower of debris was raining down.

'IED!' yelled Tim, extricating himself from his vehicle and scrambling down onto the ground.

He readied his assault rifle and scanned the surrounding desert for possible attackers; he could see none. He turned his gaze to the upturned vehicle ahead; there were four men in there – were they all dead? Tim began cautiously to make his way towards the wreckage, his rifle at the ready, all the time scanning his surroundings for any further threats. The other three men who had been travelling with Tim were now also getting out of the vehicle and readying their weapons. There was still no sign that the enemy was present; maybe the bomb had been triggered automatically as the armoured car passed over it and not by someone observing the patrol.

Suddenly, he saw movement ahead. One of the soldiers was scrambling out of the vehicle; it was Jim Archer. There was blood streaming from a gash to his forehead and he was unsteady on his feet. Thankfully, though, he didn't look to be seriously injured. He was followed by their commanding officer, Steve Salt, who was clutching his elbow in obvious pain. Tim looked around once more for any signs of danger; still there seemed to be none. Nevertheless, he signalled for the three men he had been travelling with to stay by their vehicle before he began to advance at a slow trot towards his injured comrades. After the deafening sound of the explosion, the silence was now total, save for the ringing still echoing in his ears.

Suddenly, the silence was shattered as the air was rent by the vicious chatter of automatic weapon fire. He watched in horror as Steve Salt pitched face-forward onto the sand. Alongside him, Jim Archer's body was jerking and twitching like some bizarre, life-sized marionette, before he too fell to the ground. All around the two of them the sand erupted in little fountains as the hail of bullets struck. Tim looked in the direction from which the shots had been fired and there at the top of a ridge, about a hundred and fifty yards away, he could see the muzzle flashes and the silhouettes of around six or eight turban-clad heads. He raised his weapon and fired a long burst at the attackers, causing them to take cover and providing a momentary lull in the onslaught.

'Cover me!' he yelled to the three men crouching behind their vehicle; in unison, they stood up and unleashed a withering volley of fire at the insurgents.

Tim rushed towards the two fallen men, all the time raking the top of the ridge with his own ferocious, but randomly-aimed stream of bullets. In spite of the volume of fire trying to keep them pinned down, the enemy were still returning fire sporadically, and Tim's heart was pounding furiously as he reached his stricken comrades.

One glance was enough to tell him that Jim Archer was dead: his face, neck, and chest riddled with bullet wounds, his eyes staring vacantly skyward. Steve Salt was clutching his blood-soaked leg with one hand while trying, without success, to drag himself across the sand with the other, his face contorted with pain.

Tim fired one more burst towards the insurgents on the ridge before pitching his rifle aside and using both hands to grab Steve under the armpits, dragging him towards the cover of the upturned vehicle. It seemed to take forever – Steve was a big man, and in his current condition he was virtually deadweight. Another short burst of fire thudded into the sand inches from Tim's feet followed by the metallic ping of several more rounds hitting the wrecked armoured car. How the hell had they escaped being hit?

But then Tim's luck ran out; he felt a shockingly hard blow to the front of his shoulder, and at the same time an intense ripping sensation at the back as the bullet passed right through his body. The pain which followed a moment later was excruciating. Somehow, he maintained his hold on the injured man and, with one last superhuman effort, he dragged Steve behind the upturned vehicle, collapsing alongside him, too exhausted to speak or even move. The furious firefight continued raging out of their sight; they were powerless to do anything but lie there listening.

But then the wall of sound subsided, dwindling first to intermittent and randomly-spaced shots, before stopping completely. The silence was surreal, overwhelming, after the fury of the preceding battle. They waited for what seemed an age, before two of their comrades appeared, one with his rifle still at the ready, the other carrying a medical kit; the latter immediately knelt down to tend to Steve's leg. He took a knife from his belt and ripped open the fabric of the uniform.

'How is he?' gasped Tim, grimacing with pain.

'Looks like … yes … two bullet wounds in his thigh.'

'How serious?'

'Not sure …' He felt gently with his fingers around the wounds. 'I think his femur is broken.'

Steve was lapsing in and out of consciousness as the other man bound his leg.

'OK … now you,' said the soldier, turning towards Tim. He cut away the fabric from Tim's shoulder and examined the wound. 'You're lucky … the bullet passed right through without hitting the bone.'

Tim managed a small smile. 'Hurts like a bitch though.'

'I'll bet … I'll give you a shot of morphine.'

Within seconds of the injection, Tim could feel the powerful drug coursing through his system, dulling the pain almost immediately.

'Better?' said the soldier as he bandaged the wound.

'Better,' confirmed Tim. 'So what's the score out there?'

'We got four of them – the rest have melted away into the desert.'

'What about our guys?'

'The other three from this car are all dead.'

Tim said nothing. He already knew that Jim was dead and he was expecting the worst for the other two but the news still hit him like a pile driver. He felt numb, stunned. This was the reality of war: one moment everything could seem calm, boring even, but then, in a heartbeat, tragedy could strike.

The third soldier from Tim's car appeared, carrying a field radio. 'OK – chopper's on its way … should be here in about 5 minutes.'

The first man finished dressing Tim's wound. 'When the helicopter arrives we'll get you and Steve on board and to hospital ASAP. The rest of us will get the Coyote back to base.'

Tim heard a groan as Steve Salt regained consciousness. He placed a bloody hand on Tim's sleeve, clutching it and pulling Tim towards him.

He struggled for a moment to find his voice, but then croaked, weakly, 'Thanks, Tim … I owe you.'

Tim was still trying to frame the words to reply to this simple, but heartfelt expression of gratitude when Steve's eyelids began to flicker and then closed completely.

'Get better, Steve,' he whispered. But Steve couldn't hear him.

Chapter 1

Kandahar Province, Afghanistan – six years later

Tim Steele had, by now, transferred to the Special Air Service and progressed to the rank of Captain. He lay on his stomach just behind a slight ridge in the sand, propped up on his elbows as he peered through his night-vision binoculars. The desert night was almost pitch-dark but the ghostly green image of the compound, some two hundred and fifty yards away, could be clearly seen in his eyepieces, pulsating and speckling like an old analogue TV. He could discern seven separate buildings, mostly not much more than shacks, but one was more substantial: a sturdy, brick-built structure whose frontage was perhaps thirty-five feet in width. He guessed that was where the principal target would be found.

After the scorching heat of the day, the desert night was unbelievably cold; Tim shivered involuntarily as the cold gradually insinuated its way through his thick uniform, chilling him to the bone. It was eerily quiet, in a way that no urban or suburban environment can ever be, whatever the time of day or night. When the distant high-pitched bark of some unidentified desert creature broke the silence it sounded unnaturally, startlingly loud, causing Tim's heart to skip a beat.

He turned his attention back to scanning the compound, panning his binoculars from one building to the next. Nothing: no movement, no sound, and no clue as to how many people occupied the compound, nor whether the target was one of them. He was loathe to move in without some confirmation that the intelligence was correct. As Tim continued to watch and wait, he felt, deep in his gut, the old familiar feeling which always preceded a mission: a strange mixture of fear, excitement, and anticipation.

A door in one of the smaller buildings opened, the light flooding out magnified to a blinding glare by the image intensifiers in Tim's binoculars. He quickly lowered the binoculars, blinking as he tried to allow his eyes to readjust. As the door was closed, extinguishing the unexpected deluge of light, Tim raised the binoculars once more. A figure had emerged, his white robes and turban showing up brightly as the image intensifiers picked up the light reflected from his clothing. His face, however, was impossible to see clearly: the skin tone was too dark compared to the brilliance of his clothing. He was moving slowly, unhurriedly as he raised both hands in front of his face. He was holding something, but Tim couldn't make out what it was. He was instantly on the alert.

Suddenly there was a fierce flare of intense light which seemed to emanate from right in front of the man's face, instantly obliterating the entire image. Tim instinctively ducked down behind the ridge as he anticipated the bullet which would follow a split second after the muzzle flash. Even as he did so he realised that, at this relatively close range, his reactions could never be fast enough.

Nothing happened. No pulverising impact to his face or head, no whine of a bullet speeding past, no delayed gunshot crack: nothing.

He let go of the breath he had been holding and tentatively lifted his head above the ridge once more. As he peered through the night-vision binoculars his racing heartbeat began to settle back; he realised that the blinding light had been the result of nothing more sinister than the man lighting a cigarette. The flare of the match had been amplified many times over by the image intensifiers, creating a blinding light in the eyepieces of his binoculars.

The man bent down and picked something up which had been leaning against the wall of the building, just outside the door. As he took a draw from his cigarette, the tip glowed brightly, illuminating the front of the man's face and upper body as clearly as if a floodlight had been shone on him. The object he had picked up was an AK47 assault rifle. Tim's heart jumped again. This was the confirmation he needed that the intelligence was accurate. This could not be just a hamlet occupied by innocent desert dwellers.

The target was one Mohamed Asheed, third from the top of Al Qaeda's chain of command. He had evaded British and American forces for years, but now the British SAS had finally tracked him down. Tim's orders were clear: Asheed had to be eliminated at all costs. Collateral damage was to be avoided as far as possible but the number one priority was to kill Asheed.

He stowed away his binoculars and pulled down over his eyes the non-magnifying night-vision glasses attached to his helmet. He raised his hand and signalled to the twelve men lying on the sand behind him before taking his assault rifle in both hands and wriggling over the ridge on elbows and knees. The rest of the troop followed.

They had advanced to within around a hundred and fifty yards of the cluster of buildings when the man with the AK47 began making a slow circuit of the compound, occasionally stopping to peer into the blackness of the desert, but as he had no night-vision equipment it was doubtful that he could see much beyond ten yards or so. Tim and his men continued cautiously edging forward. As the sentry passed around to the far side of the compound, Tim signalled to his men who, as one, scrambled to their feet and advanced at a crouching run. Tim's heart was pounding now, partly due to the exertion of running with the heavy pack on his back, but mainly due to the anticipation of imminent action.

Around twenty seconds had elapsed when the glow of the man's cigarette reappeared around the edge of one of the buildings. They all dropped onto their bellies once more. Tim made another hand signal indicating that they should remain prone and motionless; they were too close now to risk even crawling forward lest the sentry should spot them. They waited patiently until he disappeared again, continuing his slow circuit around the compound. At Tim's signal they sprang to their feet and resumed the crouching run. This was it: the assault started now.

Suddenly, the silence was shattered by the spiteful chatter of automatic weapon fire as a pulsating series of muzzle flashes appeared in the window of one of the outbuildings. Tim heard a scream to his right and turned to see the man nearest to him go down. He raised his weapon and fired directly into the window where he had seen the muzzle flashes. There was a loud cry and a short burst of automatic fire rent the air, the flashes arcing upwards just before the man's weapon spun from his grasp as he collapsed.

'Go, go, go,' yelled Tim. There was clearly no point in attempting any further stealth. As the troop surged forward, the original sentry came running around the edge of an outbuilding, his AK47 blazing. Tim cut him down with a burst of fire from his own weapon, before he could hit anyone.

The mayhem stopped as abruptly as it had started; silence reigned. Tim gave the signal for a house-to-house scouring to begin and the troop split up into four groups, each cautiously approaching a separate building.

Suddenly, a black-robed figure appeared, rushing directly towards Tim, brandishing a curved sword. Another short burst of fire from Tim's rifle dropped the man before he could do any damage.

Then all hell broke loose. Another burst of automatic fire came from the doorway of the largest building and suddenly there were people rushing at them from all directions, screaming and brandishing various weapons. Tim made for the largest building, ducking and weaving to avoid the gunfire from the figure in the doorway. He dropped to one knee and returned fire, silencing the assailant. He stopped at the doorway, prodding the prone figure with his toe to make sure he posed no threat before cautiously stepping over the body and entering the building.

Then he saw it: a black-robed figure with a long black beard. Was it Asheed? It certainly looked like him. He had studied the photographs over and over but in the gloom, and in the brief moments he had available in which to decide, it was impossible to be sure. His finger tightened on the trigger as he grappled with the decision as to whether or not to fire. There was a sound of sudden movement off to the side and, as Tim glanced sideways to ascertain its source, the black-robed figure made a lightning-fast grab for something on the table alongside him. In an instant, Tim realised that the man was raising a handgun. As he made the decision to fire, a second figure lunged across in front of the man with the gun. Tim's burst of automatic fire cut them both down as a single shot from the handgun whistled past his ear.

As he lowered his weapon, he realised that all had fallen silent outside. It was over as quickly as it had begun. He flipped up the night-vision glasses and switched on the lamp attached to his helmet. As he swept the beam back and forth, he spotted an oil lamp on the table; a box of matches lay alongside it. It took him three attempts to strike a match, such was the degree to which his hands were shaking. Eventually he succeeded in lighting the lamp, turning up the wick until the room was fully illuminated by the guttering flame, before going to investigate the two prone figures. The face of the first was obscured by a black headscarf. As he pulled it back, he gasped; the face which stared back at him was that of a young woman, probably in her late twenties. One of her eyes was missing, replaced by a pulped, bloody pit, streaming blood down the side of her face. As he tried to pull the body to one side, what he saw made him stop breathing for a moment as he sank to his knees in shock. The child which she had been holding to her under her robe was barely more than a baby, probably no more than two years old. Tim gazed in horror at the three bloody bullet wounds which desecrated the tiny body: one in its neck, one in its chest, and one in its hip. He couldn't move, couldn't breathe properly, couldn't think straight. He just remained motionless, staring at the tiny, mutilated body.

At length, he gathered his wits sufficiently to pull the bodies of the mother and child to one side in order to inspect the man's body. There were four bullet wounds to his chest and abdomen, but his face was unmarked. He pulled the photograph from his pocket and held it alongside the dead man's face. His heart nearly stopped; there was a resemblance, to be sure, but this was not Mohamed Asheed.

One of Tim's men appeared in the doorway. 'Are you OK, sir? Any more hostiles in here?'

Tim dragged himself wearily to his feet; his throat was so dry that he could hardly speak. He swallowed, trying to moisten his parched mouth. When he eventually found his voice, he said, 'I'm OK, sergeant. There are three dead here: one man, one woman, one child. What's our own casualty count?'

'We have one dead – Terry Blake – and two injured. All the ragheads are dead: eleven men, six women, four children … plus the three in here.'

Tim glared at him. 'If I hear you use the term "raghead" once more, I will personally beat the living shit out of you.'

The other soldier shrank back. 'Yes, sir. Sorry, sir.'

Tim took a few seconds to control his simmering anger before continuing. 'Is Asheed among the dead?'

'No sir. I think this set-up must have been a decoy, to divert our attention from where the real Asheed is hiding.'

Tim's heart sank. So much carnage, and for what?

'Get out of here and leave me alone for a few minutes will you?' said Tim.

'Yes sir.' The sergeant beat a hasty retreat.

Tim Steele sank to his knees once more and began quietly to weep.

***

The Chinook helicopter had been waiting for them in the desert a few miles from the scene. When Tim's radio operator called the pilot, the aircraft arrived within a few minutes, its massive rotors churning up dense clouds of orange dust as it settled onto the sand.

As soon as it touched down, Tim ordered two of his men to help the injured to board the aircraft. Chris Parker had suffered a bullet

11

wound to his arm – very painful, but not life-threatening. Simon King, however, was in a bad way: he had taken a bullet in his stomach which was now bleeding profusely, soaking the field dressing which had been applied with a deep crimson stain. They needed to get him to Camp Bastion fast for proper medical attention if he was to survive.

As soon as the injured men were on board, Tim ushered his men forward. One by one, they advanced at a crouching run, covering their faces as they tried to avoid the choking clouds of dust swirling around the aircraft. Finally, Tim climbed aboard and took his seat alongside the pilot.

'OK, go,' he said, but the pilot was already spinning up the rotors and almost as soon as he uttered the words he felt the aircraft begin to lift.

As the helicopter gained height and began to gather forward momentum, Tim stole a last glance out of the window at the scene of the battle. One of the buildings was ablaze, a dense pall of black smoke curling skyward, and everywhere there were bodies lying on the ground, limbs protruding at unnatural angles, many surrounded by dark stains seeping into the sand. He felt sick to his stomach.

'Did you get him?' asked the pilot, but as soon as Tim turned towards him he must have read the expression on Tim's face. 'Hmm – I guess not. What happened?'

'He wasn't there … just a passable double, some fighters, plus some women and children.' Tim paused for a moment, trying to gain control of the emotion welling up within him. 'They're all dead, Jeff … what a bloody waste.'

Jeff Patterson was Australian by birth, and still retained a slight accent. 'You couldn't have known, mate; you just had to rely on the intelligence supplied.'

At thirty-seven years old, Jeff was the oldest member of the team and this was to be his last mission before leaving the army. Tim turned towards him, but somehow could not find the words to reply.

'Don't beat yourself up, Tim,' continued Jeff. 'You did what was asked of you based on the information you had.'

Tim gave a muted shrug, finally finding his voice. 'What's done is done – I can't change it but I … well, I … Oh, shit, let's just leave it shall we?' Jeff nodded and they lapsed into an uneasy silence, punctuated by the insistent, throbbing rhythm of the rotor blades.

After some minutes Tim spoke again. 'This is your last mission isn't it?'

'Uh, huh – it's Civvy Street for me now.'

'What are you going to do?'

'Flying's the only thing I know, so it's fortunate that I've been able to land a job as a commercial pilot.'

'What … scheduled passenger aircraft?'

'No, I've got a job with a company which charters executive jets to businessmen and wealthy individuals. The money's good, and I get to carry on doing what I like best.'

Tim nodded. 'I'm pleased for you Jeff. You'll keep in touch won't you?'

Jeff glanced across at Tim, the skin at the corners of his deep blue eyes creasing as a hint of the old smile returned to his face. 'Sure thing.'

They lapsed into silence once more. Tim knew he would miss Jeff – his warm, laconic manner and dry sense of humour were a welcome counter to the sometimes overly boisterous, macho approach of some of the younger guys in the team. He was glad that Jeff's future was mapped out clearly; but what about his own? Today's events had scarred him – he wasn't sure if he could carry on doing this much longer. He needed time to think, to process what had happened, to rationalise his emotions.

His thoughts were interrupted by Jeff's amplified voice on the aircraft's tannoy system. 'OK, guys – we'll be at Camp Bastion in two or three minutes. Prepare for landing and make sure you're ready to get the injured to the medics ASAP.'

'Too late, I'm afraid,' came a voice from behind Tim. 'Simon's dead.'

Tim felt strangely devoid of emotion – he just felt numb, drained. Maybe he just had no more tears left to shed.

Chapter 2

Best Western Hotel – Shenzhen, southern China

Chuck Kabel was feeling jittery as he finished packing his case, ready to head for the airport; his meeting with Chang Wei on Friday had unsettled him, and the sooner he could get home the better.

Chuck was Logistics Director for the UK-based company, Gatmarsh Automotive, which made dashboard instrument clusters for luxury cars. He had just completed a three-week fact-finding visit to their subcontract manufacturing company, Sotoyo Electronics, based in Shenzhen, and he didn't like what he had seen. There were some strange anomalies in the financial records, and when he had tried to discuss these with Plant Manager, Chang Wei, Chang had made it very clear that he didn't appreciate Chuck's prying. Sotoyo's financial arrangements, he had insisted, were a matter for Sotoyo. He had also made it clear that he did not expect Chuck to discuss this aspect of his visit with his boss when he returned to the UK. Chang was an intimidating character, and during their meeting, his manner had been aggressive, almost threatening. Yes, Chuck was feeling distinctly edgy as he prepared to leave.

He put the last few items into his suitcase and closed the lid, before turning to his laptop, quickly checking for any new emails which had arrived that morning. There were only four, none of which were of any great significance, so he switched the machine off before folding down the screen and slipping it into its shoulder bag. He took a last look around his hotel room to make sure he had left nothing. The room was like that in any other three or four-star hotel: comfortable enough, but cold and impersonal with its regulation mock-mahogany furniture and generic decoration, especially once all Chuck's clutter and personal photographs had been cleared away and consigned to his suitcase. It had been his home for the last three weeks, but he was more than glad to be leaving it now.

He grabbed his bags from the bed and laid them on the floor just by the door. He unlatched the security catch before opening the door a little to poke his head out and take a quick glance left and right down the corridor; there was no-one around. He picked up his bags, stepped out into the corridor, and made his way down to reception. The smiling, almond-eyed girl on reception – who spoke near-perfect English – was effusive in her enquiries about how his stay had been and in her wishes for his journey home to be a wonderful experience. *Some chance*, thought Chuck as he contemplated the very long journey crammed into economy class with barely enough room into which to fold his long legs. Nevertheless, he was anxious to be on that plane just as soon as possible.

After checking out, he made his way across the car park towards his hire car – a dark blue Toyota. He set his bags down behind the car and delved in his pocket for the remote control to unlock the car, but as his thumb hovered over the unlock button, he suddenly felt nervous. He looked around the car park, not wishing to look foolish for what he was about to do. There was no-one around, so he bent down and looked under the car. Everything looked normal – not that he really knew what *was* normal for the underside of a Toyota. He worked his way right around the car checking the underside from every angle, but could see nothing untoward.

At length, he stood up and brushed the dust from the knees of his trousers. Everything looked fine, but he still felt – probably irrationally, he thought – nervous. He looked around the car park once more; there was still no-one around. He picked up his bags and walked away until he was around fifty feet from the car before finally summoning up the courage to press the unlock button on the remote. There was a reassuring 'clunk' and the hazard lights flashed twice. So far, so good. He pressed another button and the boot lid swung smoothly upward.

He shook his head, chiding himself for his foolishness, and walked briskly over to the car, dropping his bags into the boot and slamming it shut. He slipped into the driver's seat and fastened his seat belt before inserting the key into its socket. As he prepared to start the car, he was once again seized by a sense of foreboding. He applied just a little twisting force to the key, then a little more – as if turning the key very gradually like this might mitigate whatever was to come.

The starter motor whirred, and with a subdued roar, the engine burst into life.

He let out the breath he had been holding and his heartbeat began to settle. *I must have been watching too many Hollywood movies,* he thought, smiling, as he selected first gear, released the handbrake, and moved smoothly away.

By the time he arrived at the airport he was in a far more relaxed mood as he contemplated the prospect of returning to the now-familiar surroundings of Birmingham, England, away from this hostile environment. Even at this early hour the airport was bustling: a heaving, writhing throng of humanity, where every person seemed intent on moving in a different direction to every other person. Most of them looked thoroughly miserable. The days when air travel was considered glamourous were long gone.

The queue to check in seemed interminable; as he craned his neck to observe the progress at the front of the queue, each group of passengers seemed to take longer than the last to process. The family which was currently at the desk had evidently not taken the precaution of weighing their bags before arriving at the airport for they were now engaged in opening up each of their cases and spreading the contents on the floor, apparently selecting certain items to be discarded. Chuck cursed under his breath. He looked at his watch; at this rate it would be the best part of an hour before he reached the desk. He consoled himself with the thought of that first gin and tonic once he was finally on board.

All of a sudden, he felt a short, sharp stabbing pain in the back of his thigh, as if he had been stung. He whirled around but could see nothing untoward.

The small, wiry Chinese man behind him had his nose in a paperback book – as he had done since joining the queue. He looked up when Chuck turned around. 'Impossibly slow isn't it?' he said, smiling, in heavily accented English.

Chuck nodded. 'Yes it is,' he replied, absently, still none the wiser as to what had caused the sharp pain.

The man returned to his book, and Chuck turned back. He put his hand down to massage the point where he had felt the pain; it was still stinging, but less so now. What the hell was it, though? Maybe an insect bite. He pressed his hand hard against his trouser leg and rubbed it back and forth in an effort to crush any nasty little bug that might be lurking in there. He couldn't feel any evidence of such an intruder, though.

As he edged forward, excruciatingly slowly, he began to feel a little hot and feverish; he would get a bottle of water as soon as he was through to the departure lounge. He felt a trickle of perspiration run down the side of his temple, and wiped it away with his handkerchief. At least there were only a handful of people in front of him now.

Finally he made it to the front of the queue.

'Good morning sir,' said the young girl behind the desk, in perfect English with barely a trace of an accent. 'What is your destination?'

'London … H … Heathrow,' he stammered. He felt a wave of nausea, and his sense of balance began to falter. As he swayed, unsteadily, he clutched the edge of the counter for support.

'Are you alright sir?' asked the girl, concern evident in both the tone of her voice and the expression on her face, which Chuck now contemplated through blurred vision. 'Would you like me to get some help?'

'Y … yes. I think I … I need …' His throat felt swollen and his tongue could no longer form the words which his brain instructed.

A dark veil descended and his legs buckled. As he hit the floor, his vision returned and he saw a blurry outline of a middle-aged woman in the queue behind stepping forward to try to help. There was no sign of the man with the book who had previously been behind him. The concerned face of the woman kneeling over him was the last thing Chuck ever saw on this earth.

Chapter 3

It was Monday morning, and Roy Groves, Managing Director of Gatmarsh Automotive, had just entered the main entrance of the factory. As he walked through the corridor from Reception towards the main office area, his footsteps echoed loudly in the deserted building. It was just 6.00 a.m. and, as the first production shift was not due to start work until 7.30 a.m. the building was unnaturally quiet. As he stepped through into the main open-plan office area he noted that, even at this hour, he was not the first in the building. There were two people already at their desks in the Finance department, no doubt because it was 'that time of the month': the first working day after the close of the monthly accounting period, when everyone in the Finance department had to work crazy hours to get the monthly accounts completed within the timescale expected.

Roy called out a cheery 'Good morning' to Christine and Mark before making his way across the open-plan office towards his own individual office. He had a busy week ahead of him and wanted to catch up on a little paperwork before the hustle and bustle of the working day began in earnest. He fired up his computer and went to get a cup of coffee from the vending machine to help kick start his day.

When he returned to his desk, he set down the steaming cup and clicked on his emails. As he scanned the list of headers, his eye was immediately drawn to one from Chang Wei in Shenzhen; the header read 'Chuck Kabel – tragic news.' A cold wave of concern swept through him as he clicked to open the email.

To: Roy Groves
From: Chang Wei,
Subject: Chuck Kabel – tragic news

Mr, Groves,

I have just received some shocking news. It seems that Mr Chuck Kabel collapsed at Shenzhen airport before boarding his flight back to the UK. He was rushed to hospital but was pronounced dead on arrival. As yet I have no news about what caused this tragic event.

I will let you know as and when I have any further information, but for now please accept my sincere condolences for the loss of your valued colleague.

Regards,
Chang Wei

Roy sat staring at his screen in a stunned stupor, unable to take it in; it just didn't seem real. How could this have happened? Chuck had been just thirty-eight years old, fit, healthy, and with absolutely no history of health problems. People don't just keel over and die for no reason, do they? Maybe the medical people in China would be able to provide some answers in due course.

My God, he thought, *is it ever going to end?* He grappled to rationalise this latest twist in the bizarre chain of events which had unfolded over the last few years.

Some seven years previously, Roy had set out, together with five colleagues, to buy the company they worked for – with the backing of venture capitalists – from its parent company, in a management buyout or MBO. They had all had to borrow money, putting their homes on the line as security, in order to invest in the venture, but their shared conviction was that, freed from the stifling constraints of corporate intervention, they would be able to grow the company more quickly as well as, eventually, making some serious money for themselves.

Corporate politics and personal vendettas had conspired almost to wreck the MBO bid, and the subsequent journey to floatation of Romotive plc on the London Stock Exchange. Blackmail, theft, and even murder had been committed in an attempt to thwart the team's plans, but in the end, against the odds, they came through it OK – some of them at least.

Most of the team had made some decent money out of the venture, but once Romotive became a publicly-quoted company, even those who had survived the journey thus far became so disillusioned with the direction they were forced to take that, one by one, they all resigned.

Roy decided to retire early rather than seek another executive position. Over the next couple of years, however, he watched in horror as his old company, previously so vibrant and successful, was gradually brought to its knees due to a series of disastrously ill-judged strategic decisions by the new management. Just two and a half years after the floatation, the company was about to go bust and was bought for a fraction of its previous value by Gatmarsh Corporation, an American corporation headquartered in Philadelphia, Pennsylvania. Romotive was subsequently renamed Gatmarsh Automotive.

Cary Woods, CEO of Gatmarsh Corporation, and Roy Groves knew each other of old, and Cary invited Roy to come out of retirement and take on the challenge of restoring his old company to its former glory. He didn't really need to work again, but he was still only fifty-two years old, and the prospect of putting right some of the wrongs which had been inflicted on his old company proved irresistible, so Roy accepted the position of Managing Director of Gatmarsh Automotive. He even managed to re-hire some of the original management team to help him tackle the task ahead. Chuck Kabel, however, wasn't one of the original team; he was an

American who had been transferred from elsewhere within Gatmarsh Corporation to help Roy sort out the logistics operation, which was in a real mess.

One of the first things which Roy had asked Chuck to do was to visit the subcontract manufacturing facility in China where the company's products were now assembled and tested. The decision to outsource manufacturing to Sotoyo Electronics in China – it had originally been done in-house in Birmingham, in the West Midlands of the UK – was one of the things that the recent management had got disastrously wrong. On-time delivery performance had deteriorated badly, inventory levels had gone through the roof, and the costs of frequent write-offs of obsolete stock had become crippling.

Chuck's brief was to assess the situation and make a recommendation as whether these problems could be solved by working with Sotoyo to mend the system, or whether they would have to embark on the complex and costly project of bringing the manufacturing operation back to the UK. Roy was expecting to receive Chuck's report that very day.

But now Chuck was dead. Roy felt numb. He needed to talk to his management team about this shocking news, but it was too early just now. He decided to fill the time until everyone else arrived by dealing with some of his other emails. This turned out to be a futile plan though: with thoughts about Chuck's untimely death swirling around his mind, he just couldn't concentrate on anything else.

**

At 9.00 a.m. Roy picked up the phone, and dialled the number of Mick McNulty, Financial Director. 'Mick, could you come over to my office for a few minutes? I've just received some bad news which we need to discuss urgently.'

'What's up?' said Mick, in his broad Belfast accent, as he sat down opposite Roy. 'Ya sounded worried as hell on t' phone, so ya did.'

Mick was a tall, but slight figure. He was in his late forties, but with his boyish features he looked younger, in spite of the fact that his abundant shock of dark wavy hair was now starting to go grey at the temples. He wore spectacles with thin bronze-coloured rims, which he pushed up his nose as he leant forward to hear what Roy had to say.

Roy puffed out his cheeks and blew air through pursed lips as he prepared himself to break the news. 'I'm afraid I've just heard from Chang Wei that Chuck's dead.'

'Dead?' gasped Mick. 'But he can't be. He's ... well he's supposed ta be back in t' UK by now.'

'I know,' said Roy, 'but apparently, he never made the flight. It seems he was taken ill and collapsed while waiting to check in at the airport, and by the time they got him to hospital he was dead.'

Mick placed one elbow on the desk and rested his forehead in the crook between thumb and forefinger, sighing deeply as he digested the news. After a few seconds he looked up, shaking his head in disbelief. 'Do they know what caused it?'

'At this stage, no. I guess there may well be a post-mortem to establish the cause of death, so maybe we'll learn more then.'

'Unbelievable,' said Mick, still shaking his head. He was silent for several seconds, apparently struggling to come to terms with the shocking news. Then his expression changed subtly: his eyes narrowed behind his glasses and his mouth puckered as he pursed his lips. 'Did Chuck talk ta ya about any o' his findings before he died?'

'No. I was expecting his report today. Why do you ask?'

'I spoke ta him on t' phone a couple o' times during his visit, and he thought there was something fishy about Sotoyo's finances. He was due ta talk ta Chang about it before he left.'

'And did he?'

'I don't know.'

'Hmm,' mused Roy, 'have you seen a copy of his report?'

24

'No. Like you, I was expecting ta see it today.'

Roy exhaled noisily. 'I think I need to call Chang Wei, but I'm going to leave it until tomorrow. He's a slippery customer and I want to think carefully about how I approach him.'

'That he is,' said Mick with a wry smile. 'In any case it'll be' – he looked at his watch – 'around 4.30 p.m. out there by now. You wouldn't have much time ta get yer thoughts organised before they'd be going home. It'll be best ta call first thing in t' morning.'

Roy nodded. 'I'll let you know what I find out.'

A few moments after Mick had left, Roy's phone rang. He picked up and answered. 'Hello – Roy Groves.'

The woman on the phone answered with an American accent. She sounded distraught.

'This is' – her voice caught in her throat – 'Gabby Kabel, Chuck's wife.' She started to sob. 'Have you heard what's happened?'

His stomach clenched; he wasn't ready for this conversation. What could he possibly say? Anyway, there was no opportunity to prepare now. His reply was faltering.

'Er …yes I have … just this morning. I can't tell you how sorry I am.'

'I can't believe it,' she sniffed. 'Chuck's never been sick in his life. How could this just happen out of the blue?'

'I don't know,' said Roy. 'I was absolutely shocked to hear what had happened.'

'I got a call around lunchtime yesterday from the hospital in China, and they … well, all they could tell me was that he had collapsed and died. How could he … how could he just … *die*? They wouldn't tell me anything about what caused it. Why won't they tell me? I'm his *wife* for God's sake.'

She began sobbing once more. Roy waited while she regained her composure, unsure what he could possibly say that would help.

Eventually she continued. 'I was wondering whether … well, whether *you* had any more information.'

'I'm sorry,' he replied, gently, 'I don't know any more than you do.'

'Oh' – she sounded defeated – 'I just hoped that … well, that you might know something more.'

'Look,' he said, 'I'll try and find out a bit more and call you back the moment I learn anything.'

'Thank you,' she sniffed. 'I'll wait to hear from you then.'

Roy was about to put the phone down when something odd struck him. 'Oh, Gabby, just one other thing …'

'Uh … yes, what?'

'What time did you say the hospital phoned you?'

'Oh, I don't know exactly. I was just preparing a sandwich for lunch … about midday I guess.'

'OK, thanks. I'll be in touch again soon.'

As he put the phone down, Roy considered the implications of what Gabby had just told him. Chang's e-mail was sent at 10.45 a.m. Sunday, Shenzhen time – that would have been 3.45 a.m. UK time. How come *he* had been informed about Chuck's death some eight hours before Gabby had? Surely she should have been the first person to be informed? He added this to his mental list of things which would need teasing out when he spoke to Chang.

Chapter 4

'Hi, how was work today?' called out Donna from the kitchen, as Roy closed the front door behind him. He walked through to the kitchen where she was busy preparing dinner.

'Pretty awful, actually,' he replied.

She turned her head and looked at him enquiringly. Donna was forty-nine years old, tall, slim, her pretty face framed by dark-blonde hair, streaked with grey in places; she had, so far, steadfastly refused to resort to colouring it. In any case, Roy rather liked the multi-coloured streaks which punctuated her hair; they lent it an agreeable depth of texture.

'Why? What's happened?' she said.

'Chuck Kabel has died.'

'What?' she gasped, laying down the knife she had been holding and turning fully to face Roy.

'He was just on his way back from a visit to the subcontract manufacturer in China and he collapsed at the airport while he was queuing to check in. By the time they got him to hospital he was dead.'

'Oh Roy ... how awful.'

'Yes,' he sighed, shaking his head, still struggling to come to terms with what had happened, 'and completely unexpected. Chuck was in perfect health and peak physical condition.'

'So, what caused it then?'

'They don't know yet. I'm guessing they'll want to do a post-mortem to try to establish the cause of death.'

'I guess so,' she murmured, her brow wrinkling in a frown as she considered this thought. 'Oh, Roy, you look absolutely shattered. Go and sit down ... do you want a drink?'

'I could certainly use one.'

She reached behind her waist and loosened the tapes of the apron, slipping it over her head and placing it on the worktop before making for the fridge.

Roy stepped into the hall and shrugged off his jacket, hanging it over the post at the bottom of the stairs before loosening his tie and undoing the top button of his shirt. He moved through to the lounge and sank into the sofa with a deep sigh. Donna followed a few moments later carrying two glasses of wine.

'Thanks,' he said, accepting one of the glasses and taking a long, grateful swallow. He set the glass down on the coffee table before exhaling a heavy sigh. 'I'm going to call the plant manager in China first thing in the morning, and see what else he knows.'

Donna sat down alongside him. 'What about Chuck's family?'

'He's married, but I don't think there are any children. His wife, Gabby, only moved over to the UK a few weeks ago. Before that she was still in the USA while Chuck was in a rented house over here in the UK. Actually, she called me today to see if I knew any more than she did about what happened – which unfortunately I didn't. She sounded – understandably – completely distraught.'

'Oh, poor woman. She probably doesn't have any friends over here to turn to for support.' She paused for a few moments looking thoughtful. 'Do you want me to give her a call and see if I can do anything to help?'

Roy smiled – for the first time that day. 'You really are the good Samaritan aren't you?'

'Well, I just ...' She was cut off in mid-sentence as Roy leant over and kissed her full on the lips.

When their lips parted, Roy said, 'That's a wonderful gesture, but I really don't know whether she would actually want to talk to anyone just now. I hardly know her at all, and in any case who knows how *anyone* will be under these circumstances.'

'I know,' she said. 'She might prefer to be on her own, but ... well, if she *does* want to talk to someone, I'd be more than willing to meet her.'

'Look,' he replied, 'I have to call her myself as soon as I have any more news about Chuck's death. I'll try to find an opportunity to mention it to her then.'

Donna smiled. 'OK, thanks. I only hope I can be of some help.'

Roy hoped that Donna would get an opportunity to talk to Gabby. If she did, he was quite sure that she *would* be able to help. Donna had an uncanny ability to bond with other women – even total strangers – when they were going through periods of grief or distress.

***

The following morning, Roy was in his office by 6.00 a.m. He did not want any interruptions or distractions during his phone call to Chang Wei. He took a sip from the steaming cup of coffee, which he had just brought back to his desk from the vending machine, as he ran through in his head, once more, the questions to which he needed answers. Yes, he was now as ready as he was ever going to be.

Chang answered on the third ring, and began by offering effusive, but not terribly sincere-sounding condolences for Chuck's death. Roy listened politely, but what he really wanted was specific answers to some specific questions.

'Do you know if they have established the cause of death yet?'

'Not as far as I know, Mr Groves, but I don't suppose the authorities will disclose such information to me anyway; after all I am not a member of his family. It will probably be best for you to talk to Mr Kabel's widow about that. I would think she will be the first to be informed of any findings.'

'I'm sure you're right,' said Roy – not mentioning that he had already spoken to Gabby – 'but what you have just said begs another question. How is it that you were informed of Chuck's death before his wife?'

There was a moment's hesitation before Chang replied. 'Well … ah yes, I believe the paramedics who attended to Mr Kabel at the airport found one of my business cards on his person. They thought that perhaps he worked for my company, so they called me first – my mobile number was on the card as well as my office number. He was apparently pronounced dead at around 9.00 a.m. which would be 2.00 a.m. in the UK, so I assume they decided to wait until a more appropriate hour to call Mrs Kabel.'

'I see,' replied Roy, pausing for a moment as he digested this reply. Gabby had not been informed until around midday; under the circumstances, would the hospital *really* have delayed informing a dead man's wife for around *ten hours*? He chose not to query the point just now.

'There's something else which has been puzzling me,' Roy continued. 'Chuck was, as far as I know, completely fit and healthy, so it came as a complete shock that this could happen. Did he seem to be in good health when you last saw him?'

'Well I only saw him at the beginning of his visit, but yes, he seemed fine then.'

'So he didn't discuss any of his findings with you before he left.'

'Unfortunately, no.'

'But I assume he will have left you a copy of his report?'

'No, he didn't. Maybe he hadn't finished it.'

'Then he would have had it in his possession when he collapsed, either on his laptop or on a memory stick, and possibly as hard copy too. How can I get access to these items?'

'Well,' said Chang, smoothly, 'I understand that the authorities will keep hold of all the personal possessions which he had with him until they have concluded their investigations. I believe they will then be released to Mrs Kabel. I suggest you speak to her about this.'

'I will,' replied Roy.

'Is there anything else I can help you with?'

'Not right now. Just let me know if you find out any more.'

'Of course. Well, once again, let me offer my sincere condolences.' He hung up

Roy slammed the phone down in frustration. *So,* he thought, *Chang claims he doesn't know what caused Chuck's death, he never saw or spoke to Chuck before he left, he doesn't know anything about Chuck's findings, and he hasn't seen the report.*

The creeping sense of unease deep in Roy's gut began to grow. Something didn't ring true here.

Chapter 5

'Len Douglas,' said the person answering the phone. Roy chuckled inwardly as he noted how, in just those two words, Len's unmistakeable Geordie accent came through loud and clear.

'Len, it's Roy here … Roy Groves.'

'Roy?' Len replied, his tone lifting when he heard Roy's voice. 'This is a bit of a surprise. How the hell are y'?'

'Oh, OK I guess. How about you?'

'Not so bad.'

'And Daphne?'

'She's fine. She's actually got another job now, running the warehousing and distribution operations at a local furniture manufacturer. Makes me feel like a bit of a fraud, what with her working while I sit around the hoose doing nowt.'

Roy laughed. 'Actually that was the main reason I called: to see what you're up to work-wise these days.'

'Not much,' replied Len. 'I do a bit of consultancy from time t' time, and the odd short-term contract, but mostly I'm still living on me payoff from Romotive.'

Len had previously been Logistics Director at Romotive, and a member of the original MBO team, but an unfortunate and shocking series of events during the run-up to the stock market floatation resulted in Len being fired. Shirley Stevens, CEO and core MBO team member was a talented and popular leader, but she was unexpectedly and tragically struck down by cancer before the floatation. The venture capitalists who had provided much of the finance for the MBO brought in a new CEO from outside the company. It was he who took the ill-advised decision to fire Len, believing that if manufacturing was subcontracted to the Far East then Len's services could be dispensed with. Len had received a decent payoff, but not enough to retire on – not that he would have wanted to anyway, Roy guessed.

'OK,' said Roy, 'well in that case I have a proposition for you.'

'Sorry,' said Len, 'you're a lovely fella and all that, but y' know that I prefer the ladies, and in any case, I'm married now.'

'Oh shut up you idiot,' replied Roy, chuckling in spite of himself – he had always found Len's jocular manner endearing, even though it sometimes emerged at the most inappropriate moments. 'Can't you ever be serious for more than a few minutes at a time?'

'Sorry, it's just that me ready wit is too precious not t' share. OK – shoot. I'm listening.'

'Do you want your old job back?'

Len seemed lost for a flippant reply; he was silent for a few seconds.

'What? Y' mean at Romotive … or whatever it's now called?'

'Uh, huh,' replied Roy. 'And, by the way, it's Gatmarsh Automotive.'

Len was silent for a few seconds. 'Uh, yes … I did know that. But what about the American guy who was brought in from Gatmarsh Corporation?'

'That's why I'm calling you. Chuck has unexpectedly collapsed and died.'

'Died? But how … what caused it?'

'No-one knows yet; we're waiting for the results of the post-mortem. Look, before you give me an answer I need to explain what Chuck was doing before he died and what I'd want you to do if you accept the offer. You might just decide that you don't want to get involved.'

'OK, I'm listening.'

Roy proceeded to relate the whole story, including his concerns about the dearth of information coming from China, the missing report, and Chang's somewhat evasive manner. Len stopped him frequently to ask questions.

Eventually, when Roy had finished, Len asked, 'So are y' saying y' think there's summat fishy about Chuck's death?'

'I honestly don't know,' said Roy. 'There's probably nothing untoward going on but I just have an uneasy feeling about the whole thing. That's why I wanted you to have all the facts – such as they are – in front of you before you make a decision. If you take the job I'll need you to pick up where Chuck left off.'

'Hmm … OK, look, I need to talk it over with Daphne and I'll get back t' y' within the next few days.'

'Thanks, Len. Oh, and give my love to Daphne.'

'And mine t' Donna.'

***

Chang Wei smiled a thin, humourless smile as he addressed the man sitting on the other side of the desk. 'Five million Yuan is a great deal of money just to clean up a laptop, lose a few papers, and modify some medical findings.'

The man opposite took a deep draw from his cigarette, holding his breath for several long seconds before exhaling slowly, blue tendrils of smoke curling upwards, starkly illuminated as they passed through the shaft of sunlight coming through the tiny window set high in the wall of the otherwise dim and gloomy office.

Zheng Bao was the chief of the local police force, a small, wiry man with a thin face ravaged by pock marks and bearing a small scar above his right eye. He contemplated the precariously balanced projection of ash on the end of his cigarette stub, and tapped it to dislodge the ash into the ashtray, before finally stubbing out it out with an exaggeratedly slow and deliberate circular grinding motion.

'The thing is,' he said, looking directly into Chang's eyes, 'what you get with me is a one-stop-shop, so to speak. I'll take care of everything: the police, the coroner, the hospital, everything. It will be as if the gentleman simply suffered an unfortunate heart attack.'

'Nevertheless, the price you are asking is exorbitant.'

'You need to understand that I have expenses: other people to pay.'

Chang exhaled loudly and raised a forefinger, pointing directly at Zhang's face. 'And *you* need to understand that my … associates … are becoming weary of your increasingly outrageous demands. I need hardly remind you that you only hang on to this job as a result of their patronage. They can easily find someone else to replace you, and if they get *really* upset with you, it could be more than your job that you lose. Do you understand me?'

A little of the colour drained from Zheng's already pallid complexion; his Adam's apple bobbed up and down in his scrawny neck as he gulped involuntarily. Chang knew he had the other man where he wanted him.

'Well, given our long-standing and productive partnership,' spluttered Zheng, 'I will make a special concession … a gesture of goodwill: four million Yuan.' He smiled an insincere-looking, ingratiating smile and spread his hands outwards. 'I can't be fairer than that, can I?'

Chang stared back at him, his expression unchanging; he said nothing. A slight twitch appeared alongside Zheng's right eye as he met Chang's gaze.

After a silence lasting several seconds Chang said, 'three million.'

'But … but that won't even cover my costs,' protested Zheng. 'I couldn't possibly go any lower than three and a half million.'

Chang leant forward and placed both hands palm-downward on the desk. His slanting eyes narrowed as they bored into Zheng's. 'Perhaps you do not understand me. The price is three million.'

Zheng looked desperate, hunted. There was a slight tremor in his voice when he replied. 'Chang Wei, my friend, we have always worked so well together. Surely we can work out something mutually acceptable here?'

Chang puffed air noisily through pursed lips. 'Am I to understand that you wish me to report back that you refuse to accept my generous offer? If my associates have to find someone else at short notice to deal with this matter, I cannot imagine that they will be too pleased.' Zheng's shoulders slumped in a gesture of defeat. 'Well?' persisted Chang.

'Three million then,' muttered Zheng.

Chang smiled, before picking up his briefcase from the floor and laying it on the table. He slid the latches to the sides and the locks popped open. He opened the lid in such a way as to hide the contents from Zheng's gaze and withdrew three million Yuan in cash, sliding it across the desk to the disconsolate-looking policeman, who quickly scooped the bundles of banknotes up and put them in his desk drawer.

Chang closed the briefcase and stood up, extending his hand. 'As always, a pleasure doing business with you,' he said, smiling broadly.

Zheng muttered something which Chang couldn't make out as he stood up and accepted the hand proffered.

'I'll see myself out,' said Chang, cheerfully.

As he slipped into the seat of his car and laid the briefcase on the passenger seat, Chang sighed contentedly; it had been a very good meeting. He had been authorised to pay up to six million Yuan, and that was the sum of money which had been inside the briefcase. He had been told, however, that if he could negotiate a lower figure he could keep fifty per cent of the amount he saved. He had just earned himself one and a half million Yuan for half an hour's work.

He had fleetingly considered telling his boss that the figure agreed was higher than three million so that he could keep even more. If he had claimed that the price agreed had been, say, five million he would have been able to pocket the two million difference plus fifty percent of the remaining million. That would have netted him a very handsome two and a half million in total. It was tempting, but he had swiftly dismissed the idea as too dangerous; the risk that he would be found out was too high. When a member of the Triad double-crossed his superiors, the outcome was never *ever* good.

Chapter 6

It was 11.00 a.m. Monday morning. Roy had spent the last couple of hours catching up on some routine paperwork, but the issue of Chuck's untimely death was weighing heavily on him. It was now a full week since Roy had heard about Chuck's death and he had heard absolutely nothing more since then. He decided to phone Chuck's wife, Gabby.

The voice on the other end of the phone was dead, lifeless. 'Hello, Gabby Kabel.'

'Gabby, it's Roy Groves.'

'Oh, hello.' She sounded distant and disinterested. Roy wasn't sure how to start the conversation.

'Look, I said I'd call you when I had any more information, but that's the thing … I'm afraid I know absolutely nothing more than I did when we spoke last week.'

'Oh, well that makes two of us then.'

'Haven't they told you anything either?'

'They've told me plenty, but I still know *nothing*.'

Her frustration and simmering anger were palpable, transmitting themselves through the telephone as clearly as if she were sitting opposite him. There was a tense silence for a second or two, and then Gabby burst into floods of tears. The anguished sobs tore at Roy's heart, but there was nothing he could do or say to comfort her. At length, her sobbing subsided and she appeared to regain her composure.

'I'm sorry,' she said, 'but I still can't take it all in. Why can't they tell me what happened?'

'No need to apologise,' said Roy, as gently as possible. He paused for a second or two. 'But can you tell me what they *have* actually told you?'

Roy heard the deep intake of breath as Gabby sought to settle herself sufficiently to reply. 'Apparently it was a heart attack.'

'I see,' said Roy. He paused for a few moments before continuing, 'Look, I know this must be very difficult for you, but … well … did Chuck have any prior history of heart problems?'

'No,' she replied, 'he never had *any* health problems … he hardly ever even used to catch a cold.' She caught her breath, clearly struggling to retain her composure. 'He kept himself in such great shape; he used to go running every morning before work, and worked out at the gym at least twice a week. I just don't understand. It seems so … well … *unfair*.' She began sobbing once more.

'I'm so sorry,' said Roy. It seemed a wholly inadequate response, but he just didn't know what else to say.

When her sobs eventually subsided, Roy asked, 'Have they sent his things back yet?'

'Yes, I received them on Friday.'

'Do you think I could possibly take a look at his work things: his laptop and his work-related papers?'

'Why? What do you want with Chuck's things? He's *dead*. What does any of it matter now?'

Roy realised he had pushed too hard, too soon.

'I'm sorry, Gabby. There's no hurry … take your time to go through everything yourself and we can talk later.'

He heard her breath catch in her throat. 'Oh, what the hell? Take his damned papers; they are in his briefcase … and he only used his laptop for work, so you may as well keep that too.'

'Thanks,' said Roy, gently. 'I do appreciate it.'

'I just wish he'd never ever taken this damned job … that we'd stayed in Boston … that we'd just …' – she started sobbing once more – 'that things could just be as they were.'

Roy's heart went out to her. They had been a relatively young couple with everything to live for; she didn't deserve to be enduring this anguish. But a heart attack could strike at anyone, any time. There was no reason to suppose that Chuck's new job, or the move to England had anything to do with it. This was not the time, though, to be having that conversation.

'I'm so sorry,' said Roy, once again acutely conscious at the total inadequacy of his words.

She did not reply, but he could hear her uneven, ragged breathing as she struggled to regain control. He waited until he judged that it was OK to continue.

'Gabby ... I really am very grateful for your allowing me to take a look at Chuck's work things. I don't suppose it will help shed any more light on what happened but it could be important in other ways. Would it be OK if ... well, if I sent someone round to collect them this afternoon?'

'Oh, I guess so,' she replied, sniffling. 'I'm not going anywhere.'

'Look,' said Roy, hesitantly, 'I know this must be an incredibly difficult time for you ... do you have friends here who can offer a bit of help and support?'

'Well, no ... not really. I only moved over here to England three weeks ago. Before that Chuck was just staying here on his own while I was still back in Boston, until we could find a nice house in England.' Her voice caught in her throat, and it was a few seconds before she was able to continue. 'We were so looking forward to making a new life in England and ...' She couldn't finish the sentence.

'I can only imagine what you must be going through,' said Roy. 'Look, I'll ask my wife, Donna, to come round and collect Chuck's work things, and if you want someone to talk to, I know she'll be happy to stay as long as you like. She's a very good listener.'

'Thanks,' she replied in a faltering voice, 'but I really don't feel like talking to anyone right now.'

'OK … I understand,' he replied. 'Well, anyway, I'll get Donna to come round today to pick up Chuck's work things.'

'Sure,' was her cryptic response.

'Well … goodbye then. I … I'm so sorry for your loss.'

'Sure,' she repeated, her voice dull and lifeless. 'Bye then.'

After Roy had hung up, he sat for several minutes reflecting on their conversation. Chuck had been relatively young and super-fit, with absolutely no history of health problems, so how likely was it that he would suddenly suffer a fatal heart attack? The truth was, Roy had no idea; maybe it was perfectly possible – after all, heart attacks were not that uncommon.

Roy was very keen, now, to get his hands on Chuck's report and all his papers. Maybe they would shed some light on how the visit had gone, and on the reasons for Chang's evasive manner. In truth, Roy had no evidence that Chang had behaved at all improperly, or that Chuck's death was anything other than a tragic misfortune.

And yet, perhaps irrationally, the tendrils of suspicion continued to snake through his mind.

***

That evening, Roy stepped through his front door at around 6.30 p.m.

'Hi, I'm in the lounge,' called out Donna.

He shrugged off his jacket and hung it over the post at the bottom of the stairs, before moving through to the lounge, where Donna was sitting with a glass of wine in her hand, reading the local newspaper. She set down her glass and folded the paper before getting up to kiss Roy. He pulled her to him, perhaps more tightly than usual, savouring the warmth of her breasts against his torso and the scent of her infiltrating his senses. He held her like that for several seconds before easing back a little, his hands still resting lightly on her hips.

'Hey, what's got into you?' she asked, tilting her head to one side, her expression quizzical.

'What … can't a guy kiss his wife when he gets home from work?'

She didn't reply to his question. 'Tough day, then?'

'Yes,' he said, managing a small smile, 'tough day. Anyway, did you see Chuck's wife?'

'Uh huh.'

'And did you get his things?'

She nodded, inclining her head to indicate the armchair in the corner of the room. Lying on it were a black leather briefcase and, on top of that, what looked like a laptop computer case.

'Thanks for that,' he said, finally letting go of her completely.

He went over and picked up the laptop case, setting it down on the floor – the computer could wait until he took it onto work the following day. He turned his attention, instead, to the briefcase, sliding the catches sideways to flip up the lid. He began rifling through its contents.

'Shall I get you a glass of wine while you do that?'

'Mmm, that would be nice,' he said, smiling at Donna.

She disappeared into the kitchen while Roy inspected the contents of the briefcase: a mobile phone, an address book, a paperback novel – by some tragic irony, entitled 'Death in the Orient' – and a few papers, none of which appeared to be related to Chuck's visit to China. Certainly there was no sign of the anticipated report. Roy puffed out his cheeks and exhaled heavily.

'Dammit!' he muttered under his breath.

'I guess you didn't find what you were looking for,' said Donna, as she entered the room and set down Roy's drink on the coffee table.

'No, there seems to be hardly anything in here.'

'What about his laptop?'

'I'll take it into work tomorrow; I can't face ploughing through all his files tonight. In any case, I'd prefer to have my IT people go through the computer thoroughly to make sure we don't miss anything.' He sank into the sofa and took a grateful sip of his wine, before setting the glass back down 'So how was Gabby?'

Donna sighed. 'She's absolutely shattered; her whole world has just fallen apart.'

Roy shook his head. 'Poor woman.'

'She and Chuck were planning to start a whole new life here, but now this ... well it's changed everything.'

'Yes, I guess it has,' he sighed. He picked up his wine glass once more, swirling the contents gently as he gazed contemplatively into the glass. 'So what's she planning to do now?'

'Well, she's having Chuck's body flown back to Boston: that's where her family and friends live and that's where the funeral will be held. She really hasn't thought much beyond that; I think she's still in a state of shock.'

Roy took a sip of his wine, holding the glass for a few more seconds while he considered what Donna had said. He set the glass down before asking, 'When's the funeral?'

'Next Tuesday. I said I'd go and see her again before she goes; she doesn't have any friends or family here in the UK.'

'That's nice. I'm sure she'll appreciate it.'

Donna shrugged. 'I'm not sure I can really do anything to help, but at least she'll have someone to talk to.'

Roy leaned over and kissed her on the cheek. 'You're something special, you know.'

She smiled and nuzzled her head against him. 'Not really ... just trying to help.'

'I guess she told you about the cause of Chuck's death?'

'Uh, huh ... heart attack, apparently. She can hardly believe it when he was so fit and relatively young. Still, that's what the post-mortem showed, so I guess it was just one of those horrible unlucky chances.'

'Hmm,' said Roy ... 'I guess so.'

Chapter 7

The next morning, Roy was looking across the large oval boardroom table at Len Douglas. As always, Len was immaculately turned out; he wore a pale grey designer suit teamed with a cream shirt and blue silk tie. It seemed that his time away from the corporate world had not dulled his sense of sartorial elegance. His full head of hair – previously a salt and pepper mix – had now turned a distinguished uniform grey colour, while his neatly trimmed moustache had somehow retained its medium brown tone, and contained no grey at all. He had always kept himself in good physical shape, and still looked lean and fit.

'It's great to have you back on the team, Len,' said Roy, smiling.

Mick McNulty, who was also attending the meeting, echoed Roy's welcome. 'It's almost like old times, eh?'

'Well, I was doing nowt useful at home and t' be honest it's been driving me nuts just hanging around and trying t' think up things t' fill me time. It'll be champion t' get back in the saddle again.'

Roy smiled as he observed Len's eager expression. 'Well, I can't think of anyone better to pick up where Chuck left off.'

'So what exactly was his brief?' asked Len, leaning forward and placing an elbow on the table, taking his chin between thumb and forefinger.

'Well, as you already know, outsourcing the manufacturing operation to China has proven to be an unmitigated disaster. On-time delivery performance has fallen through the floor, inventory levels have skyrocketed, and stock write-offs have reached epidemic proportions.'

'Well, it's nothing that we didn't foresee,' commented Len.

'That's true,' said Roy, with a wry smile, 'but the real irony is that even the cost savings which were supposed to flow from outsourcing to the Far East have failed to materialise. Anyway, in answer to your question, Chuck's brief was to try to figure out what's going wrong and come up with a plan to fix it.'

'Well,' said Len, 'the obvious answer which springs t' mind is just t' pull the manufacturing operation back here t' England … but that's not so simple is it?'

'No it isn't. Clearly it would have been best if the decision to outsource manufacturing to China had never been taken in the first place, but what's done is done. Any decision to now bring it back here to the UK cannot be taken lightly. The idiots running the company, before Gatmarsh bought it, had fired the entire manufacturing workforce – almost four hundred people, sold off all the production equipment, and disposed of the previous factory in favour of this smaller facility in which we now sit.'

'Arseholes,' said Len, summing up his view in his usual forthright manner.

'Quite,' said Roy. 'Anyway, my point is that it would be a very complex and costly project to reverse all those actions.'

Len nodded, stroking his chin, thoughtfully.

Mick chipped in. 'For that reason, we asked Chuck ta go out there and make an assessment of what would be needed ta fix t' various problems we're struggling with. If we can implement some changes ta make t' current setup work, then that may be t' best solution, but if needs be, we'll have ta pull t' manufacturing operation back ta the UK and suffer t' upheaval and costs which Roy just outlined.'

'So can y' give me a bit more detail on what's going wrong?' said Len, leaning forward and placing his elbows on the polished rosewood table top.

Roy gave a wry smile. 'I hardly know where to begin …'

'Well, just the main points then.'

'OK,' said Roy, laying the forefinger of his right hand on the little finger of his left. 'The first point is that delivery performance has gone completely to pot. Every time we receive a delivery from China, around half the items we ordered are missing, and in their place there are hundreds of items we didn't order. This is forcing us to hold substantial buffer stocks of the most popular products here in the UK, but even so we are letting many of our customers down badly when we just don't have the products they have ordered.'

Roy sighed, pausing as he raked the fingers of his right hand back through his hair.

'The second problem,' he continued, laying the forefinger of his right hand across two fingers of his left, 'is that Sotoyo keep billing us for massive stock write-offs. Every time we phase out an older product to introduce a new one we discover that they're sitting on huge stocks of the older product which can no longer be sold. They claim that they've only built ahead of purchase orders according to our latest forecasts, but even allowing for less-than-perfect forecasting that just *cannot* be true.'

Roy paused again, shaking his head in frustration.

'What else?' encouraged Len.

'Well,' continued Roy, 'I guess a lot of what I just outlined was predictable … to a certain extent, at least.'

'Aye, it was,' agreed Len. 'Y' pretty much told 'em as much before y' quit.'

Roy nodded, smiling grimly. 'Anyway the main point of outsourcing to the Far East was to save money. They convinced themselves that the savings would be so great that it would be worth dealing with any delivery performance and stock control problems which might arise, in order to achieve those savings.' He paused again, before looking Len directly in the eyes. 'The thing is, we're just not getting those savings. Every time we introduce a new product the actual manufacturing cost seems to end up at least twenty per cent higher than we forecast.'

Len held up his hand. 'OK y' don't need t' go on; I get the picture.'

'So,' continued Roy, 'Chuck's brief was to investigate what was behind all these problems, and recommend an action plan to fix them – one way or another.'

Their discussion was interrupted by a knock on the door. The face which poked around the door was that of Chris Williams, head of the IT Department. He was a studious-looking man with a thin face, circular glasses, and an unruly mop of brown curly hair. 'Can I interrupt?' he asked.

'Sure, come in,' said Roy, beckoning him to enter.

He came in, clutching a laptop.

'Come and sit down,' said Roy.

He did so, laying the laptop on the table in front of him.

'You know Len of course,' said Roy. 'He's going to be rejoining the company to replace Chuck Kabel.'

Chris nodded. 'Hello Len. Good to see you again.'

'Likewise,' said Len. 'I'm looking forward t' getting back t' work.'

Roy looked across at Len. 'Chris has been checking over Chuck's laptop to try to find anything related to his visit to China.' Len nodded.

Roy turned to Chris. 'So what have you found?'

Chris cleared his throat and shuffled awkwardly in his chair. 'Well, there's a folder in his documents area entitled "Sotoyo visit".'

'Ah, good,' said Roy leaning forward and planting his elbow on the table. 'What's in the folder?'

'Well, there's a file called "Visit Plan" which contains what looks like an outline of the investigations he planned to make and the people he needed to talk to, together with a timetable for these actions.'

'Uh, huh,' said Roy. 'What else?'

'There's another file labelled "Must see". It seems to be a list of places he wanted to see during his free time. For example …'

Roy cut him off. 'I'm not really interested in how he planned to spend his weekends,' he said, a touch irritably. 'What else?'

Chris recoiled slightly at Roy's uncharacteristically brusque interjection. 'Well, nothing else, really.'

'What – no sign of a visit report or anything like that?'

'Sorry, no.'

Roy clasped his forehead in his hand and sighed heavily. 'Goddamit. No papers, no memory sticks and nothing on his computer. What the hell's going on here?'

No-one answered his rhetorical question, but Chris said, 'Look, I've only had a superficial look so far, but I have a feeling – no more than a suspicion, mind – that some material has been erased. If that *has* been done there may be traces of it deep in the system. I'll keep digging to see if I can find anything.'

Roy slowly raised his head. 'OK, you do that, and let me know if you find anything.'

Chris nodded, but looked distinctly unsettled as he glanced nervously from Len, to Mick, and then returned his gaze to Roy. 'Er, well shall I go now then?'

'Yes … oh, and thanks for your help. Sorry if I was a bit sharp.'

'No problem,' replied Chris. He gathered up the laptop and headed for the door.

When Chris had left, Len spoke up. 'It does sound a bit fishy doesn't it? I mean he had just finished a three-week trip, and apparently there's absolutely nowt about the visit recorded.'

Mick chipped in. 'He definitely told me that we would have his report on t' Monday after he returned ta work, so it's bloody weird that's there's no sign o' it amongst his things.'

Roy looked across at Len. 'I don't like the look of this. Are you sure you still want to do this?'

Len sounded resolute. 'Aye, I'll find out what's been going on.'

'Well, take care,' said Roy.

After the meeting, Roy returned to his desk, and for the next ten minutes, just sat there in silence, turning over in his mind what he had learned. In truth he had learned practically nothing, but still he felt desperately uneasy.

Chapter 8

The young woman who was just about to lower herself on to Len's straining member had the most perfect breasts he had ever seen: full yet pert, with proudly protruding nipples. For a second or so he managed to tear his eyes away from these wondrous objects in order to look up at her face. It was the kind of face which graced the covers of upmarket women's magazines: dark, almond-shaped eyes with impossibly long lashes beneath elegantly curved brows, sharply defined cheekbones, and full sensuous lips, glistening and moist. He grasped her slender waist, encouraging her as she settled herself onto him. She gave a soft moan, like the purr of a contented animal. Her long, straight, jet-black hair brushed against his face as she began, slowly, to move back and forth.

Len was in that strange intermediate stage of consciousness: neither awake nor fully asleep; dreaming, yet somehow knowing he was dreaming. He really, really didn't want to wake up.

Suddenly, the insistent drone all around him eased off and he felt a strange sensation in his stomach – a kind of gradual weightlessness; he dimly registered that they had started their descent. He fought hard to stay in his dream, but it was no use – harsh reality insisted on intruding. Gradually, he began to surface from his trancelike state, and said a reluctant goodbye to … well, she didn't actually have a name, but he was nevertheless very sorry to have to say goodbye to her. As he returned to full consciousness, his thoughts turned to his marriage, which could not be more different to the fantasy dream world which he had just left behind.

Daphne was his fourth wife; all three of his previous marriages had been wrecked by his own infidelity. Indeed, it was his affair with Daphne which was responsible for the breakdown of his third marriage. At the time Daphne had seemed so exciting, so desirable, and he had wasted little time in marrying her after his divorce had come through. What had happened to that exhilarating feeling? Within a few short years his marriage had become boring and dull; even the sex – previously wild and adventurous – had lapsed into a mechanical and predictable routine. How he craved the excitement which had crackled and sparked during the early part of their affair.

What was he to do, though? He knew full well that it was his own roving eye which had been responsible for the breakdown of his previous marriages; he could not, in all conscience, place the blame on any of his ex-wives. Daphne had done nothing wrong, either; certainly she did not deserve to be cast aside just because he had become bored, and in any case he could not face the thought of going through yet another messy separation. Maybe now that he was working again, that would put a little spark back in his life. He doubted, though, that this could replace the thrill of pursuing, and ultimately capturing, an exciting new sexual partner. But how long could he carry on like this? In his mind, he was still the virile young man that all the ladies wanted to bed, but somewhere deep down he knew that those days were slipping away now.

He felt suddenly chilly, and grabbed the blanket from his lap, pulling it up around his shoulders and nestling his head against the side pod of the headrest. He tried to put his domestic dilemma out of his mind and get a few minutes more sleep; maybe his fantasy lover would still be there, waiting for him.

'Cabin crew, ten minutes to landing,' announced the electronically-distorted male voice, far too loudly.

Len gave up on his efforts to re-enter the elusive dream. He rubbed his eyes and turned to raise the window blind a little, squinting against the bright light which flooded in. He blinked and turned away to give his eyes a few moments to adjust.

The captain's voice on the tannoy was replaced by a soft female voice. 'Ladies and gentlemen, as you can see, the captain has turned on the seatbelt signs. Please ensure your trays are folded away, your seatbacks are in the upright position, and your seatbelts are securely fastened.'

As Len's eyes became adjusted, he opened fully the window blind and peered out. Below lay the massive industrial sprawl of Shenzhen, viewed through a brownish haze of pollution. He wondered what was waiting for him down there.

***

The following morning, Len met Chang Wei for the first time. Chang was a short, stocky figure in his late forties. His jet black hair was swept back and slicked down, accentuating his widow's peak hairline. His nose was crooked and lopsided: probably the legacy of a badly-healed break.

'A pleasure to meet you, Mr. Douglas,' said Chang, in perfect English. He spoke with an accent which was half-American, half-Asian. As he shook Len's hand, his exaggerated smile revealed a perfectly even set of pearly-white teeth which seemed strangely at odds with his rugged countenance and crooked nose. *I wonder how much they cost him*, wondered Len. Chang sat down behind his desk and indicated the chair opposite, where Len should sit.

'Likewise,' said Len.

'It was a terrible tragedy … the fate of your colleague, Mr. Kabel.'

'Aye, that it was. As far as we knew he was in perfect health.'

Chang's brow creased in puzzlement as he grappled to decipher Len's Geordie accent.

Len chuckled. 'Sorry, I'll try to tone down me accent a bit. Even some of the folks in the South of England struggle t' understand me sometimes.'

Chang flashed his perfect set of tombstones once more. 'No problem, I am sure we will soon come to understand each other perfectly.'

Was there a double meaning in that statement? Something in Chang's insincere-looking smile and his dark, intense eyes, made Len shiver.

'So, what exactly is the purpose of your visit?'

'I've come t' pick up where Chuck left off.'

'But I understood that Mr Kabel had completed his investigations before his unfortunate demise.'

'So did I,' replied Len, 'but he never got the chance t' tell us what he'd found or what actions he recommended.'

'Ah, I see … most unfortunate.'

'And when we went through his things, there was no visit report. In fact there was nowt at all about t' visit.' Len paused and looked into Chang's dark eyes. 'A bit strange don't y' think'

'Nowt?' repeated Chang, a puzzled frown creasing his brow once more.

'Sorry, I mean "nothing" … there was nothing about his visit among his papers or on his computer.'

'Ah,' said Chang, understanding dawning, 'yes, that is strange indeed.'

'I don't suppose he discussed his findings with you?'

Chang shook his head. 'Sadly, no – I hardly spoke to Mr Kabel all the time he was here. Like you, I was waiting for his report.'

'Hmm,' said Len, unconvinced. 'Well, anyway, that's why I'm here: t' repeat Chuck's work and come up with some recommendations as t' how we can improve things.'

Chang was no longer smiling. 'Improve what things exactly?'

Len shook his head in exasperation. 'I'm sure y' are already well aware of our concerns, but just in case there *is* any misunderstanding I have written 'em down for you.' He reached for his briefcase and placed it on the desk. He opened it, withdrew a sheet of paper, and handed it to Chang.

'As y' can see, the principal areas of concern are poor delivery performance, excessive stock write-offs, and unexpectedly high product costs.' Chang was scanning the paper back and forth as Len spoke. 'There's plenty of other stuff there, but I'll be starting with those.'

Chang studied the sheet of paper in silence, his jaw clenched tight. Len did not interrupt him. After a minute or so, he raised his head slowly, his eyes narrowed, and his mouth set in a thin, straight line.

'Just what exactly are you trying to prove here, Mr Douglas?'

'I'm not trying t' prove owt … I mean "anything"; I just want t' understand what's causing these problems so that we can come up with a plan t' fix them.'

Chang looked unconvinced; he fixed Len with a withering stare. 'Are you trying to build a case to withdraw your business from my company? Because if you are, I should warn you that you are contractually bound ...'

Len cut him off by raising his hand. 'Look, all I'm interested in is figuring out how we solve t' problems I just outlined. If we can do so while maintaining our existing business relationship, then that'll be best for all concerned. The cost and hassle involved in moving manufacturing back t' the UK would be horrendous.'

Len paused a moment to allow his words to sink in. Chang said nothing, but just continued to stare back at him, unblinking.

Len continued. 'However, y' should understand that we are prepared to do whatever is necessary t' fix the problems. If we can't do so in co-operation with your company we are indeed quite prepared t' pull manufacturing back t' the UK and face up t' the cost and difficulty of doing so.'

Chang's yellowish complexion began to change tone as the blood surged to his cheeks. He leaned forward and extended a forefinger towards Len. 'I already warned you that you are contractually bound to use Sotoyo as your exclusive manufacturing supplier for at least a further five years. If you renege on the contract there will be serious consequences.'

'Look,' said Len, 'it is our considered opinion that your company's failure t' meet the performance standards set out in the contract already amounts t' breach of contract.' He paused before adding, 'Under these circumstances we are perfectly entitled to terminate t' contact without notice.'

Chang stood up and placed both hands on the desk, leaning forward, glaring furiously downwards at Len. 'You really don't want to pick a fight with me, Mr Douglas,' he snarled.

Len remained seated. His voice was calm and level when he replied. 'No I don't. I just want t' fix the problems ... so I hope we can work together constructively t' do so.'

Chang exhaled loudly and sank back into his chair. He took several seconds, apparently trying to control his anger, before continuing. 'So what exactly do you want to look at?'

'I'm not sure yet ... it'll depend on where the investigation takes me. I'm sure I don't need t' remind y' that, under the terms of the contract, y' are required t' give reasonable inspection access to any authorised representative of my company.'

Chang's fists were clenched, resting in clear view on top of the desk, and when he replied, it was a petulant hiss. 'Just make sure you keep me fully informed of exactly what you are doing at all times.'

'Of course,' replied Len. 'Now, I think a good starting point would be a factory tour ... just to familiarise myself with the shop floor operations here.'

Chang glared at him for several more seconds before picking up the phone and stabbing a few keys, using far more force than was actually necessary. 'Hello, Pang' – then a pause for a few seconds – 'yes I know I am speaking in English, you idiot. I have an important guest here who requires a factory tour' – another pause – 'yes, right now. Please come to my office at once.' He slammed the handset down.

'Thanks *so* much for your assistance,' said Len. He was smiling, and his voice was calm and pleasant, but inside, his heart was pounding like a jackhammer.

*****

By the time Len arrived back in his hotel room – it was the very same hotel where Chuck had stayed before his unfortunate death – he was exhausted. He had been given a very detailed factory tour, but had formed the distinct impression that he was being shown only what they wanted him to see. He had been closely chaperoned all day, and had been afforded very little opportunity to explore anything outside of the guided tour. He would have to find a way of shaking off his minders and sniffing out the information he needed without someone constantly looking over his shoulder. Maybe after a few days they would lose interest in what he was doing, allowing him to pursue his investigations more freely.

He yawned – the jetlag hadn't worn off yet – and decided to get something to eat via room service before turning in for an early night. Before doing so, though, he fired up his laptop in order to check his emails. There were twenty-seven unread messages but, as Len scanned through the headers, his gaze settled on one from Kevin Brethan. Kevin was Technical Director at Gatmarsh Automotive, responsible for all design and development activities. He was widely regarded as Roy's number two. The message was entitled, 'Urgent – Sotoyo substituting inferior components.' Len clicked to open the email.

To: Len Douglas
From: Kevin Brethan
Subject: Urgent – Sotoyo substituting inferior components

Len,

I've been investigating a higher-than-expected field failure rate on some of the products manufactured by Sotoyo and I've discovered that they are not fitting the specified components. The substituted components are functionally similar, so that the products basically work OK, but their specifications don't include the safety margins which we designed in for good reliability. They are therefore prone to failing prematurely.

They have obviously done this to save money, which makes it all the more surprising that the prices we are paying them are nearly always higher than the original estimates.

Can you dig into it from your end and try to find out more about this issue? I'd like to make sure we have all our ducks in a row before we confront Chang.

Regards,
Kevin

Great, thought Len. *One more thing to add to the list.*

Chapter 9

It was one of those rare occasions when Roy and Donna were able to have both of their daughters over for Sunday lunch. Both of the girls were grown up and had long since flown the parental nest; naturally enough, they had busy lives of their own to lead now. When there *was* time for the whole family to get together it was a treat to savour.

Roy had just laid the table and poured two glasses of red wine. He walked through to the kitchen, where Donna was busy preparing the meal, and passed her one of the glasses. They clinked the glasses together.

'Well, here's to a nice Sunday with the girls,' he said.

Donna wiped her free hand against her apron and pushed aside a stray tendril of hair which had fallen across her cheek. 'Yes, it doesn't happen often enough. Funny thing is, it was actually Beatrice who suggested it this time – now that's pretty unusual, don't you think?'

'Oh, well yes … I guess. Was there any special reason?'

'Not that I know of, but you know Bea; she doesn't generally …'

The doorbell rang.

'I'll go,' said Roy, smiling. When he opened the door, he hardly recognised his younger daughter, Raquel, standing there. Her previously very long, straight, blonde hair had been cut short in a choppy, feathered style which barely reached her collar. The colour was now a glowing, rich reddish-chestnut tone.

The young man standing behind her laughed when he saw Roy's dumbstruck expression. 'I told her to leave it alone,' said her boyfriend, Tim, 'but she never listens to me. Actually though, I quite like it.'

'Come on in,' said Roy, hugging his daughter and then shaking Tim's hand. 'Come and show Mum.'

Donna emerged from the kitchen and Raquel performed a little twirl, flicking up her hair at the back of her neck with her hand. 'So what do you think of the new look, Mum?'

Donna smiled. 'I love it,' she said. Then moving forward she took one of her daughter's hands. 'And what about these nails!'

Raquel spread her fingers wide, offering her new acrylic nails for inspection. They were a midnight blue colour and each bore a moon symbol and several tiny stars. 'Cool, eh?'

'Er, yes … cool,' said Donna, laughing. She kissed her daughter on the cheek.

Raquel stepped back. 'And what about this?' she pulled up the front of her sweater to reveal a gold ring piercing her navel.

'Now *that's* a step too far,' declared Roy, his brow puckering in a disapproving frown.

'Oh for goodness' sake,' scolded Donna. 'She's young; that's what they all do these days.'

Roy shook his head and shrugged his shoulders. 'I guess I must be a bit behind the times. Anyway, why don't you come on through and sit down? What do you want to drink? A white wine for you Raquel?'

She nodded. 'Thanks.'

'How about you, Tim?'

'A beer will be just fine thanks.'

'Go on through and sit down,' said Roy as he disappeared into the kitchen to fetch the drinks.

Just as Roy returned and handed the two of them their drinks, the doorbell rang again. He went to answer it. Standing on the

59

doorstep were his elder daughter Beatrice, and her husband Rick. At least Beatrice looked the same as usual: blonde, shoulder-length hair, styled in soft waves, framing her pretty, child-like face.

'Come on through,' said Roy. 'Raquel and Tim are already here.'

Before long, they were all sitting and chatting together in the lounge. Ten minutes later, when Donna announced that the starters were ready, everyone moved through to the dining room.

The discussion over lunch seemed to centre largely on a lengthy debate about the talent show, 'New Megastar' which had been shown on TV the previous evening, and every other previous Saturday evening for what seemed to Roy like many months. Roy and Donna rarely watched it, but both of the girls were avid followers.

'The judges are idiots,' declared Raquel. 'How can they put "Pentagon" bottom of the leader board? It's the best new boy band for *ages*.'

'I agree,' said Beatrice. 'And what about "Melissa"? She's rubbish – yet they've put her second.'

'Oh, I quite like her,' said Raquel, 'but I must admit I can't see how she justifies second place.'

'Well, hopefully the public vote will save "Pentagon",' said Beatrice.

Tim and Rick stayed dutifully silent as this debate continued. It was pretty clear that neither of the men shared their partners' enthusiasm for the show. Roy had very little idea what the girls were talking about, but like Donna, smiled and nodded when it seemed appropriate.

Finally, as desserts were being served, there was a lull in the conversation.

'Come on Bea,' said Donna, smiling. 'What's up?'

'What do you mean?' replied Beatrice, her expression inscrutable.

'Well first of all you actually suggest Sunday lunch all together and then every time you stop talking about that wretched talent show for a few seconds, you adopt a sort of self-satisfied smirk.' Donna leaned forward and placed her elbow on the table and her chin in her hand, inclining her head to one side. 'I'm your mother. Do you think I still don't know you? So what's up?'

Beatrice's face broke into a broad smile. 'Well I was going to wait until after lunch but … well actually, I'm pregnant.'

Donna stood up and rushed around the table to hug her daughter. 'That's wonderful news. How long?'

'Three months,' she replied, beaming.

'Boy or girl?' said Raquel.

'Well, I don't know yet … and actually, I don't think I want to. I'd like it to be a surprise.'

'This calls for a toast,' said Roy, as he leaned forward to top up everyone's glasses. 'To Bea and Rick, and their new baby.'

Everyone raised their glasses and toasted the forthcoming addition to the family.

For the next half hour or so, the conversation revolved around the subject of the new baby. Inevitably, Roy and Donna recalled various incidents which had occurred when Beatrice and Raquel were themselves babies.

'*Muuum,*' complained Raquel, 'enough … please. Not in front of Rick and Tim.' The two men chuckled.

Eventually, the conversation began to slow down and Raquel took the opportunity to say something that *she* had evidently been waiting for the right moment to add.

'Actually, we have some news as well … not as cheerful as Bea's I'm afraid.'

'What's that?' said Roy.

'Tim's leaving the army.'

There was a stunned silence for a few seconds. Roy and Donna had always understood that Tim loved his career in the army. He was often rather evasive about exactly what his role was, but Roy knew that he had risen to the rank of Captain at the relatively young age of twenty-seven and he had always assumed that by the time Tim was too old for front-line duties he would have achieved a senior command rank.

'But why?' asked Roy, looking at Tim.

Tim looked down at the table, encircling his glass with thumbs and forefingers of both hands, slowly twirling it between them. 'It's … complicated.'

'I don't understand,' said Roy.

'Look, I know I've never told you much about my duties in the army, and actually it's probably best if I still don't. Let's just say I've seen and done some things which I never thought I would … and I just can't do it anymore.'

It was abundantly clear that Tim did not wish to discuss any further the reasons for his decision.

'But what are you planning to do now?' said Roy.

Tim sighed. 'I haven't decided yet, but I'm sure something will crop up.'

And that was it. The conversation was killed stone dead, overshadowing Beatrice's happy news and bringing about an abrupt and unexpected change to the previously upbeat atmosphere.

After ten more minutes of stilted and forced conversation, both the girls, and their men, made their excuses and left.

Chapter 10

Len had been in China for just over a week. After the initial tense confrontation with Chang Wei, he had been careful to keep a low profile and avoid any unnecessary friction while carrying out his investigation. As he had hoped, Chang and his immediate managers were now paying him far less attention, and once he was able to start talking to some of the more junior management and supervisory staff – who, for the most part, seemed far less touchy than Chang – it was becoming a little easier to gain access to information.

He had already established that the finished goods warehouse contained huge stocks of product, including considerable quantities of obsolete product which would no doubt soon become the subject of another dispute between Sotoyo and Gatmarsh Automotive. He wasn't too surprised by this, but today he wanted to dig in to *why* Sotoyo's build program was so far at odds with his own company's actual requirements. He was, therefore, sitting in the office of Liang Bo, Production Control Supervisor.

Liang Bo was an amiable character, with a round face and eyes which always seemed to convey a hint of a smile. Like most of the managers Len had met, he spoke very good English.

'So can y' explain t' me exactly how y' construct the build schedule for the production line?' asked Len.

'Well,' said Bo, swivelling his computer screen round so that Len could see it clearly, 'we use this program. We input two main pieces of information: first the latest orders from your company, and second the capacity constraints of the production line.'

Len nodded, 'Ok, so can y' show me?'

'OK, let's do the schedule for next week.'

Bo spent around ten minutes inputting the data while Len observed; sure enough he appeared to be using the correct data from Gatmarsh and inputting it without modification. So far, so good. When he had finished entering all the orders, he clicked the mouse a couple of times and within a few seconds the build schedule appeared on the screen. Len leaned forward to inspect the schedule, comparing it with the purchase orders from Gatmarsh.

'But this schedule bears very little resemblance t' our actual requirement,' said Len, a puzzled frown creasing his brow. He slid the list of purchase orders in front of Bo in order to emphasise his point.

'Ah,' said Bo, 'this is because our production scheduling program takes certain other things into account.'

'I don't understand,' said Len, his frown deepening.

'Apart from the line capacity, the other main constraint is availability of components.'

'Go on,' said Len, cautiously.

'Well, once your purchase orders have been entered, the program works out what components are needed to build the requested products … if we have the parts in stock then these products are included in the build schedule. The products for which there are some components unavailable are omitted from the schedule.' He looked at Len and added, in his most reasonable tone, 'After all there's no point in asking the production people to build something if they don't have the right parts is there?'

Len did not respond to this rhetorical question, but scanned the build schedule again. 'What about this product?' he said, pointing at the screen. We have not ordered *any* of these, yet you have scheduled the line to build five hundred and seventy of them.'

'Ah, this is the other clever feature of our program,' replied Bo. 'If the capacity of the line has not been fully utilised, the program looks at which other of your products *can* be built with components which are in stock and schedules these so as to fully employ the available capacity.

Len's jaw dropped as he digested this information. No *wonder* there were always missing products in each shipment which arrived in England, no *wonder* there were always unwanted products in those shipments, and no *wonder* there were so many crippling write-offs of obsolete product.

Bo sat there smiling; quite clearly, he could see nothing whatsoever wrong with this production scheduling methodology.

Len did not want overtly to raise his concerns. Bo had been very open and accommodating and Len didn't yet want to say anything critical that might get back to Chang Wei. No, having grasped the significance of component shortages in this sorry state of affairs, he now wanted to dig into the question of *why* they were so often short of the components they needed. And he wanted to do so without attracting undue attention. This seemed like the right time to conclude his session with Liang Bo and move on to the next stage of his investigation.

'Well, thanks for your clear explanation,' said Len, smiling.

'You are most welcome.'

'Uh, I'd really like t' spend a little time with your purchasing people now. Could y' set up a meeting for me?'

'Most certainly,' he said reaching for the phone. 'I will call our purchasing manager ...'

'Oh, there's no need t' bother him,' interjected Len, wanting to keep his enquiries as low-profile as possible. 'If I could just talk t' one of the more junior people in the department, I'm sure they could show me what I need t' see.'

'Of course,' replied Bo.

He picked up the phone and, after a few seconds, spoke to someone in the strident tones of his own language. When he replaced the handset, he said 'I have arranged for you to meet with the buyer who deals with most of the components used in your products. His name is Wu Kang, and he can see you at 3 p.m. today. He speaks very good English'

'Thanks,' said Len, pushing his chair back. He shook Liang Bo's hand. 'You've been most helpful.'

Bo gave a little bow. 'You are very welcome, Mr. Douglas.'

***

Wu Kang was a small, wiry, serious-looking individual, who peered through spectacles which looked as though they had been designed at least thirty years ago: perfectly circular lenses set in a heavy-looking, thick black frame. In spite of his rather stern countenance, Len sensed no hostility or suspicion in his manner. He was in the middle of explaining to Len how he arrived at his purchasing decisions.

'The production control people enter the finished product requirements into the Material Requirements Planning Program. You understand this kind of program?'

Len nodded, 'I'm very familiar with MRP.'

Wu Kang continued. 'Well, MRP gives us a list of recommended purchase orders, taking into account EOQs ...'

'EOQs?' interjected Len. 'You mean economic order quantities?'

'Quite so. Now ...'

Len stopped him again. 'Could I possible take a look at this week's MRP output?'

'Of course.' He hefted a weighty-looking wad of computer printout onto the desk and pointed out the relevant section.

Len scrutinized the sheet and pointed at one particular line. 'Now this component shows a requirement of just over nine hundred, yet t' purchase order quantity indicated is zero.'

Wu Kang leant forward and peered at the sheet. 'Look,' he said, pointing at one of the figures on the sheet, 'the EOQ is five thousand pieces.'

'So?' enquired Len, puzzled.

'So we don't order any until we have a requirement for over five thousand.'

'But that's not how EOQ is supposed to work,' protested Len.

Wu Kang's brow furrowed in puzzlement as he pushed his heavy-rimmed spectacles up the bridge of his nose and tilted his head slightly to one side in silent enquiry.

Len continued. 'Look, surely if your actual stock of the component is lower than the quantity required for the build program, you *have* to place an order. The point about EOQ is that when you place that order you place it for' – he glanced at the sheet again – 'five thousand pieces, rather than just the nine hundred that you need right now.'

Wu Kang shook his head, 'No, that's not the way we do things: we run a lean operation here, and we don't want to fill the stock room with parts which are not going to be quickly used up.'

Len grasped the skin on his forehead between the fingers and thumb of his right hand, squeezing it and causing it to pucker as he struggled to process the logic of what he had just been told. 'What about safety stocks? Surely the MRP system has a field in which to enter a safety stock figure for each component, quite apart from the quantities needed to satisfy the actual build requirement?'

'It does,' confirmed Wu Kang, 'but we don't use it ... we set the safety stock figures to zero. As I said earlier, we run a lean operation here.'

Len's jaw dropped; this was madness. In an instant it was clear why they were always running short of components.

As Len struggled to frame his response to these disclosures, the phone rang. Wu Kang picked it up and spoke in his own language for a few seconds.

When he replaced the handset he turned to Len and said, 'Can you excuse me for a few minutes? This is something I really must attend to at once.'

Len nodded, still reeling from the revelations which had just unfolded.

So now he found himself alone and unobserved in Wu Kang's office. This was a golden opportunity to see if he could unearth any other useful information. He turned to the computer on the desk and nudged the mouse. When the screen sprang to life he could see that it was displaying a Bill of Materials – or BOM – for one of Gatmarsh's products. Fortunately all the main headers were in English – he guessed it was probably an American program. He began scrolling up and down and exploring links to other documents. Suddenly, he came across one labelled 'Shadow BOM'. He clicked on the link and was immediately taken to another document, which at first glance appeared to be very similar to the one he had just left. As he studied this document he realised that it was a version of the BOM he had just been looking at, but this time there were alternative components listed alongside many of the originally specified components. The alternatives were, in every case, cheaper. He scrolled down to the bottom of the document where he found summary costing information. The original BOM resulted in a total material cost for the product of six hundred and ninety Yuan, whereas the shadow BOM resulted in a cost of five hundred and seventy-two Yuan.

This was dynamite: it explained Kevin's findings, back in the UK, of inferior components being fitted, and no doubt had something to do with the irregular costing information that Mick had been complaining about. He looked at his watch. Wu Kang had been gone for six minutes; Len couldn't risk digging any further right now. He pulled from his pocket a USB memory stick and plugged it in to the computer before copying all of the folders which appeared to relate to BOMs and product costing. He hurriedly withdrew the memory stick and slipped it back into his pocket before attempting to navigate back to the screen which the computer had originally been displaying.

He couldn't find it! Desperately, he fumbled with the mouse as he dived this way and that, trying to retrace his steps, but getting increasingly lost. He heard footsteps approaching – he was out of time now. As he looked up, anxiously, he saw the door handle rotate and the door start to open.

Chapter 11

In desperation, Len yanked the power cord from the back of the machine; the screen went blank just as Wu Kang stepped through the door.

'So sorry about that,' said Kang as he sat down. He glanced at the computer, his brow creasing in a puzzled frown.

'Er … terribly sorry,' said Len, 'but I accidentally caught t' power cord and pulled it out of the machine while reaching down for me briefcase.'

A momentary shadow flitted across Kang's rodent-like features, but in a moment it had passed, to be replaced by a toothy smile. 'No problem Mr. Douglas.' He plugged the cable back in and restarted the computer. While his machine was booting up, he turned back to Len. 'Now where were we?'

'Well, t' be honest, I thing we've covered more or less everything I wanted t' see for now, but maybe I can talk t' y' again if anything else comes up?'

Kang's eyes narrowed for a moment and his mouth puckered. Was he suspicious? In a heartbeat, though, the fleeting expression had evaporated.

'Of course,' he said, smiling once more. 'I'm glad to have been of assistance.'

Len gathered his things together and stood up, preparing to leave. Kang's expression was inscrutable behind his heavy-set spectacles as he stood up and shook Len's hand.

'If you need anything else … anything at all, please don't hesitate to let me know.'

'OK,' said Len, anxious to get away as quickly as possible, 'and thanks again.'

His heart was pounding and he felt a cold prickle of sweat down his back as he stepped out of the office. Had the little man realised what he had been doing? Something in his demeanour bothered Len.

***

It was just after midnight. Tim and Raquel sat in the back of the taxi, a dim yellow glow coming and going erratically as they passed under the streetlamps. Raquel was an English teacher, and they had been out to dinner with a group of the teachers from Raquel's school, together with some of their other halves. The occasion was a leaving do for Sandra Baker, the PE teacher, who was getting married soon and would be moving to Plymouth where her fiancé lived and worked. Raquel was to be a bridesmaid at the forthcoming wedding.

'She's pretty isn't she?' said Raquel.

'Who?' replied Tim, in the most innocent tone he could muster.

'Oh, right … like you didn't notice … Sandra of course.' Her tone was playful and light-hearted.

Of course Tim had noticed. Raquel's friend had striking model-good looks: large, deep-blue eyes; finely sculpted cheekbones; and full, sensuous lips. Her jet-black, straight, shoulder-length hair was full and glossy. The fact that she had chosen to wear a dress with a low-cut neckline, displaying a glimpse of cleavage, had made it all the more difficult for Tim not to keep glancing across at her.

'Oh, yes I suppose she is pretty, but you know I only have eyes for you.'

'Liar!' exclaimed Raquel, her eyes widening and her eyebrows lifting in an expression which conveyed incredulity at Tim's audacity in pretending he hadn't noticed her friend's striking good looks. She gave him a playful punch in the ribs.

'Alright, she is a bit of a stunner, I admit ... but not a patch on you.'

Raquel giggled. 'You are a liar, Tim Steele ... but I love you for it.'

Tim leaned over and kissed her neck, his hand sliding slowly up her thigh, insinuating its way under the hem of her skirt. She clamped her hand over his, halting its progress.

She wriggled away from him before putting her lips to his ear and whispering, 'Tim, not here. Look ... the driver can see us in his mirror.'

'Can't help myself,' whispered Tim back. 'You're looking soo sexy tonight.'

'Behave yourself!' she said, trying to keep her voice to a whisper. 'Look we're nearly home now.'

Tim did as he was told, removing his wandering hand from her leg and sitting up straight in the seat. Raquel smoothed her skirt down and adjusted her position so as to sit as primly as possible. Tim caught a glimpse of the cabbie's face in the mirror; he was clearly trying to stifle a smile. Tim felt a little embarrassed and swiftly moved to turn the conversation to other subjects.

'Your dad's face was a picture when you showed him your piercing,' he said. 'I don't think he approved, do you?'

Raquel laughed. 'Oh he's alright ... a bit old-fashioned maybe, but he always comes around in the end. I think he sometimes forgets I'm a grown woman now and no longer his little girl. He's just a bit over-protective on occasion.'

'Nothing wrong with that ... it shows he cares. He's a good dad, Raquel.'

'I know,' she said, smiling.

The cab pulled up outside their house with a faint squeal from the brakes. Tim paid the cabbie and they stumbled out of the car – a little unsteadily, for they had both had quite a bit to drink that evening. As the cab pulled away they looked at each other and exchanged a knowing smile before both stealing a glance at the window of the house next door. Sure enough the curtain – which had clearly been held a little to one side – swung back into place, swaying for a second or so before coming to a standstill. They looked at each other and burst out laughing, clutching each other for support.

'Wow! She's up late tonight,' said Tim, still laughing. 'OK, let's give her something to look at.' He gathered Raquel in his arms, pulling her to him and smothering her with a long, passionate kiss, his left hand sliding up and down over her buttocks.

Raquel was clearly feeling as eager as Tim was, but after a few seconds she extricated herself from the clinch. 'Tim, that's *so* mean. Beryl is a good neighbour, she's just ... inquisitive, that's all.'

'If you say so,' replied Tim, grudgingly. In his opinion Beryl Perkins was just *too* damned nosy, but she was harmless enough, and he had to admit that her incessant curtain-twitching was actually a subject of constant amusement to the two of them.

'Come on,' said Raquel, taking Tim's hand and flashing him a mischievous smile, 'I'm ready for bed.'

Tim didn't need to be asked twice.

Chapter 12

Roy, Kevin, and Mick were seated around the large oval table in the boardroom, discussing the interim report which Len Douglas had sent, detailing his initial findings.

'So,' said Roy, 'it's easy to see why their delivery performance is so poor and how we keep getting hit with these horrendous stock write-offs. Basically their purchasing and production control methods are geared up to minimise their component costs and maximise the utilisation of their production facilities. They are making practically no attempt at all to meet our actual delivery requirements.'

'What's more,' added Mick, 'we are stuck wit' a contract which makes *us* liable for t' cost o' any stock write-offs, even though they're almost entirely caused by Sotoyo's incompetence and contempt.'

Roy nodded. 'Hmm … how the hell the previous management allowed *that* clause to be included, Christ knows.' He puffed out his cheeks and exhaled through pursed lips in exasperation.

Kevin, who had not spoken so far, offered his opinion. 'I think we can get out of this contract if we want to.'

'Go on,' said Roy, his interest piqued.

'The substitution of inferior, non-specified components,' continued Kevin, 'is a clear breach of contract. They have quite

74

callously compromised the performance and reliability of our products in order to save money.'

'Hmm,' said Roy, 'that may indeed offer us a way to get out of the contract, but you can bet they would contest it vigorously. Nevertheless I agree we probably do have enough evidence to prove breach of contract if we decide to go down that route.'

'I think so too,' said Mick.

'OK, let's park that one for a moment,' said Roy, 'because your mention of cost savings, Kevin, brings me to the next point I wanted to explore. I want to know what's happening to these supposed cost savings, because we're sure as hell not seeing any benefit from them.' He turned to Mick. 'Have you had any luck untangling all the files that Len sent you?'

Mick nodded, a grim smile on his face. 'I sure have, and you're not going ta like this.'

'Go on,' encouraged Roy.

Mick swivelled his laptop around so that Roy and Kevin could see the screen. 'OK,' he said, dragging his finger across the track pad and tapping it to bring up the document he wanted to go through. 'Len had already identified that they have two different versions o' t' Bill o' Materials.' The other two nodded. 'Well actually they have *three*.'

Roy was puzzled. 'Three? Why the hell would they do that?'

'First they have this one,' said Mick pointing at the screen. 'They call it their "Costing Bill". It seems ta assume that all t' components are bought in tiny quantities – and hence at the highest prices. This is t' one they use ta determine the cost charged ta us.'

'OK ...' said Roy, cautiously. 'What's the second one?'

Mick brought up a new document. 'This is t' "Production Bill". It's similar ta the first one except that it includes much larger minimum purchase quantities, and consequently many o' t' components are much cheaper.

'And the third,' said Roy, 'must be this "Shadow Bill" that Len discovered.'

'Yes, this one also contains t' larger minimum purchase quantities, but in addition, cheaper, non-specified components have been substituted for many o' t' original items. I assume that this is t' one used ta determine their actual purchasing and production practices.'

'So,' said Roy as he tried to process and summarise what he had been hearing, 'they have been charging us an inflated price based on unrealistically small component purchase quantities?'

'Yes.'

'Then they actually apply very much higher minimum component purchase quantities to get the best possible component prices?'

'Yes they do … ta the detriment of delivery performance and write-off costs.'

'And then, wherever they can, they substitute inferior, non-approved components to save even more money?'

'That's about t' size of it,' agreed Mick.

Roy leaned forward and placed both hands palm-downward on the table. His jaw was grimly-set as he declared, 'The bastards … I won't let them get away with this.'

'It gets worse,' said Mick.

'Worse?' interjected Kevin. 'How could it be worse?'

'I've been trying ta figure out where these "savings" actually go.'

'And?' said Roy.

'Well, it looks as though t' savings made by applying very large EOQs – Economic Order Quantities – go straight inta Sotoyo's coffers.'

'As you'd expect,' said Roy.

'But here's the really sinister bit.' said Mick, glancing from Roy to Kevin in turn. 'It seems that the further savings due to substituting inferior components go into an entirely separate bank account … completely detached from the company's finances.'

'So what exactly are you saying?' said Roy, but even as he uttered the words he realised what the answer must be.

'What I'm saying,' replied Mick, 'is that someone – possibly Chang Wei – is creaming off huge sums of money for their personal gain.'

Chapter 13

Len sat alone at the bar in his hotel, nursing a single malt whisky. It was very quiet tonight. Idly, he twirled the glass between thumb and middle finger, watching the amber liquid swirl around, clinging to the sides of the glass for a moment before trickling back down, until he decided to disturb its equilibrium again by twirling the glass once more. He glanced up at the shelves behind the bar, the myriad bottles of various liqueurs illuminated by the subtle blue glow of concealed lighting. Maybe he would work his way through the entire selection tonight.

He was a little disappointed that the attractive barmaid who was usually on duty – with whom Len felt he had struck up quite a rapport – had been replaced by a tall, thin, unsmiling man who seemed disinclined to engage in any conversation, even though he spoke pretty good English and Len was just about his only customer that evening.

He took a small sip of his whisky, swirling the spirit around his mouth slowly, savouring the sharp, smoky, peaty tang for several long seconds before swallowing and letting the fiery liquid course down his throat. He exhaled a long, contemplative sigh as he set down the glass and began running over, in his mind, what his investigation of Sotoyo had so far revealed.

He now he knew why the deliveries which arrived in the UK invariably bore little resemblance to what was actually required. He had also confirmed the deliberate substitution of inferior components, compromising the reliability of his company's products, and he had discovered serious irregularities in product costing. He had been unable, however, to figure out exactly what happened to the money saved by substituting the cheaper components. Maybe Mick would be able to figure it out when he trawled through the files which Len had sent back to England.

'You look bit sad,' came the heavily accented female voice from his left, startling Len from his introspective musing.

He turned to see that a small, slim Chinese woman, aged perhaps around thirty, had occupied the bar stool alongside him; lost in his private thoughts, he hadn't even registered her arrival. Her pointed chin, Cupid's bow lips, well defined cheekbones, and dark, slanted eyes lent her a sultry oriental beauty which immediately grabbed Len's attention. Her hair was swept back from her face and piled up on top of her head, secured with what looked like long wooden dowels. Unbidden, Len's eyes roamed swiftly up and down her body. She wore a blue and green patterned silk dress with a slit in the side which showed an enticing length of her slim, well-toned thigh as she adjusted her position on the bar stool to swivel around and face Len more directly. In an instant, the problems with which he had been wrestling evaporated from his mind.

'Uh, yes … I guess. Well, not exactly sad … just thinking about some business issues.'

'Oh, you here on business?' Her voice had an attractive lilt to it, rising and falling in pitch as she formed the words in slightly halting English.

'Aye, I've been here for a couple of weeks.'

'You got funny accent … you Australian?'

Len laughed. 'Well you got funny accent too.' She giggled, raising an elegantly manicured hand to cover her mouth and dipping her head, shyly. 'No, I'm from England … North East actually; we all talk funny up there.'

Her face broke into a luminous smile, with little dimples appearing in her cheeks. She extended her small, dainty hand. 'My name Bao Yu. You call me Yu.'

Len shook her hand. 'Len Douglas. Pleased t' meet y'.'

'I here on business too – cosmetics – my company based in Beijing, but we got suppliers here in Shenzhen.'

'Are you here on your own then?'

'Yes, for three days.'

'I see. Well … in that case, can I get y' a drink?'

She smiled prettily and swivelled round a little further towards him on the barstool, in doing so exposing another inch of thigh. 'You most kind man. I like Gin Tonic.'

Len motioned to the barman. 'A double Gin and Tonic please, and I'll have another whisky.' The man nodded disinterestedly in acknowledgement of the request, and turned away to prepare the drinks.

When the drinks arrived Bao Yu leaned forward and clinked glasses with Len. Her neckline was high – right up to her neck – but the silk fabric was closely tailored around her small, pert breasts and the nipple outline was plain to see. With a considerable effort, Len raised his eyes and focussed on her face.

She smiled that enigmatic smile once more. 'How you say? Cheers?'

'Yes, Cheers,' he responded, smiling, now quite captivated by this enticing little sexpot.

She took a sip of her drink before asking, 'So you stay here in hotel?'

'Yes … you?'

'Yes, I stay here too.'

Len's heart gave a little jump, and he felt an involuntary tingle in his loins. They were both staying alone in the same hotel and Daphne was thousands of miles away. His next words came almost without conscious thought.

'Er … have you eaten yet?'

'No.'

'Well, as we are both on our own, would y' like t' join me for dinner?'

She placed one elbow on the bar and propped her chin on the back of her hand, tilting her head to one side. 'That be lovely. I hungry … I got big appetite.'

As she said it, the tip of her tongue appeared between her lips and she ran it back and forth over them, leaving a glistening sheen. The gesture was subtle – nothing too overt – but Len was sure the *double entendre* was intentional.

'Do y' know any nice restaurants nearby?'

She shook her head. 'Why not just hotel restaurant? I not want to be too late to bed.'

There she goes again, thought Len. He drained his glass and stood up – a little awkwardly, as he was now trying to conceal the erection within his trousers which was growing by the minute. He hadn't had sex for more than two weeks – which was a very long time indeed by Len's standards – and this little minx had, by now, sent his hormones into overdrive.

'After you,' he said, offering her his hand to help her down from the tall bar stool.

She slid from the stool and smoothed down her silk dress which had ridden up a little while she was seated. She wriggled her hips slightly from side to side, running her hands down over the thin fabric, removing the horizontal creases which had formed while she had been seated.

'There, that better,' she said, smiling. 'Let's go eat.'

***

Two hours later they were making their way – a little unsteadily, as they were both rather drunk – to Len's room; Len was clutching a half-empty bottle of champagne. As he fumbled to insert the key card into the slot, Yu leant her body against his back and her hand snaked around his waist, finding his erection and massaging it gently through the fabric of his trousers. This did nothing to help Len's aim with the key card.

'Ooh,' she cooed, 'you big boy. What you thinking about then?'

Len didn't answer; he was desperately trying to concentrate all his efforts on persuading the wayward key card into its slot. Finally he succeeded and they both stumbled into the room, Len closing the door behind them with a kick of his foot.

Yu was tiny, and as she wrapped her arms around his neck she had to stand on tiptoe while he bent forward as she kissed him full on the lips, her tongue curling and thrusting within his mouth. As he pulled her to him, and ran his hands over her firm, toned buttocks and tiny waist he was acutely aware of the striking contrast with the feel of Daphne's body, with her full, voluptuous figure, generous breasts, and soft, yielding flesh.

She stepped away from him and turned her back towards him, looking over her shoulder with a mischievous smile. 'You help with zip?'

With fumbling fingers, he slid the zip down. She turned to face him; slowly and deliberately, she allowed her dress to slide to the floor, stepping out of it wearing only a tiny black thong. Len's mouth was dry as sand as his eyes roamed over the figure in front of him. She had the body of an athlete: wiry and muscular, yet still feminine and alluring. Her breasts were small and firm, yet the nipples were large and stood out proudly, their dark colour contrasting starkly against the pale, waxy tone of her skin. She then began pulling the wooden dowels from her hair, allowing it to fall over her shoulders and almost down to her waist.

'You like?'

Len nodded, dumbly.

'You want see what's in here?' she said, hooking a forefinger in the top of her thong and pulling it slightly away from her body, looking downward as if taking a surreptitious peek herself. Len swallowed, but did not reply. 'Oh, I see you do,' she said, looking down and pointing at the straining bulge in his trousers.

She slid the tiny panties down, wriggling her hips from side to side as she did so, before stepping out of them. Her pubic hair was jet black, neatly trimmed to a thin vertical strip which led his eye down to the pink lips below, just visible as she stood with her legs a little apart. She walked slowly toward him and knelt down in front of him.

'We need get this out,' she said, unbuckling his belt. 'Looks like something burst otherwise.'

She reached forward and unzipped his trousers, releasing his straining member from the confines of his clothing. 'Wow, you really are big boy,' she said, laughing, as she tried to encircle his penis with her tiny hand, unable to make thumb and middle finger meet around its girth. She began artfully flicking her tongue back and forth across the tip, evoking from him a deep, husky groan. She looked up at him from beneath long lashes and took him fully into her mouth, keeping her tiny hand wrapped around the base as she began moving her head slowly back and forth, occasionally moving back and teasing him again with her tongue. Len put his hands behind her head, pulling him to her, encouraging her, but after a few more seconds she let go of him, stood up, and stepped back. He groaned in dismay and frustration.

'Not too fast,' she said, 'I not want you come just yet.'

She stood up and picked up the bottle of champagne from the table, raising it in front of her and slowly tilting it, allowing the liquid to pour over her breasts and down her torso. As the champagne trickled over her stomach, the sheen created picked up the light, accentuating the toned, symmetrical muscle pack. Len was mesmerised, and completely oblivious to the rapidly spreading puddle of champagne on the carpet.

She fixed him with a mischievous smile. 'You want suck champagne off my tits?'

Len very much wanted to suck champagne off her tits.

He pushed her back until she was sitting on the edge of the bed and knelt down in front of her, taking one of those large, swollen nipples in his mouth. The taste of her blended with the taste of the champagne to create an intoxicating cocktail. She gave a little moan of pleasure, placing her hand behind his neck and pulling him to her. She guided him to her other breast where he greedily sucked the champagne from her once again. After a few more moments she gently pushed him away from her breast.

'You want fuck me now?'

Yes, Len was very sure he wanted to fuck her now. He eased her back onto the bed and spread her legs apart as he moved forward and on top of her. Quite suddenly, and with surprising strength, given her diminutive stature, she flipped him over to one side and moved on top of him, straddling him.

'You naughty boy. I want be in charge tonight.'

With that, she grasped his penis with one hand and guided it into her as she slowly lowered herself onto him. He placed his hands either side of her tiny waist, pulling her down gently as he settled her into position.

'Now you let me do it all,' she said, her voice now low and husky, in contrast to its previously higher-pitched lilting tone.

And she did. She moved with easy confidence, squeezing him and teasing him as she moved back and forth, her hips undulating, her long silky hair falling carelessly across his face and chest, occasionally obscuring her own face completely. Len was in seventh heaven. Before long he was begging her to bring him to the point of release.

Just when he was nearly there, she eased herself off him. The urge to pull her back down and finish it was almost irresistible but she was very much in charge now, and he did not do so.

'Now you suck my pussy,' she said, moving up, walking on her knees until she was in position to gently lower herself onto his face. This invitation went a long way towards mitigating his disappointment at the way she had lifted herself off of him just when he was almost ready to let go.

He began probing and licking her, and as her moans became louder and more urgent, it spurred him on to more and more enthusiastic tongue gymnastics. Gradually her moans turned to screams, louder and louder until at last she gave a prolonged, almost feline wail, sliding slowly back from his face, now straddling his chest. She fixed him with an intense cat-like stare from those dark, slanting eyes.

'You still ready fuck me?' she said, panting furiously. She wriggled back down until she was on top of his thighs, grasping his penis and giving it a few encouraging strokes up and down.

Len didn't need much encouragement; he was still very much ready, as once again she guided him into her and sank down on him.

She skilfully brought him nearer and nearer to the point of release once more before slowing her movements right down and saying, in hushed tones, 'You ready now?'

Len didn't need to answer. She smiled that mischievous smile once more and began moving her body urgently back and forth until Len finally let go, with a loud groan. She eased herself off him and slid down alongside him.

The last thing he remembered before drifting off to sleep was the feel of her tiny hand massaging his now-flaccid member and her teeth nibbling gently at his earlobe.

***

He wasn't sure what exactly had woken him, but he was aware of soft shuffling noises gradually impinging on his consciousness. He rolled over and extended his arm, expecting to find Yu's firm little body within his reach, but there was nothing there; the bed where she had lain was still warm though. Tentatively, he opened his eyes, just a crack, to see that the soft light of dawn was diffusing though the gap around the edge of the curtains at the window. He closed his eyes, but became suddenly aware, through his closed eyelids, of a sudden flash of light. He propped himself up on one elbow and forced his eyes fully open. The first thing he saw was the back of Bao Yu's naked body as she hunched over the desk in the corner of the room. The sight of her taught, toned buttocks, and the fleeting glimpse of plump lips between her legs as she bent forward, evoked a pleasant tingle in his groin, even at this time of the morning. But what the hell was going on here?

'Yu, what are you doing?' he croaked, through parched lips.

She whirled around and froze, like a startled rabbit caught in the headlights of an approaching car. Her hand shot behind her back as though she was concealing something. 'Nothing … I just got up to use toilet.'

Len jumped up and approached her. His briefcase was open on the desk and there were papers strewn everywhere.

Chapter 14

Roy and Donna were going out for dinner at their favourite restaurant. *El Girasol* was an authentic Spanish restaurant and they had been coming here for years. They didn't often eat out midweek, but it was Donna's fiftieth birthday, so that evening they made an exception. Donna had steadfastly refused to entertain the idea of a big party on her fiftieth, but the idea of a nice intimate dinner – just the two of them – suited her just fine.

As they stepped through the door the proprietor, Emilio, came rushing up to them. *'¡Hola Señores! Bienvenidos de nuevo,'* he gushed.

They smiled and shrugged off their coats, passing them to Emilio, who laid them over his arm.

'Hola Emilio ¿Qué tal estás?' said Roy.

This was, in fact, the entire extent of Roy's knowledge of Spanish but Emilio was effusive in his praise. *'Muy bien, Señor Groves.* So now you speak my language like a native, I think.'

Donna giggled. 'I don't think so; he's been practicing that for the last hour or so.'

'No pasa nada – para mi es perfecto,' enthused Emilio.

Initial Greetings over, Emilio showed them to their table. They sat down and surveyed their surroundings: dark wood panelling; evocative paintings of flamenco dancers and toreadors; and subdued, intimate lighting. The décor never changed, but Roy and Donna never tired of its gentle charm.

The waitress who came to take their drinks order was also Spanish. Her black hair was scraped tightly back from her face and tied in a ponytail. Her fine, almost Arabic-looking, features and olive-coloured skin lent her a striking, sultry beauty. Her face broke into a warm smile as she spoke. Her English was near-perfect, though heavily-accented. *'Hola Señores.* It is very nice to see you again.'

'Hello Elvira, how are you?' said Donna.

She gave a little nod. 'I'm very well, *gracias*. And you?'

'We're fine,' replied Roy.

'We don't often see you in the middle of the week,' said Elvira. 'Is it a special occasion?'

'Well, yes it is actually … it's Donna's birthday.'

'Oh, ¡feliz cumpleaños!' exclaimed Elvira.

'Thanks,' replied Donna, smiling.

'What would you like to drink?' said Elvira.

'Well, as it's a special occasion I thought perhaps a bottle of champagne?' said Roy, looking enquiringly at Donna.

'Mmm … yes please,' said Donna.

'A bottle of Verve Clicquot, then,' said Roy.

Elvira nodded, smiling, and withdrew to get the champagne.

As Roy gazed across the table at his wife, her face illuminated by the flickering glow from the single candle in the centre of the table, he was struck – as he often was – by how kindly the years had treated her. Her delicate features, finely shaped nose, and soft brown eyes lent her a gentle beauty which was barely dimmed by the passage of time. Apart from a few fine lines around the eyes and at the edges of her mouth, and a little grey in her dark-blonde hair, she looked much as she had when he had first met her, some thirty years ago.

'What?' she said, her expression quizzical, as she picked up on Roy's wistful gaze.

He smiled. 'I just can't believe you're fifty.'

'Neither can I … I always regarded fifty as positively ancient. Yet here I am.'

'Here you are,' repeated Roy, 'and you look as beautiful as ever.'

'Oh, for goodness' sake …' she began, laughing, but she didn't finish her sentence; Elvira had returned with the champagne.

Roy took a sip and nodded his approval. Elvira filled their glasses and then took their food orders.

They raised their glasses and clinked them together. 'I meant what I said,' declared Roy.

'Flatterer,' she replied. 'But thanks anyway.'

The restaurant was starting to fill up now, and the many separate quiet conversations began to meld together creating that gentle background hum which, far from intruding on their conversation, created a blanket of privacy, ensuring they could chat without being overheard.

They had been reminiscing about their student days and their early married life, but when they had finished their starters, Donna changed the subject. 'I saw Gabby again today.'

Roy dabbed his mouth with his napkin. 'Chuck's wife? How's she holding up?'

'Not very well I'm afraid. She hardly knows anyone here in England; I'm now probably the nearest she's got to a friend here.'

Roy reached across and squeezed her hand. 'It's really good of you to get involved and to try to help her.'

'It's what anyone would do in similar circumstances.'

'No, it really isn't … not *anyone* … in fact, not most people. It's a really kind thing you have done.'

She gave a little shrug. 'Well anyway, Chuck's body has been flown back to the USA. The funeral's in Boston on Tuesday. She's flying on Friday and she's decided to stay out there.'

'What … permanently?'

'Uh, huh … she's given notice on their rented house here and she's having all her things crated up and sent back to Boston.'

'It's a very sudden decision … I mean even before the funeral has been held. She must still be grieving. Do you think she's rushing into it too fast?'

'I don't think so,' opined Donna. 'All of her family and friends are out there, after all.' She paused for a few moments, absently twirling her wine glass, holding its stem between thumb and index finger. 'She was really looking forward to making a new life in England, but she says that now there's no point … without Chuck.' A tear began to well up in the corner of Donna's eye. 'There's nothing for her here now that …' Her voice caught in her throat.

Roy reached across and took her hand. 'Oh Donna, you've done everything you can. What happened to Chuck was tragic, but it's done – nothing can bring him back. Gabby will have to try to rebuild her life as best she can, and I'm sure you're right – the best place for her to do that is in familiar surrounding among family and friends.'

Donna dabbed her eyes with her napkin. 'I know that, but well I'd like … I'd like to do one last thing for her before she resettles in the States.' She looked at Roy with an expression which was almost one of pleading.

Roy inclined his head to one side, curious. 'What's that?'

'Could I go with her?'

For a second or so, Roy did not quite understand what Donna was saying. 'Go with her?' he said, '… to Boston?'

'I mean travel with her … just until she meets up with people she knows. Then I could come straight back.'

'Well, yes, I suppose if that's what you want to do …'

'The thing is, she's absolutely in pieces. I'm worried about her making that long journey on her own with no-one to talk to … no support.'

Roy smiled. 'Of course you can go with her. That's a wonderful thing to do.'

'I know the flights will be expensive at short notice but …'

'Shhh … don't worry about it.'

Her face broke into a luminous smile and she stretched both hands across the table to grasp Roy's. 'Thanks. I knew you'd understand.'

Roy was silent for a few moments as he thought about what Donna had just told him. Then he said, 'Look, it's only right and proper that someone should represent the company at the funeral. I'd go myself if things weren't so hectic at work just now, but I wasn't particularly close to Chuck and I really don't know Gabby at all. Why don't you attend the funeral on my behalf?'

'Well, I … I'm not actually part of the company am I?'

'You're the managing director's wife. That's good enough isn't it?'

'Well … yes, I suppose it is.'

'In any case, you can't just fly straight back without giving your body a few days to get over the jetlag.'

'Well, that's true.'

'And I'm sure you'd feel much happier knowing that Gabby was properly settled back with her friends and family before you say goodbye.'

Her face relaxed and she smiled. 'I would. Thanks so much.'

Roy was gratified to see the weight of anxiety slip from Donna's shoulders as her mood began to lighten and, once again, the conversation began to turn to happier subjects.

Roy had his own anxiety to deal with, though he was trying desperately to conceal it. The moment was fast approaching when he would have to confront Chang. First, though, he had to get Len home; he feared for Len's safety if he were still to be in China once Roy had fully revealed his hand.

Chapter 15

Len stepped forward and grabbed Yu's shoulder with his right hand, whilst moving his left around her waist and seizing her wrist, which was held behind her back.

'What are y' hiding there?'

As he forced her hand around in front of her, he could see that she was holding a tiny camera. He snatched it away from her and laid it on the desk.

'Are y' photographing my papers?' he demanded, now gripping her wrist tightly.

As she struggled to break free of his grip, her small breasts, with their still-protruding nipples, jiggled from side to side, and in spite of himself, Len felt another surge in his groin; he did his best to ignore it. Yu said nothing, but the expression in her eyes was desperate, pleading.

'What are y' doing?' he insisted, now twisting her wrist until she cried out in pain.

'Sorry, sorry. They make me do it.'

'Who? Who's making you do it?' He gripped her wrist more tightly and twisted it a little further. She gave a sharp yelp.

'OK, OK ... it's Chang Wei ... he got my little girl. He say he hurt her if I not do what he says.'

'Chang's kidnapped your daughter?' said Len, incredulous. He relaxed the pressure on her wrist.

She nodded, sobbing now, her eyes full of fear. 'He say I got to copy all your papers so he can see what you up to.'

Len's mind was reeling now. Chang had appeared to lose interest in him after the first couple of days, but if he was prepared to go to these lengths then nothing could be further from the truth. He released her wrist. She massaged it with her other hand.

'Get dressed and get out,' he ordered.

Yu began gathering up her clothes from where they were carelessly strewn on the floor, but she was sobbing desperately now.

'What?' said Len, moved by her obvious distress, in spite of her duplicity.

When she replied she sounded terrified, hysterical. 'If he knows you found me out and I have nothing for him, he … he…' She was hyperventilating, her breath coming in short, desperate gasps.

'What?' he demanded. 'What will he do?'

She took several seconds to gain enough control of her breathing to reply. 'My little girl … he hurt her bad. Maybe me too.'

Maybe it was her pretty face, or maybe the desperate look in her eyes, but Len was inclined to believe her. Bao Yu was being used, cynically, by Chang Wei; she was just an innocent victim dragged into this affair solely because she had the obvious assets to entrap a man easily.

'OK,' he said, 'here's what we're going to do …' She looked up at him, attentively, wiping tears away with the back of her hand, sniffling and nodding weakly. 'First, I want to see you delete everything you have copied so far.'

Yu abandoned the bundle of clothes which she was holding to her breast and deposited it on the bed. Still sobbing, she moved towards the desk and picked up the camera. With fumbling hands, she erased everything on the memory card in her camera. Len checked the camera carefully to make sure she had done so. He then shuffled through all the papers on the desk and in his briefcase, sorting out those which gave no clues as to what he had uncovered regarding Sotoyo's illicit practices.

'Right,' he said, passing the pile of papers to her, 'y' can copy all of these. Y' tell Chang that everything went according t' plan and we had a nice breakfast together. This was all y' could find t' photograph. Understand?'

She nodded, still sniffing back tears.

'I'm going t' give y' something else too,' he said, sitting down at the desk and lifting the lid of his laptop. 'Get dressed and take your photos while I do this.'

Obediently, she gathered up her clothes from the bed and began dressing.

Once the computer sprang to life, Len began re-organising his files, creating what looked like a master document folder, but which excluded all the incriminating evidence pertaining to Sotoyo. While he was doing this, Yu busied herself photographing all the papers which Len has given her.

It took Len about fifteen minutes to finish what he was doing; he plugged in a USB memory stick and copied the newly created folder.

He turned to Bao Yu and handed her the memory stick. 'Tell him this is what y' managed t' copy from me computer.'

She smiled, sweetly. 'Thank you. You save my little girl.' She turned her back to him and looked over her shoulder. 'You do my zipper?' Len obliged, once again feeling a tingle of arousal as his fingers brushed the ridged outline of her spine.

She gathered together all the papers she had copied and slipped them into her shoulder bag. As she prepared to leave, she said, 'Thank you. You nice man – I would have fucked you anyway … and you got big cock.'

'Oh, get out,' said Len waving her away, dismissively. Actually though, he rather liked the compliment.

When Yu had left, Len decided to check his emails to see whether there was any news from England regarding the various files he had sent back. He immediately settled on one from Roy headed 'Urgent recall to England.'

To: Len Douglas
From: Roy Groves
Subject: Urgent recall to England

Len,

The files you sent back indicate serious financial irregularities at Sotoyo. We have reason to believe that Chang may even be involved in fraudulent criminal activity. I think you have probably already unearthed everything we need and I want to confront Chang as soon as possible. However I am concerned for your personal safety if I do so while you are still out there.

I therefore suggest that you take the first available flight home, and don't say anything to Chang until you are safely back.

Regards,
Roy

Given everything else that had just unfolded, Len did not need to be told twice.

Chapter 16

It took Len less than thirty minutes trawling the airline websites to find and book a flight to Heathrow. It was early Saturday morning, and his flight was due to leave the following day so he wouldn't be missed until Monday.

With his flight safely booked, he began to think about Bao Yu's daughter. What sort of bastard would stoop to kidnapping and threatening a little girl just to get hold of copies of the documents which he had in his possession? Len was concerned now that when Chang learned that he had cut short his visit and returned to England he might well realise that Yu had been found out. What might he do then?

As he mulled over this question, he became increasingly concerned for the safety of Yu's daughter, and that of Yu herself. Notwithstanding the fact that she had tried to entrap and betray him, he felt a compelling desire to protect her. He wasn't really sure why – other than that she had just given him one of the best sexual experiences of his life. But then Len was the first to admit that he was rather prone to allowing his dick to rule his head.

After some minutes' deliberation, he turned back to his laptop and composed an email.

<u>To: Chang Wei</u>
<u>From: Len Douglas</u>
<u>Subject: Early return to UK</u>

Wei,

I'm afraid I have had to cut short my visit due to an unexpected family bereavement. I have to return to England immediately and unfortunately will be unable to meet with you before I go. I will, however forward my report and conclusions on my visit as soon as possible, and if it is deemed necessary to make any further investigations, I will be in contact to arrange a further visit.

I would like to take the opportunity to thank you for your hospitality and co-operation during my visit. Please extend my thanks also to your staff who assisted me while I was there.

Regards,
Len Douglas.

He hoped it would be enough to convince Chang that his departure was nothing to do with Yu's visit.

He moved the cursor over the 'send' button, but as his finger hovered over the track pad, he hesitated. He changed his mind and hit 'Save draft' instead. He didn't want Chang to read this until he was home and safe. He would delay sending it until after he arrived back in England.

***

Chang Wei did not go into work on Monday morning; he had an important meeting which was best held away from the factory. He sat in a comfortable, low-slung, white leather sofa in his opulent, western-style home. He took one last draw on his cigar, and extinguished the stub with a slow, deliberate grinding action against the base of the grey, smoked-glass ashtray on the arm of the sofa. Bao Yu sat facing him on the opposite side of a low, glass-topped coffee table. She no longer wore the kind of traditional Chinese clothing and hairstyle that she had when she had met Len. Now she wore skin-tight blue jeans and a stretchy, white tee shirt which clung to her small, firm breasts. Her hair fell carelessly down over her shoulders, long and straight. She hooked it back behind her ears before leaning forward and sliding the sheaf of papers across the table towards Chang. He thought he detected a slight nervousness in her eyes, but it was gone in an instant.

'So,' he said, 'did everything go OK?'

'No problems,' she replied, smiling. 'I copy everything in his briefcase, and' – she delved into her handbag and produced the memory stick – 'I got lot of stuff from his computer.'

He paused for a moment before asking, 'And he really didn't suspect anything?'

'No, he too interested in fucking me.'

'Yes,' said Chang, his eyes drawn irresistibly to her nipples, protruding prominently beneath the thin, clinging fabric of her tee shirt. 'I imagine he was.'

'You pay me now?'

Chang stood up and moved towards a sideboard, opening a drawer and withdrawing a thick brown envelope. He sat down once more and placed the envelope on the table, keeping his hand on top of it. He fixed her with a penetrating stare for several long seconds.

'And you are completely sure he suspected nothing?'

Yu did not flinch from eye contact as she replied, 'I sure – when have I ever let you down?'

He slid the envelope across the table towards her. 'Twenty thousand Yuan, as agreed.' She leaned forward to take it but before she reached it, he clamped his hand over hers, fixing her with a penetrating stare.

'What wrong?' she said. 'I did everything you want me to.' She chewed her bottom lip anxiously as she looked up at him, fear now clearly evident in her dark, slanted eyes.

Chapter 17

Chang Wei stared into Bao Yu's frightened eyes for several seconds, his hand clamped over hers. Then his face broke into a slow smile.

'Nothing is wrong, my flower. I was just wondering if you'd like to earn another ten thousand.'

As he looked into her eyes, he could see understanding dawning – she was, after all, very adept at understanding how most men think. Her fearful expression dispersed and her face broke into a knowing smile.

'Ah,' she said, '*you* want fuck me too.' Chang said nothing; he didn't need to; the hungry look in his dark eyes was enough.

She stood up, crossed her arms in front of her and grasped the hem of her tee shirt, pulling it over her head in one fluid movement. Chang licked his lips as he drank in the sight of her finely muscled torso, her small, firm breasts, and those enticingly prominent nipples. She unzipped her jeans and wriggled out of them, shimmying her hips from side to side as she extricated herself from the tight-fitting garment. When she finally stepped out of the crumpled jeans, she was wearing only a tiny red thong. The fabric was very thin, and semi-transparent; it clung to the contours of her body, accentuating the cleft between her legs. Chang's eyes were fixed on her, unblinking. His Adam's apple bobbed up and down in his throat, involuntarily.

She moved around the coffee table and sat down beside him, placing her hand over the growing bulge in his trousers, massaging gently.

'Only ten thousand?' she said, unzipping his trousers and sliding her hand inside.

'Don't be greedy, Yu,' he growled.

But she was very much in charge now. She took the tip of his penis between thumb and forefinger and began gently stroking up and down. 'Oh, I think you can do bit better than ten thousand.'

Chang was past the point of no return now. 'Alright ...' he gasped, 'twelve.'

Yu smiled, wickedly. 'Well ... make it fifteen and you get blow job *and* fuck ... if you can manage both, of course'

Chang roared with laughter. 'That's my Yu ... always the negotiator, but always value for money ... OK, I'll make it thirteen.'

'Thirteen then,' she said, moving around in front of him and kneeling on the floor between his splayed legs, looking up at him with a mischievous smile.

He settled back into the sofa, pushing his hips forward. Yu unfastened his trousers completely and bent down, hooking her long, black hair behind her ears before taking him into her mouth.

***

Chang was puzzled. After Bao Yu had left, he spent over an hour sifting through all the papers and computer files which she had given him, and there was absolutely nothing to suggest that Len Douglas had unearthed anything untoward during the two weeks he had spent at the factory. Yu had been quite definite that Douglas had suspected nothing when she picked him up at the hotel, and she was equally sure that she had managed to copy everything in his briefcase. It was possible, of course, that he had some other papers or memory sticks hidden away somewhere in his room, but it seemed very strange that there was just *nothing* amongst the material which Yu had procured.

He pushed his chair back a little from his desk and leaned back in his chair, interlacing his fingers behind his neck and exhaling through pursed lips. As he sifted, in his mind, through the various possible explanations for this strange state of affairs, his puzzlement began to turn to suspicion: was it possible that Bao Yu was lying to him? No, she had always been a reliable associate in the past, and in any case, surely she would be well aware of the severe consequences which would ensue if she crossed him and was found out. A more likely explanation was that Len Douglas had been very careful to hide anything incriminating which he had in his possession. Then again, maybe Douglas really *hadn't* found anything – he didn't strike Chang as the sharpest of individuals. He did, however, seem to be a stubbornly persistent bastard. The truth was, Chang just didn't know. To make matters worse, he had just learned that Douglas had unexpectedly returned to the UK on a pretext which he found totally unconvincing. Something didn't smell right here.

He glanced at the phone on his desk; a prickle of sweat broke out down the centre of his back. He couldn't leave it any longer; he really had to make the call today. He took a deep breath, picked up the phone, and dialled the number.

'Ah, I was expecting to hear from you,' came the familiar, high-pitched, sing-song tones of the man on the other end of the line. 'So what is the situation regarding these troublesome people from the English automotive company?'

'No problem, Peng. The American they sent first found out too much but we took care of him … permanently.'

'You tied up all loose ends?'

'Yes. As far as anyone knows it was a heart attack … and we retrieved all the evidence he had collected before he could tell anyone. I can assure you that nothing he found out will ever see the light of day.'

'Good … and what about the second person they sent?'

'He discovered nothing. I've been through all his papers and his computer and there's nothing there.'

There was a short silence, lasting just a few seconds, before the voice replied, 'How long has he been there?'

'Two weeks.'

'Two weeks? And he's found *nothing*? Am I to believe that they are sending idiots now?'

Chang's brow broke out in a dense mass of beads of perspiration. He loosened his tie as he struggled to sound calm and confident in the face of the obvious scepticism evident in that whining high-pitched voice.

'Really, Peng, he has found nothing. I give you my personal assurance of that.'

The phone went silent for several long seconds. Chang held his breath, waiting anxiously for a response. A rivulet of perspiration trickled down his forehead and into the corner of his eye, stinging and burning.

At last the other man broke his silence. When he spoke, his words were slow and deliberate. 'I do hope, for your own sake, that you are right Chang Wei.'

With that, he hung up, quite abruptly.

Chang exhaled a loud sigh, grabbing a bunch of tissues from the box on his desk to wipe away the stinging perspiration which was now running freely down into both of his eyes. He sat there motionless, for a full minute, while his breathing settled and his pounding heartbeat began to slow down a little.

Mao Peng was the top man in the Shenzhen Triad. He was a small, insignificant-looking figure, and the high-pitched voice added to his innocuous persona. He was, however, utterly ruthless, and Chang knew full well that if he fouled up on this, then his years of loyal service to the Triad would count for nothing. He was in no doubt whatsoever that his death would be slow and painful.

Chapter 18

It was 7.30 a.m. Roy had already fully debriefed Len the previous day and now he was as ready as he would ever be to have the difficult phone conversation with Chang. Given the seven-hour time difference, he had decided to go into the office early and make the call his very first job of the day. He dialled the number and Chang picked up on the second ring.

'Ah, Mr Groves. What a pleasure to hear from you.' His tone was sickly sweet and, in Roy's judgment, totally insincere. 'So sorry to hear of the unfortunate family bereavement which cut short Mr. Douglas's visit. Please offer him my condolences.'

'Thank you … I will,' said Roy, stiffly, 'but this is not a social call. I have some serious business issues to discuss with you.'

'Of course.' The tone of Chang's voice hardened a little. 'So, what can I do for you?'

Roy was blunt and to the point. 'I know what you have been doing.'

'I'm sorry,' replied Chang, 'but I really don't quite understand what you are getting at.' His tone was one of puzzlement, but Roy was sure he knew exactly what the subject for discussion was.

'OK, well let me enlighten you,' continued Roy. 'What about ignoring our delivery requirements; falsifying pricing information on our products; deliberately substituting inferior, unapproved components; and creaming off money from your own company, as well as from mine?'

Silence: several long seconds of ominous silence. When Chang finally responded, the veneer of civility to his voice had evaporated; his tone was hard and menacing.

'These are very serious allegations Mr Groves. I assume you have some evidence to support these outrageous statements?'

'Do you honestly think I'd be making this call if I didn't?'

'I really don't know,' replied Chang, his voice dripping with sarcasm. 'Your English ideas of correct business practices are something of a mystery to me.'

'Correct business practices?' spluttered Roy. 'I didn't realise you had such an ironic sense of humour.'

'Listen to me ...' began Chang, but Roy cut him off.

'No, *you* listen to *me*. I have all the evidence I need to prove gross breach of contract on the part of your company, not to mention fraudulent activity by person or persons unknown against your own company.' Roy paused to let the meaning of 'person or persons unknown' sink in. 'I'm not interested in the criminal activity which has clearly been perpetrated against your own company, but I can tell you, here and now, that I am not prepared to allow *my* company to continue to be exploited in this way.'

Chang paused for a moment before replying. 'Mr Groves, I do hope you are not planning to pick a fight with me. That would be most unwise.'

'I'm not planning to pick a fight with you, or with anyone else. I am simply telling you, clearly and unambiguously, that our business relationship is over. I intend to bring our manufacturing operations back to England.'

'You can't just do that without warning – you are contractually bound ...'

Roy cut him off. 'I can, and I will. If you want to contest the legality of this action in court then be my guest. I can assure you that with the evidence I have collected, you don't stand a chance. And, by the way, I expect full co-operation with my team when it comes to organising the transfer of manufacturing back to the UK. If not, I may be forced to hand over certain items of evidence which I have to the Chinese authorities.'

There were a few seconds of silence before Chang replied, his voice now a low, menacing growl. 'You are making a very big mistake, Mr Groves ... one which you will live bitterly to regret.'

'I don't believe we have anything else to discuss right now,' said Roy, and he put the phone down, without further comment.

As he sank back in his chair, Roy became aware that his heart was pounding and he was drenched in perspiration. However much he had endeavoured to present a confident front, he had to admit – to himself at least – that Chang Wei *scared* him. He didn't yet realise just how well-founded was that fear.

Chapter 19

Tim Steele leaned forward and laid down the newspaper – still open at the 'Situations Vacant' page – on the coffee table. He ran his fingers through his dark wavy hair – it was getting longer now, since he had left the army – and sighed heavily. Another week had gone by and there was still no sign of a suitable job. But what was a suitable job anyway? Unlike his old comrade, Jeff Patterson – who could fly anything from a helicopter to a large passenger plane – Tim didn't have a specific skill which was easily transferable to civilian life. All he really knew was how to track down and kill his quarry, while trying to avoid being killed himself.

He picked up the bottle of Corona beer from the table and pushed the slice of lime down through the neck of the bottle, idly studying the pattern of bubbles which swirled from it as it entered the liquid. He took a deep swallow before setting down the bottle and easing himself back in the sofa, interlacing his fingers behind the back of his neck and gazing at the light fitting hanging from the ceiling above him.

One or two of the lads had opted to join the police. He thought of Steve Salt, his old commanding officer, who had almost been killed in the ambush in Afghanistan. Steve had eventually recovered from his injuries sufficiently to walk unaided, but he was no longer fit enough for frontline duties in the army. Steve had, instead, forged for himself a very successful career in the police. The last Tim had heard, Steve had achieved the rank of Detective Inspector. Maybe Tim should also try to get into the police force. For some reason, though, the idea just didn't appeal.

Maybe he had acted prematurely in abandoning his previous career. He was only twenty-seven years old and had already attained the rank of Captain. Furthermore, he knew that SAS officers often went on to reach the very highest echelons in the British Army. But then the memories of that bungled attempt to assassinate Mohamed Asheed came flooding back: the young woman's face, her eye smashed to a bloody pulp; her baby with three gaping bullet wounds desecrating its tiny body. Twenty-six people had died that day, many of them women and children. And Asheed? Even now he was still at large.

Tim shook his head in an effort to dispel the horrifying image. No, he *had* made the right decision: there was no way he could carry on after that day. And yet he missed the buzz: the knot of fear in his stomach before a mission, the heightened senses, the excitement. He missed the tight bond with his comrades, on whom his life often depended, just as theirs did on him. And now ...

At least he had come out of the army physically – if not mentally – intact. Some of his friends had lost limbs, and one – Adam Sharp – had been blinded, his face horribly disfigured by a grenade blast. At least the poor devil could not look at his own ruined features in a mirror. Tim realised that he could easily be much worse off. He knew he had to snap out of this morose mood which had taken him. He was at least physically able to take another job, even if it turned out not to be the most exciting and fulfilling.

He took another long swallow of his beer and wiped the froth from his lip with the back of his hand. He resolved, at that moment, to get serious about job hunting and stop sitting around drinking beer in the middle of the afternoon. And he needed to get back in shape. Not so many weeks ago he had been in the peak of physical condition – the arduous training routines which were a regular feature of life in the SAS had seen to that. Now though, little by little, he felt himself getting sluggish and – by his standards – flabby.

He lifted the hem of his tee shirt and ran his hand over his torso. Yes, no doubt about it: the musculature was starting to lose definition. It was time to do something about it.

He looked at his watch: 3.02 p.m. Raquel would probably be home at around 4.30 p.m. As a teacher, she was usually able to leave work early enough to get home before the worst of the daily rush. An hour and a half was long enough, Tim decided, and he had to start sometime, so he decided to go for a run before she got home. As he made to stand up, Raquel's little dog – a grey and white Miniature Schnauzer, named Sammy – started, awoken from his slumbers by the sudden movement. He had been curled up on the sofa alongside Tim for the past hour.

'Sorry to wake you, little fella,' said Tim, ruffling the fur at the little dog's neck. Sammy cocked his head on one side as though listening intently. 'I'm going for a run. You might as well go back to sleep.'

Sammy stretched, yawned, and did as Tim had suggested, nuzzling into the cushion as he made himself comfortable.

***

As Tim settled into his stride he began to feel better. His feet pounding on the pavement beat out a comforting rhythm; his breathing had settled into that steady aerobic state which signalled a pace which he knew he could keep up for a considerable time. The wind in his face cooled him; the physical exertion invigorated him; he began to experience that slightly lightheaded feeling, almost like a mild version of the effects of drugs or alcohol.

Tim knew this route well, and as he rounded the corner, passing through the patch of shade cast by the huge oak tree in the adjacent garden, he knew there were just under three miles to go of the total ten-mile circuit. He still felt good, so decided to up his pace a little. As he moved beyond that comfortable aerobic state, he began to feel the burn in his calf muscles, but pushed on – only a mile to go. Then he began to feel the stitch in his side; he knew he was pushing too hard now, but he was only a few hundred yards from home so he did not slacken his pace.

When he reached the front gate he leant on it, bending over and holding his side until the pain began to subside and his breathing to settle. Raquel's red Mini was already in the drive; maybe she had gotten out of school a little early today. He checked his watch: 4.38 p.m. She wasn't early; he was late. He had taken an hour and fifteen minutes to run ten miles – pathetic! He should have been able to do it in an hour and five, or even less. He resolved to keep training until he could once again crack one hour five minutes.

He slipped the key into the lock, opened the door, and stepped inside. He was surprised that Sammy did not come bounding up to greet him. He called out to Raquel, but there was no answer. Neither was there the familiar thunder of tiny paws which signalled Sammy bounding down the stairs when awoken from a snooze on the bed. Raquel must have decided to take Sammy for a walk.

Tim went to have a shower and change. As he closed his eyes and threw his head back he relished the feel of the warm jets pummelling his face. The physical exercise had had a cleansing effect on his mind, just as the shower had on his body. He had broken free of the clouds of gloom which had enveloped him; he was going to make a fresh start. By the time he had towelled himself off and slipped into his clean clothes, he was feeling good.

He went downstairs and moved through to the kitchen to make some coffee. As he listened to the strangled spluttering and gurgling noises emanating from the filter coffee machine, he glanced at his watch again: 5.25 p.m. Raquel must have taken Sammy for a longer-than-usual walk. He smiled as he imagined them trotting along with, more often than not, Sammy dictating the pace as he zigzagged this way and that, seeking out the most interesting sniff. Raquel loved that little dog, and so did he.

He poured the coffee, inhaling deeply as he savoured the pleasant aroma. Then he heard it: *tap, tap, scratch*. What was it? He picked up his coffee and made to move through to the lounge. He heard it again: *tap, scratch, tap, tap, scratch*. As he entered the lounge, he realised the sound was coming from behind the curtains at the patio door – they had been drawn together to ward off the afternoon sun. He drew back the curtains to see Sammy's little face, his front paws tapping and scratching at the glass. He opened the door and Sammy came jumping up to him, licking and scrabbling furiously. But it wasn't Sammy's usual greeting: there was something different … *frantic* … in his demeanour.

Then Tim saw it: the lead trailing from his collar. He stepped outside and called out to Raquel. No answer.

He picked up the phone and dialled her mobile. No answer; he was put through to her voicemail. His growing sense of unease coalesced to form a tight knot in the pit of his stomach. Where was she?

Chapter 20

Roy had just arrived home after a particularly gruelling day at work, most of which had been taken up with a board meeting, whose purpose was to rough out a plan for the complex and challenging task of pulling manufacturing operations out of China and back to the UK.

The management team had estimated that the project would take over a year to complete and cost somewhere in the region of five million pounds. This was money which the company could ill afford to spend but they had estimated that the investment should pay for itself within two years, given the scale of the malpractice which they now knew had been taking place at Sotoyo. After that, the savings would be considerable.

They were still considering how much compensation to claim from Sotoyo on the grounds of breach of contract. If they kept their claim modest, perhaps they could reach an out-of-court settlement with the Chinese company, but if they over-cooked their demand and had to go to court, it could drag on for years, racking up colossal legal bills in the process. In the end, exhaustion had set in before they had covered all the topics which needed to be addressed, and there were still several key decisions outstanding. It was clear that they could not complete the planned agenda in a single day, so Roy had adjourned the meeting with the agreement to convene a further session on another day to complete the work.

Roy had heard nothing more from Chang since their acrimonious phone conversation a few days earlier, and he therefore assumed that Chang did not intend to challenge his decision to pull manufacturing operations back to the UK. At least that was one less thing to worry about.

The house seemed strangely empty as Roy stepped into the hallway that evening. Donna was still in the USA with Gabby Kabel; Chuck's funeral was to take place today. Roy looked at his watch: 6.55 p.m. It would only be 1.55 p.m. in Boston: too early to call Donna; she would still be at the funeral. He resolved to call her just before he went to bed.

As Roy shrugged off his jacket and hung it on the post at the bottom of the stairs, his thoughts turned to food. The board meeting had been so fraught that they had all skipped lunch and just worked through into the afternoon. His stomach was growling as he opened the freezer to see what he could find. Cooking was not Roy's *forte*, but fortunately Donna had provided for him before leaving, and there were several pre-prepared individual dishes covered in aluminium foil and neatly labelled. He smiled at her thoughtfulness. After a few moments deliberation, he selected the dish labelled lasagne, laying it on the worktop to begin thawing, before turning on the oven. He grabbed a bottle of beer from the fridge, flipped off the cap, and took a long swallow, before exhaling loudly and wiping the froth from his upper lip with the back of his hand. He moved through to the lounge, taking the bottle with him, before switching on the TV in order to watch the evening news while the oven warmed up.

The news was depressingly familiar: yet more unrest in the Middle East; a strike by air traffic controllers in Spain; at home in the UK, another round of worsening economic data, capped off by the news that the FTSE was down by over one hundred points on the day. Roy had quite a bit of money invested in various bonds which, in spite of their supposed diversity, all seemed pretty much to follow the FTSE up and down. *I wonder how much money I lost today,* he pondered. All in all, he concluded, there was absolutely nothing to feel good about in today's news.

As he took another sip of his beer, he heard the letter box clang, followed a moment later by the gentle slapping sound of something landing on the doormat. Strange, he thought, that the post should arrive so late. With a sigh, he levered himself out of the armchair and walked through to the hall, where a padded brown envelope lay on the mat. He bent down and picked it up; he was surprised to see that there was no postage stamp and no name or address on the envelope.

He heard a car start up outside and then a chirrup of tyres as it set off. He opened the door just in time to see a dark blue Audi disappearing around the corner at some speed. He had no idea what that was all about but for no rational reason which he could discern, he felt a shiver of unease ripple through his body.

He closed the door and looked again at the envelope: no writing, no label, nothing. His sense of disquiet increased. He slid his thumb under the flap of the envelope and ripped it open. Inside was a small package wrapped in white paper kitchen towel with an elastic band around it. He removed the elastic band and began unfurling the paper towel. As the first couple of layers were removed he noticed several brownish-red stains appear. As he continued to unwrap the package the stains became larger. He felt a tight knot forming in his stomach.

Finally, the last layer of paper was removed; what he saw made his heart skip a beat and his breath catch in his throat. He let out an anguished wail and sank to his knees, staring in disbelief at the severed finger with its midnight blue fingernail, decorated with a pattern of a moon and tiny stars.

Chapter 21

He remained motionless for well over a minute, on his knees, staring at the grisly object which he was holding. A cold prickle of sweat had broken out down his back and time seemed to stand still. His brain just refused to process the information which his eyes were providing. Eventually, as the shocking reality set in, he was enveloped by an involuntary shudder which shook his whole body. He tried to swallow but his mouth was too dry.

When, at last, he succeeded in breaking free of the stupor which had enveloped him, he began, slowly and tenderly, wrapping the severed finger once again in the kitchen towel. His hands were shaking so badly that it took him several attempts before he was able to replace the elastic band. He went to put the package back in the envelope, but as he did so he realised there was something else in there: a plain white piece of card covered with small pieces of paper cut from a magazine or newspaper. He picked everything up, rose unsteadily to his feet, and staggered through to the kitchen, where he laid the envelope and all its contents on the worktop. His mouth was now so dry that it felt as if his tongue was stuck in his throat. His hands were shaking as he grabbed an upturned glass from the dish drainer alongside the sink and filled it with water from the tap. He held the glass with both hands to try to steady it as he gulped down its entire contents in three deep swallows.

He turned back and picked up the card before reading the message spelled out in mismatched snippets of paper stuck to its surface.

We have your dAUghteR. Back Off **fro**m **yo**Ur ıll aDViSed pLAns noW **A**ND You will get thE Rest o**f** her back SAFE. PERSist anD She diES. **IF** yoU INVoıvE The police s**he** dIEs.

Chang: it had to be Chang who was behind this. Who else could it be? He already knew that Chang was an evil bastard, but this…? Was there no limit to the lengths to which this animal would go?

He rushed out to the hall and grabbed his mobile phone from his jacket pocket. With trembling fingers, he scrolled through the address book. He found Chang's number and rang it. No answer. Of course not: It would be around 2.30 a.m. in Shenzhen, and there would be no-one in the office. He wasn't thinking clearly.

He scrolled through the address book again and found Chang's home number. When he rang the number there was a long delay before an answering machine cut in, the strident Mandarin tones incomprehensible, but part-way through the recorded message, Chang picked up.

'What have you done you bastard?' blurted Roy, before Chang could say a word.

'Excuse me, but to whom am I speaking?' Chang's accent was unmistakeable, his tone calm and unhurried.

'You know damned well who it is. What have you done with my daughter?'

'I'm sorry, but I have no idea what you are talking about. Who is this?'

Roy exhaled heavily in exasperation. 'You know who it is … it's Roy Groves. What have you done with her?'

'Ah, Mr Groves … always a pleasure, but this is very late to be calling. I was already in bed.'

Smug, slimy bastard. Roy fought to control his temper, struggling to keep his voice level when he continued.

'Listen to me. I'll do whatever you want but just send her back to me safely.'

'I really have no idea what you are talking about. Do I take it that there is some problem with your daughter?'

'Look, I'll call off the plans to move manufacturing back to the UK ... whatever you want.'

'Well, I must say that is indeed a very wise decision.'

'Just send her back right now.'

'Do I assume, from the way that you are talking, that your daughter has gone missing?'

'Please don't play games ... just send her back.'

'Look, I have no idea what has happened to your daughter. If she has ... disappeared ... then naturally I'll do anything I can to help you find her.'

Roy sighed with relief. 'Thank you.'

'That is, after I am completely sure that your plans to take your business away from my company have been completely abandoned.'

'What do you mean?'

'What I mean,' said Chang, 'is that *I'll* decide when it's appropriate to involve myself in helping you find your daughter.'

'Please ... I give you my word.'

'Ah ... your word. Hmm ... that is most gratifying, but you know ... I always prefer actions to words.'

'No,' spluttered Roy, desperate now, 'you can't keep her.'

'I really don't think I can help you any further just now. I'm sure we'll speak again soon.'

'Please, you can't just ...'

'Goodnight, Mr Groves.'

'No ... you have to ...'

The phone went dead.

Roy laid his mobile down and put his head in his hands, stunned and completely disoriented by Chang's response to his call.

Desperately, he began trying to decide what to do next. Even if he completely abandoned his plans to pull manufacturing back to the UK, there was no telling how long Chang would keep Raquel captive, or indeed if he would ever release her. If Roy went to the police, however, he had little doubt that Chang would carry out his threat to kill her. It was an impossible situation.

Suddenly, the sight of the envelope containing Raquel's severed finger caught his eye. He tore off a sheet of paper towel from the dispenser on the wall and laid it on the worktop. With trembling fingers, he withdrew the small innocuous-looking package from the envelope and unwrapped it once again, swallowing hard as he laid the bloody finger on the paper towel. He felt the stinging surge of tears welling up in the corners of his eyes as he screwed up the soiled sheets of paper and threw them into the waste bin. Struggling to control his shaking hands, he tore off a long strip of fresh paper towel and tenderly rewrapped his daughter's finger before placing it in a plastic freezer bag and putting it in the freezer. He really wasn't sure why he was doing this, but what the hell *do* you do under these circumstances? In a daze, he trudged back into the lounge, sat down and picked up the half-empty bottle of beer, taking a deep swallow before sinking back into the armchair.

What to do next? Should he call Donna? No, not yet. It didn't feel right to break this horrifying news to her on the phone; he wanted to be there in person to try to comfort her. But what would she think if he withheld the news from her? His brain was a maelstrom of confusion; he couldn't think straight.

The phone rang. No … not now … really, *not now*. He didn't want to talk to *anyone* right now. But then his heart leapt. Maybe it was Chang again; perhaps he had reconsidered his uncompromising position. Roy grabbed the phone and picked up.

'Hello … who is it?' he barked.

'Hello … Roy? It's Tim here.' Roy's heart sank.

'Uh … Tim … uh, yes … what?'

'I'm a bit concerned about Raquel. I was out when she got home from work but now she seems to have disappeared.'

'Sit down Tim. I have some bad news ...'

Roy spent the next twenty minutes explaining the whole story – including the background as to why he and Chang were at loggerheads – to Tim, who listened, mainly in silence, as the sorry saga unfolded. Somehow though, Roy could sense his simmering anger; it seemed, by some strange means, to ooze and force its way down the phone line even though Tim had hardly uttered a word.

'So what the hell do we do now?' asked Roy.

'I don't think we should do anything too hasty,' said Tim. Although his tone was tense and grim, he sounded remarkably composed considering everything he had just learned. 'I certainly wouldn't approach the police just yet. If this Chang Wei is as much of a ruthless bastard as you describe, it could put Raquel in even more danger.'

'Well, we can't just do nothing.'

Tim was silent for a few seconds, before saying, 'Give me an hour or so to make a few enquiries at this end ... to see if I can find out anything about her kidnapping.'

'OK ... but please hurry.'

'I'll call you back.'

'Tim ...' But Tim had already hung up.

Chapter 22

The front door was of mock-Georgian design, its mahogany surface varnished to a high gloss and the brass fittings gleaming. Tim caught a glimpse of a grotesquely distorted image of himself in the highly reflective surface of the large circular doorknob: huge head, tiny legs. He reached for the heavy brass knocker and swung it twice against its stop. His heart was pounding in his chest.

Ordinarily, Tim avoided Mrs Perkins as much as possible, engaging in only the bare minimum amount of contact consistent with being a civil and considerate neighbour. Raquel was quite friendly with her, but in Tim's opinion, Beryl Perkins was a busybody and a gossip: the only thing she loved more than prying into other people's business was telling anyone else who would listen what she had discovered. Much as he disliked the woman though, this, Tim reasoned, might just be one time when her nosy nature could be of value.

When the door opened, the rounded middle-aged face which appeared was – as always, it seemed – heavily made up, the tight strawberry blonde curls which framed it lacquered so firmly in place that it would have taken a hurricane to shift them. The floral dress and knitted cardigan did a passable job of flattering Mrs Perkins' rather rotund figure. Did this woman spend her entire life dressed up and ready to go out, or to receive visitors?

'Oh, hello Tim,' she said smiling broadly. 'What a pleasure to see you. Won't you come in?'

There was no way that he was going to waste time undergoing one of Mrs Perkins' prying interrogations. His sole interest at that moment was to find out whether she knew anything about Raquel's kidnapping.

'Uh, that's very kind Mrs Perkins, but to be honest I'm in a bit of a hurry.'

The smile faded and her eyebrows arched, creating little furrows in the centre of her forehead. She folded her arms beneath her ample bosom, pushing it up and making it even more prominent.

'Well, in that case, how can I help you?' Her tone betrayed her obvious irritation at Tim's rebuttal.

Tim didn't have time to worry about Beryl Perkins' sensibilities right now. 'Raquel isn't at home. Her car's on the drive, so she's obviously been home, but she's not here now. She didn't say anything to me about her going out, and I just wondered whether she had mentioned anything to you.'

Mrs Perkins' expression changed to one of interest. She maintained the cross-armed posture but the hostility evaporated from her eyes. 'Well, no, she didn't say anything to me but I just happened to glance out of the window earlier on and saw her taking little Sammy out for a walk.'

'When was that ... roughly?'

'Oh, a couple of hours ago at least ... and she hasn't come back yet?'

Tim shook his head. 'No, she hasn't. Uh, did you notice anything ... well ... unusual?'

She unfolded her arms; all enmity had disappeared now that there was the prospect of a proper mystery into which she could poke her nose. She took a step towards him and lowered her voice to a conspiratorial whisper.

'Well, funnily enough, a little earlier, I did happen to notice a strange car parked just across the road.'

'Strange? In what way?'

'Not strange like that ... I mean one that I haven't seen before.'

'Oh, I see what you mean. So did Raquel go over to the car or meet anyone?'

Mrs Perkins now stepped right out through the door and glanced furtively to her left and her right, as though checking that they were not being observed. She lowered her voice even further.

'No, but there were two men in the car and they both sat there for over half an hour without getting out.'

He waited for her to elaborate but she didn't. Tim was starting to get very impatient at the way he had to drag each nugget of information from this wretched woman.

'So what happened?' he said, struggling to keep his irritation out of the tone of his voice.

'Well,' she continued, 'when Raquel set off up the road with Sammy' – she pointed to indicate the direction which Raquel had taken – 'the car stayed where it was for about half a minute or so and then started up and set off slowly in the same direction.'

She paused as if waiting for some reaction from Tim.

'Well go on then,' he said, rather more harshly than he had intended.

'Well, I thought it seemed a bit suspicious at the time,' she continued, 'but you know me: I'm not one to poke my nose into other people's business.'

Tim shook his head. 'No, of course not,' he said, biting his lip. 'Did you notice what kind of car it was?'

'It was dark blue.'

'Do you know what make?'

She shook her head. 'Sorry, I'm not very interested in cars.'

'Well, what type then ... hatchback, saloon, SUV?'

'A saloon I think ... oh, and it had that symbol of interlocking rings ... like the Olympic badge.'

'An Audi then ... good. Now, I don't suppose you can remember the registration number?'

'Well not the whole number, but as it happens I do remember part of it. The last three letters were B, O, B. I remember it because it sort of spells a name: Bob.'

'But you can't remember any more of the number?'

She shook her head again. 'Sorry, I'm afraid not.'

This looked like all the information Tim was likely to glean from Mrs Perkins, and he was anxious to get away now. 'Well, thank you for your help … I really do appreciate it.'

'But don't you want to come in and talk about it? I could make us a nice cup …'

But Tim was already halfway down her front path. It wasn't much to go on, but it was a start at least.

Chapter 23

It was time to call in some favours. Tim dialled the number of an old friend.

'DI Stephen Salt,' came the official-sounding response to his phone call.

'Hi Steve, it's Tim … Tim Steele.'

There was a slight delay before the reply came back. 'Tim, how the hell are you?' The tone had changed abruptly and was now upbeat and jovial. 'It's been ages … how are you doing?'

'I'm OK, I guess, but I really need …'

But Steve didn't give him a chance to finish his sentence 'I heard you've decided to leave the army.'

'Yes.'

'Well, what are you doing now?'

'Well, nothing just yet … I haven't really decided what I want to do.'

'Are you thinking of applying to join the police like some of the other lads? Because if so I could maybe put in a word …'

Tim interrupted him; he really didn't have time for this conversation. 'Look Steve, I'd love to chat, but not right now. Something really bad has happened and I need your help.'

His friend's tone immediately became more serious. 'OK … well what is it? Have you reported it yet?'

'I can't report it – not officially anyway – and I'd rather not discuss the details right now. It's ... complicated.'

'It's like that, eh?' Understanding registered in Steve's voice. 'Alright, well what can I do to help?'

'I need to trace a car.'

'OK ... give me the details.'

'I'm afraid I don't have the full registration number, but I do have a few details which might help.'

'Go on.'

'It's a dark blue Audi – I don't know which model – and the last three letters of the registration number are B, O, B. I realise there could be quite a few vehicles fitting this spec. but do what you can will you?'

'Sure thing, Tim. I'll get right on it.'

Tim was grateful that his old friend and comrade-in-arms didn't ask any questions.

Half an hour later, DI Stephen Salt called him back. 'I'm afraid there are eighty-four vehicles registered in the UK which meet that description. I don't know how you're going to narrow it down to the one you're interested in.'

This was pretty much what Tim had expected: he knew it wasn't going to be easy.

'Thanks Steve. Can you email me the details of every one of the owners?'

'Hey Tim, you know I'm not supposed to do that.'

'I know ... and I wouldn't ask unless it was important.'

'Just what the hell is this all about, Tim?'

'I can't tell you. I would if I could but ...' he sighed heavily, struggling to find a way to explain 'look, Steve, you have to trust me. I *need* you to do this for me.'

The phone went silent. Several long seconds passed as Tim waited anxiously for a response.

The deep sigh which preceded his friend's reply could be clearly heard on the phone. 'I'll send you the list within the next five minutes.'

'Thanks, Steve. I really do appreciate it.'

***

Roy waited anxiously by the phone, nursing a tumbler of malt whisky, from which he took tiny sips, swirling the fiery liquid in his mouth, savouring the pungent taste before swallowing. As each minute ticked by, the scenarios which he was imagining for his daughter became more and more alarming. He began seriously to contemplate the possibility that she might never be returned to him alive. If that happened, he simply would not be able to live with himself. Her kidnapping – and everything else which might result from it – were *his* fault: his fault for allowing his family to become innocent casualties of his business rivalries.

He took another sip of his whisky, holding it in his mouth for several seconds before allowing it to forge its fiery path down his throat. Where the hell was Tim? Why was he taking so long to get back to him?

Finally the phone rang.

'Roy, it's Tim.' Roy jumped to his feet, clutching the phone tightly to his ear. 'I've got something ...'

'What? What is it?'

'I've spoken to one of our neighbours and she's given me a description and partial registration number for the car which they used to pick Raquel up.'

'Your neighbour *saw* it happen? Why the hell didn't she do something to stop it?'

'Roy, be reasonable. She's a middle-aged woman, living on her own. What was she going to do against two heavies sent to kidnap Raquel? In any case she didn't actually realise what was happening until after I spoke to her.'

'I suppose you're right,' admitted Roy, reluctantly. 'Anyway, do you have enough to track down this car?'

'Well, unfortunately there are quite a number of cars which fit the description so I have some work to do.'

'How many?'

'I haven't counted exactly how many are on the list ... but quite a few.'

From Tim's guarded response, Roy guessed that it was a much longer list than either of them would have liked.

Something else suddenly struck Roy. 'Wait a minute ... how did you get a complete list of the suspect cars?'

'I have a few contacts in the police: ex-army mates.'

Roy's heart jumped. 'Oh God. You haven't told them about Raquel have you?'

'No ... the help I have had is purely unofficial.'

Roy felt his heart settle back. 'OK, well just supposing we can actually trace this car, what do we do next?'

'Look we're losing time here. Let me start working through the list ... I'll call you back just as soon as I get a definite lead.'

Roy felt utterly helpless, but he realised Tim was right. He sighed deeply before saying, 'OK ... let me know the moment you find anything.'

***

Tim started ploughing through the list of cars he had been given, searching for anything which might provide a clue as to the one he was looking for. Two hours later, he had reached number thirty-seven out of eighty-four and had turned up absolutely nothing. He sat back in his chair and exhaled loudly. How the hell was he going to do this? The only thing he could think of was to start visiting every one of the owners in person, and that could take weeks, by which time the trail would be well and truly cold. *Shit! Shit! Shit!*

The phone rang. 'Tim ... it's Steve Salt.'

Tim was immediately alert. 'What? What is it?'

127

'This may be of interest. About an hour ago we had a report of a stolen dark blue Audi A4 registration number RA60 BOB. We've managed to find it and have arrested the driver.'

Tim's heart skipped a beat. 'Who is he?'

'Chinese guy – says his name is Wu Min – claims not to speak much English.'

Chinese ... Yes! Surely this had to be the one.

Tim thought for a few seconds before saying, 'Steve, I need to talk to him.'

'You know I can't let you do that. It's against every rule in the book.'

'I know that ... and you know I wouldn't ask if there was any other way.'

There was a silence lasting a few seconds. 'Just what the hell *are* you involved in, Tim?'

'I can't tell you. Look, this is complicated. If I tell you what it's about you will feel obliged to get officially involved, and I just can't let that happen – if there is any sign that the police are involved the life of someone who means a great deal to me will be at risk.'

'Christ Tim ... you're not making this situation any easier. How can I *not* get involved now that you've told me that?'

Tim sighed; there was no other way now. 'Look, I didn't want to bring this up, but you owe me. Remember what happened in Afghanistan?'

The exhalation of breath was clearly audible over the phone. 'Of course I remember.'

'Well, now I'm calling in the debt. I hate to do this to you Steve, but this is important: more important than you can possibly imagine.'

The phone went silent for several seconds. Tim waited anxiously, chewing his bottom lip as he wondered whether he had pushed too hard.

When his friend finally replied, he sounded deflated, defeated. 'Get round here right now – at the Burton Road station – and ask for me. Don't get involved in any further conversation with the guy on the front desk ... just say you have an appointment with me.'

'Thanks Steve. I appreciate it.'

'Just don't overstep the mark. Understand?'

'OK ... thanks Steve.'

'Tim, I *mean* it. You can talk to him, but that's all, understand?'

Tim hung up.

Chapter 24

'So what's your name?' asked Tim, as he paced back and forth on the opposite side of the table from where the man sat silently, his hands clasped together on top of the table, his face a sullen mask of defiance.

'Give me your name, damn you,' yelled Tim, slamming his fist loudly on the table.

The man started, recoiling in his chair. 'Name Wu Min,' he muttered.

'Why did you kidnap Raquel Groves?'

'No understand. No speak English good.'

Tim was in no mood to pussy-foot around. He walked around to the other side of the table and grabbed the man by his lapels, hoisting him roughly to his feet. He pulled him forward until their noses were practically touching. The man belched; the smell which assailed Tim's nostrils was repulsive: a nauseating blend of spicy food and pungent stomach acids. Tim didn't care; he tightened his grip further.

'I *said*, "Why did you kidnap Raquel Groves"?'

The man's face wrinkled into an expression of bemusement. 'No understand.'

Tim maintained his firm hold on the man's lapels and brought his knee up sharply, rendering a crushing blow to his testicles. He screamed in pain and, as Tim released his grip, sank to his knees, gasping desperately.

He gave the man a few seconds to partially recover before hoisting him to his feet once more. 'Do you need some more help with your English?' He drew back his fist and punched the man hard in his solar plexus. This time there was no sound as the man collapsed on the floor, helpless, retching and gasping for breath, his eyes rolling back in their sockets.

Tim waited for some seconds before leaning over the prostrate figure on the floor, drawing back his fist once more, making ready to deliver a blow squarely to the man's face.

'Alright, alright,' screamed the desperate figure on the floor, holding up both of his hands in a defensive gesture. 'I paid to drive car. I don't know nothing about why she had to be taken.'

'Better,' said Tim. 'Now who else was involved?'

'I don't know other man's name.'

Tim placed his heel on top of the man's throat and began to apply pressure. 'His name ... now.'

The man was unable to speak, so Tim relaxed the pressure a little. 'His name, damn you.'

A spark of resistance registered in the man's eyes. 'Wait a minute ... you no policeman. You can't do this.'

Tim bore down once more with his heel on the man's throat. He threw up his hands, gagging as he struggled to breathe. Tim relaxed the pressure once more.

'OK, I tell you,' he gasped. 'His name Wang Dong.'

'Good. You see this is going to be much easier if you answer my questions isn't it?'

The man nodded, nervously. Tim hoisted him to his feet and dumped him back in his chair.

'Now, tell me where she is.'

'I not know.'

Tim grabbed the man's right hand and began bending back his little finger. He screamed in pain.

'Where?'

'OK, OK. I only know where I take her. Maybe she not there now.'

Tim increased the pressure a little. 'So where was that?'

The man screamed even louder. 'Please ... stop, stop.'

'Where?'

'Ninety-four Cumberland Road ... aargh ... no ... stop ... you break my finger.'

'You sure of that address?'

'Yes, I sure.'

'Who cut off her finger?' said Tim, maintaining the insistent pressure on the man's own finger.

His eyes widened in fear. 'No, no ... not me ... maybe Wang Dong.'

Tim fixed him with an unwavering stare. 'Well, just in case you are lying to me ...' He gradually increased the force he was applying, bending the man's finger further and further back until eventually the joints parted with an audible cracking sound. The scream which followed was blood-curdling.

DI Salt came crashing into the room. 'What the fuck ...?' His voice tailed off as he registered the prisoner vainly trying to coax his shattered finger back to its former attitude, whimpering pathetically as he did so.

'I think he must have hurt his finger while resisting arrest,' said Tim.

The detective glared at him, his face contorted with anger. 'This is a step too far, Tim. You never said ...'

Tim cut him off. 'We're even now, Steve.' He strode out of the room.

***

It was just after midnight. The silence was almost total, punctuated only by the regular, insistent *tick-tock* emanating from the clock on the mantelpiece. Roy stared at the phone, waiting, willing it to ring;

it stared mutely back at him, steadfastly refusing to do so. The inactivity was driving him crazy. He decided that yet another cup of coffee was in order – he had lost count of how many he had already consumed that evening. He went through to the kitchen to brew another pot, all the time willing the phone to ring. It didn't.

Having poured his coffee, he took it back into the lounge and sat once more by the phone. He sipped tentatively at the scalding liquid, occasionally blowing over its surface in an ineffectual attempt to cool it down.

Finally he could stand it no longer; he dialled Tim and Raquel's home phone number. No answer. *Damn!* Did he have a mobile number for Tim? He scrolled through the phone's address book. No luck. What about the old notebook that they used to use as an address book? He couldn't even remember where it was. He began rooting around in the drawers of the sideboard, hunting for the notebook, but failing to find it. He swore out loud in his frustration.

But then the phone finally rang; it was Tim. There was an odd reverberating quality to his voice, hard to follow clearly over the background drone. He realised that Tim was driving, speaking to him via the hands-free kit in his car.

'Well? Any luck?' asked Roy, fighting to keep the note of desperation out of his voice.

'Yes, I have a lead.'

'What? What do you have?' urged Roy.

'There's no time to explain now, but I know where they took her. I'm on my way there right now.'

'Thank God!' The feeling of relief was almost physical, but lasted only for a couple of seconds as his brain quickly moved on to the next steps. 'But wait … you're not going there alone, are you?'

'It's OK. I can take care of myself.'

'No, let me come with you.'

'There's no time, Roy. I want to get there before they move her on to somewhere else.'

'But…'

'Look, I can do this: it's what I'm trained for.'

'What do you mean?' asked Roy, puzzled.

'My army training … that's what I'm talking about.'

A sneaking realisation began to dawn on Roy. 'Just what *did* you do in the army, Tim?'

'SAS – covert operations.'

'You never told us,' said Roy, but deep down he had always known that Tim wasn't just a regular soldier.

'I wasn't allowed to … I wasn't allowed to tell anyone.'

Of course, thought Roy: it was obvious that the SAS wouldn't want the identities of their operatives to become public knowledge.

'Look,' continued Tim, 'I care for Raquel too … much more than you probably realise. You have to trust me … this is what I'm trained for.' He paused for a moment. 'This is what I do.'

In an instant Roy realised that Tim going in alone and fast probably *was* his best hope of rescuing his daughter. 'Alright, but be careful.' Even as he said it, it sounded, to his own ears, a ridiculously trite comment. He paused for a moment before adding, 'Are you … armed?'

'Yes,' replied Tim, 'but I'll try to get her out without shots being fired. Look, I'm almost there now, I need to ring off.'

'OK. Good luck, Tim. Bring her back to me.' But Tim had already hung up.

Roy sat back in a daze, overwhelmed by the way his world had been turned upside down in just a few hours. Weapons, shots … covert operations? *Surely there must be some other way.* He had spent his entire working life facing and overcoming challenging business problems, but he realised that he was entering another world entirely now, one which was way outside his own sphere of experience. The people they were dealing with now weren't just ruthless business rivals; they were vicious criminals. This was a world where Tim's background and skillset would be far more valuable than his own. He had to admit that, in this unfamiliar world, Tim probably knew best.

Chapter 25

The house was unremarkable: a thirties semi hiding inconspicuously in a long row of almost identical properties, their frontages adorned by decorative, but non-functional, black wooden beams, contrasting starkly with the uniform pale cream rendered elevations. The owners had sought, with limited success, to individualise their properties, employing looped chain fences, hanging baskets, Georgian-style front doors, and so on, in order to try to make their homes stand out from their neighbours'. But the overall impression was of an anonymous row of indistinguishable boxes. There were no lights on and all was quiet. It looked an unlikely place for a kidnap victim to be held.

Tim was hoping against hope that the thug in custody at the police station had not found some way to warn his accomplice that his identity and location had been disclosed. He doubted, though, that the man would dare admit that he had divulged this information: if these people were Triad – as Tim suspected – the penalty for grassing on one of their own was likely to be gruesome and painful. No, the chances were that he had the element of surprise on his side.

He checked his watch: 12.35 a.m. He reached into the glove box and withdrew his SIG-Sauer P226 9mm handgun. He checked that it contained a full magazine and fixed in place the silencer, rotating it slowly and carefully until he felt the reassuring resistance of it bottoming out on its screw thread. He tucked the weapon into his waistband. Next, he took out the black cloth wallet containing his lock-picking tools and slipped it into his pocket. He took one more look at the darkened windows of the house. Nothing. He opened the door of his car, stepped out, and walked unhurriedly across the road, carefully avoiding making any move which might attract unnecessary attention if anyone happened to be observing him.

He opened the front gate, slowly and carefully – anxious to avoid any squeal from unoiled hinges – and walked calmly up to the front door. He reasoned that skulking around in the back garden or climbing over fences would look far more suspicious, should anyone spot his movements, than a direct approach to the front door. In a glance he took in the pertinent details: a standard self-closing Yale lock. If it had not been deadlocked then this should be easy. He stole a swift glance all around him to check that he was not being observed; there was no sign of anyone.

He withdrew from his pocket his set of lock-picking tools, bending down and laying it on the ground before unfolding the fabric wallet and selecting two of the implements contained within it. He stood up and stole another glance to left and right; there was still no-one around. He inserted both implements into the lock and began manipulating them; in less than twenty seconds he had defeated the lock and turned the barrel. So far, so good.

He pushed the door forward a fraction of an inch, just sufficient to stop it from reclosing when he released the lock barrel. He bent back down, gathered up the fabric wallet and slipped it back into his pocket before pulling the handgun from his waistband and releasing the safety catch. Now he felt it: that buzz; the old, familiar blend of fear, excitement, and anticipation. In spite of the desperate situation in which he found himself, he felt alive, vibrant … ready.

He swung the door inwards as silently as possible, ducking down to knee height while stepping swiftly through, panning his weapon – angled upwards – swiftly from left to right, ready to face any assailant who might be waiting for him. There was no-one there. He paused for a few seconds, allowing the tension in his muscles to subside before setting about a systematic search of the ground floor, moving silently from one room to another, always with the SIG-Sauer preceding him, grasped firmly in a double-handed grip, ready for action. Nothing.

He started up the stairs, gingerly testing each one with his toe before placing his full weight on it, lest a creaking joint should betray his presence. As he reached the second-to-last step, his probing toe evoked the tiniest of creaks. He froze, heart thumping violently in his chest, finger tense as it curled around the trigger. Several seconds passed; nothing happened. He shifted the gun to a single-handed grip and reached up with his left hand to grasp the post at the top of the stairs. Very gently and very carefully, he lifted his foot and stepped right over the offending step and onto the landing, utilising his grip on the wooden post to pull himself up.

Once on the landing, he swiftly scanned his surroundings: four doors; two open, two closed. He crept forward, keeping the gun levelled in front of him, and checked the first of the open doors, stepping silently into the room with his gun levelled. The curtains were not closed, and there was enough light streaming through the windows from the streetlamps outside to see that the room was unoccupied. He turned around and stepped back onto the landing, carefully approaching the second of the open doors. This room was also at the front of the house, and similarly illuminated by the street lighting. It, too, was empty. He moved silently back onto the landing before pausing for a few seconds, listening carefully for any signs of life. Still nothing.

He approached the first of the closed doors and gently turned the knob, pushing the door slowly inwards; it was the bathroom. The light was much dimmer here, at the back of the house, so Tim withdrew from his pocket the tiny penlight he was carrying and switched it on, panning it around the small room. As he shone the narrow beam towards the bath, what he saw made him gasp involuntarily; only his years of training stopped him from crying out. The bolt cutters propped against the side of the bath were smeared with blood. A dark rivulet had run down the handle and there were several spots on the floor too. Now his heart was hammering furiously.

With trepidation, he crept slowly towards the bath and shone the beam of his torch onto it. The white towel which lay in a crumpled heap in the bottom of the bath was soaked with blood.

So this was where they had done it: severed his girlfriend's poor finger ... with *bolt cutters* for Christ's sake. Had they even given her any anaesthetic? He doubted it. He felt an overwhelming surge of anger grip him from inside. The bastards were going to pay for this ... they were going to pay dearly. But first things first: his priority was to rescue Raquel. Was she still here in the house? There was only one more room to check.

He switched off his penlight and waited in silence for over a minute, allowing time for his eyes to readjust to the darkness, and his ragged breathing to stabilise. Once again he listened intently for any sound that might betray the presence of someone else in the house. Nothing.

Careful not to make a sound, he stepped out of the bathroom and back onto the landing. He made his way stealthily towards the one remaining closed door. Holding his pistol in his right hand, he placed his left on the door knob, pausing again, straining to catch any slight sound coming from behind that closed door. Still there was nothing.

Slowly, gingerly, he turned the knob. He winced as it made a slight squeaking sound. He froze for a moment, maintaining his hold on the doorknob in its fully rotated position, fearful that releasing it might cause a further sound to betray his presence. There was no sound from within the room – still nothing to suggest that the house was occupied.

Finally he pushed gently; the door inched slowly open. He paused, waiting, listening, every sinew stretched taut. There was nothing. He began tentatively pushing the door once more, and then, when it was about halfway open, he heard – or maybe sensed – something. This, his instincts told him, was the time for action.

Abandoning all stealth, he hefted his shoulder against the door and slammed it back against the wall as hard as he could. Except it didn't hit the wall. The sound of the door slamming into flesh and bone was immediately followed by a cry of pain and the muffled thump of a heavy object hitting the carpet. In one fluid movement Tim yanked the door back and slammed the butt of his weapon into the startled face of the man flattened against the wall. He screamed and flung his hands up to his face, but did not go down. Tim raised his gun once more and swung it hard against the side of the man's head. This time he uttered a low groan and slid to the floor. Tim whirled around, his gun levelled in front of him, ready to face any other assailants, but there were none.

He turned around and bent down to examine the unconscious figure on the floor. Blood was flowing freely from his shattered nose. Tim checked his pulse; it was strong and regular. Good – at least he hadn't killed the man. He pulled back an eyelid; only the white of the eye was showing. He would be out cold for some time.

Tim scanned the rest of the room. Where was Raquel? He looked at the bed; in the dim light he couldn't tell if there was anyone in – or on – the bed. As he approached it, though, there did appear to be someone under the covers. His heart was pounding like a jackhammer as reached out with his left hand to peel back the cover, his gun poised in his right.

There was no-one in the bed: just a row of pillows. But when he peeled back the duvet a little further, what Tim saw made his breath catch in his throat. Around halfway down the bed the sheet was defaced by a large, deep-red stain spanning almost the entire width of the bed.

Chapter 26

Tim waved the smelling salts he had found in the bathroom cabinet under the unconscious man's bloody nose. He groaned and shook his head from side to side before snapping it back sharply in an attempt to evade the pungent smell. As his senses returned to him, his oriental features contorted into a vicious scowl, made all the more ugly by the blood still trickling from his damaged nose onto his mouth, chin, and shirt front. He made a vain attempt to rise to his feet but quickly realised that his arms and legs were firmly bound to the chair. He slumped back.

'You Wang Dong?' said Tim.

There was no response.

'That nose looks painful,' continued Tim, his tone casual and conversational.

The man made another attempt to break free of his bonds, only succeeding in rocking the chair slightly before it fell back to its original position. He glared venomously at Tim.

'Maybe you didn't hear my question,' said Tim, taking a step forward and bending down so that his face was only inches from the other man's. 'Are you Wang Dong?'

The man spat in Tim's face. He didn't flinch, but just calmly wiped away the warm liquid with the back of his sleeve.

'I can see we are going to have to do this the hard way,' said Tim, shaking his head slowly, in the manner of a parent expressing disappointment at the behaviour of an unruly child. He picked up the SIG from where it was lying on the bed and slowly raised it until the tip of the silencer was just an inch from the man's bloody nose. He saw fear flash in those dark, slanting eyes. 'Your name.'

'I Wang Dong. So what?'

'Who sent you to kidnap Raquel Groves?'

'Who she?'

Tim moved the gun until it was pressing against the side of the man's chin, he applied gentle pressure turning the man's head towards the bed.

'You didn't expect me to fall for the old "pillows under the cover" trick did you?' As Wang had been unconscious at the time, of course he didn't know that Tim had, in fact, fallen for it hook, line, and sinker. 'Did you think I would just rush over to the bed and let you shoot me in the back?'

Wang's lower lip turned outwards in an expression of sullen, stubborn resistance. He shrugged, defiantly, but said nothing.

'Who sent you?' insisted Tim.

'I not know. He never give me his name.'

'Not good enough, I'm afraid.'

Tim lifted the gun and pushed it forward until the cold steel of the silencer made contact with Wang's ruined nose. He tried to pull back but quickly found that the back of his head was pressed against the wall. He cried out in pain as Tim rotated the muzzle alternately one way and then the other, grinding it into cartilage and bone. The man's scream was blood-curdling, but Tim didn't react – he had seen and heard far worse.

'OK ... OK ... stop ... I tell you,' yelled Wang in a high-pitched scream.

Tim relaxed the pressure but still kept the tip of the silencer lightly in contact with the man's bloody nose. 'Well?'

'His name Chang Wei,' gasped Wang.

So Roy had been right. The man he had previously thought to be just an unpleasant business rival was indeed the vicious criminal behind Raquel's abduction.

Tim moved the gun downwards, pressing it against the Chinaman's lips, eventually forcing the tip of the silencer between his teeth and into his mouth. He moved his face right up to Wang's and fixed him with a withering stare.

'Have you killed her?'

Wang's eyes widened in fear as he tried to shake his head violently from side to side while making a strange guttural sound. Tim realised that he couldn't actually speak with the gun jammed into his mouth. He withdrew the weapon, but kept it pointing at the man's frightened face.

'No ... no ... she still alive,' Wang cried out.

Tim's heart skipped a beat as hope surged within him. *Thank God.*

'Where is she?'

'She on the way to China now ... Shenzhen'

His heart sank as swiftly as it had just lifted. *China? Oh Christ, no.*

He did his best to hide his dismay from Wang Dong. 'Where? I want an address,' he demanded.

'I not know.'

'You sure?'

'I sure. They not tell me everything.'

Tim withdrew the gun from Wang's face and took a step back; the relief on the man's face was clear to see. Tim stared at him through narrowed eyes, his mouth set in a grim, straight line as he tried to assess whether the man was lying. Wang tried to maintain eye contact but there was something – a slight flinch – which flitted across his features, alerting Tim's suspicions. Maybe he knew more than he was admitting.

Tim changed tack. 'Was it you who cut off her finger?'

'I ... I ...,' stuttered Wang.

'Did you do it?' demanded Tim, pressing the tip of the silencer to the man's forehead.

'Alright, alright,' he screamed, squirming furiously in his chair as he tried in vain to back away from the gun.

Tim withdrew the weapon by a couple of inches. 'Well?' he demanded.

Perspiration was streaming freely down the man's face, mingling with the blood flowing from his shattered nose to create a sickly deep-pink fluid which soaked into his shirt. He struggled to control his ragged breathing. 'It was orders ... orders from Chang Wei ... not my idea ... I not want to do it ... really ...'

'Shut up,' ordered Tim. Wang did so, staring back at Tim, chewing nervously at his lower lip.

Tim regarded him through cold, unblinking eyes, his mouth grimly-set, a vein pulsing in his temple. He said nothing, but after several more seconds he turned and stepped out of the room. When he returned a few moments later, he was carrying the blood-streaked bolt cutters.

Wang's eyes widened in terror. 'No ... no ... you can't ... I told you everything.'

Wang's wrists were firmly bound to the arms of the chair but his fingers were free to move. Tim reached for the little finger of Wang's left hand, prising it up from the arm of the chair as the man tried desperately to keep it clamped down. As he forced Wang's finger upward, he slipped the anvil of the bolt cutters between finger and woodwork.

'Is this how you did it?' said Tim, his voice grim and determined.

'No ... nooo ... please ... I already tell you everything I know.'

'Then you don't need to speak any more.'

Tim rolled the face flannel he had brought from the bathroom into a fat cylindrical wad and stuffed it into Wang's mouth. Slowly and deliberately, he began squeezing the handles of the bolt cutters together. The Chinaman's eyes widened further and tears sprang from their corners.

As Tim continued squeezing, Wang uttered a strangled, guttural moan which sounded barely human. Tim was surprised at just how easily the powerful tool sliced through the bone, which seemed to offer practically no resistance, but merely a faint crunching sound as the finger parted just above the first joint.

Chapter 27

The severed finger dropped noiselessly onto the carpet; Wang watched in horror as blood flowed freely from the stub where his finger had been.

Tim pulled the flannel from Wang Dong's mouth. He was whimpering like an injured animal. Tim stared into his eyes, his expression unmoving – he felt no pity for this man, nor remorse for what he had just done.

'Have you remembered the address yet?' said Tim, the bloody tool hanging at his side, held loosely in his right hand.

Wang shook his head. 'I not know no address ... really.'

Tim tightened his grip on the bolt cutters and raised them in front of Wang's eyes, which were, by now, a picture of pure, unadulterated terror. He moved unhurriedly around to the other side of the chair.

Wang started shaking violently, writhing from side to side. 'No ... nooo ... I don't know ... really ... you got to believe me ... I don't know ... I ...'

Tim grabbed his little finger and, as before, prized it up sufficiently to position the anvil of the bolt cutter beneath it. He grasped both handles and looked directly into Wang's terrified eyes. The man was sobbing uncontrollably now.

'Pleeease ... no ... I don't know nothing else.'

Tim shook his head slowly, his face a picture of regret as he removed one hand from the bolt cutters in order to pick up the makeshift gag and stuff it back into Wang's mouth. Once again, he grasped both handles of the wicked tool, looking directly into Wang's terrified eyes as he began, very slowly, the stroke which would cost Wang another finger.

Wang shook his head violently from side to side, his eyes bulging so much that they looked fit to burst from their sockets. Then, quite suddenly, his expression changed to one of abject defeat. He scrunched his eyes tight shut as he prepared himself for the searing pain which was to come. The blade closed slowly until it was pressing into the flesh. Wang clenched his jaw and screwed his eyes even more tightly shut.

Tim didn't close the handles together to complete the stroke. He just held that position, with the blade pressing lightly against flesh, until, eventually, Wang opened his eyes once more. Tim gazed into those dark eyes for several long seconds, trying to interpret what they were telling him. He could discern only fear and confusion.

'You know,' he said, 'I think you might actually be telling me the truth … maybe you really don't know any more.' Wang licked his lips and gave a small shake of his head, fear still palpable in his eyes.

Tim opened up the handles and flung the tool onto the floor. He picked up the previously severed finger and held it a few inches in front of the man's eyes. 'If you tell anyone … anyone at all … about our little discussion, it'll be your dick next. You understand?' Wang nodded furiously, causing a fresh torrent of blood to escape his smashed nose and run down over the makeshift gag and down the front of his body.

Tim laid the bloody appendage on the table, before withdrawing from a sheath at the back of his belt, a Bowie knife. As he raised the wickedly curved blade towards Wang, the frightened man's eyes once again bulged in fear and desperation. He shook his head, desperately trying to call out, but succeeding only in producing a strangled, animal whimpering noise. Tim took Wang's good hand in his own and prized it up from the arm of the chair, slipping the blade of the knife between wrist and woodwork. Wang closed his eyes and clamped his teeth firmly together.

With a swift sawing motion, Tim severed the rope which was binding the man's wrist. Wang's eyes widened in astonishment.

'You've still got one good hand,' said Tim, inclining his head towards the free hand whose fingers Wang was now flexing, 'so you should be able to undo the rest yourself. Just don't forget what I told you.'

Wang shook his head, relief flooding his oriental features.

Tim picked up the SIG-Sauer from the table where it lay and strode out of the room.

***

It was 3.18 a.m. Tim had been on the phone to Roy for the last twenty minutes, recounting what he had learned.

'So,' he concluded, 'we know that, just as you suspected, Chang Wei is the person behind this.'

'Evil bastard,' interjected Roy.

'Yeah,' agreed Tim, sighing deeply. 'Anyway,' he continued, 'we also know that she is now on the way to China – to Shenzhen – but unfortunately I have no idea where exactly they are taking her.'

'Are you sure that the guy you beat up wasn't holding something back?'

'I'm as sure as I can be.'

'How? How can you be so sure?'

'Look, I've spent a lot of time interrogating prisoners in Afghanistan; I have a pretty good idea of when a man has told you everything he knows.'

Roy suddenly grasped his meaning. He didn't know exactly what Tim had done to the man, and he didn't want to either, but he now realised that there was a hard, ruthless streak in his daughter's boyfriend which he had never previously seen. He shuddered, but did not press Tim any further.

'So what now?' said Roy. 'Chang Wei seems unwilling to negotiate, and refuses to return Raquel until *he* decides the time is right, even if I comply with all his demands. And if we go to the police, I have little doubt that he will carry out his threat to kill Raquel.'

Tim's voice was firm and resolute when he replied. 'Look, this may not be what you want to hear, but you can't negotiate with people like this, and you must never ... *never* ... give in to them.'

Roy was silent for a few moments as he processed this assessment. In his heart, he knew Tim was right.

He sighed in exasperation. 'So what *can* we do?'

'We have to fight fire with fire – start thinking like they do.'

'How? We can't just ...' his voice tailed off as a creeping suspicion infiltrated his mind. 'Are you planning to ... to go after them?'

'Only if I have your approval to do so.'

'What do you mean?'

'If I find her and attempt to rescue her, and it all goes wrong ... well, the consequences could be disastrous.'

A massive lump formed in Roy's throat, as he grasped Tim's meaning. He couldn't swallow; he couldn't breathe properly. The only thing which lay to hand which might lubricate his parched throat was the last inch of flat, stale beer in the bottle standing on the coffee table. He grabbed the bottle and drained its contents, gasping as he set the bottle back down. He spent several long seconds considering what Tim had said.

'If you go after them there's a chance she'll die, isn't there?' he said, his voice faltering.

'Yes there is.'

'But if we go to the police,' continued Roy, 'there's probably an even greater chance that she'll die.'

'Yes,' said Tim, his voice level, 'I think so.'

Roy felt a prickle of sweat break out on his face and a shudder ripple down his spine as he struggled to come to terms with the impossible dilemma facing him. He felt trapped, cornered. In business, he had never been afraid to take difficult decisions, but this was about his daughter's *life*. As he wrestled with the options – none of them palatable – he suddenly realised that there was yet another facet of this nightmarish quandary to consider.

'What about you? If you go after them then *your* life will be in danger too.'

Tim's deep sigh was clearly audible over the phone. 'Look, I've never been terribly demonstrative – to you and Donna – about my feelings for Raquel, but now's the time to say it: I love her, and I would rather die than see her come to harm. I ... well I ...'

'You don't need to say any more.' Suddenly Roy's mind was made up. 'Do it. I'll help in any way I can.'

'Don't you need to talk to Donna?'

'I will, but not now. When I tell her, she'll need time to digest what has happened and to get over the shock before she'll be able to think rationally; that's time we don't have. What can I do to help?'

'I have all the equipment that I'm likely to need.'

'Equipment?'

'Surveillance equipment, tools for breaking and entering, and weapons.'

Weapons. Roy could still hardly come to terms with this new world into which he had been thrust. He understood how to deal with the deceit, double-dealing, and blackmail which he had encountered in his business career, but violence, extortion, kidnapping? This was new territory: territory in which he had to concede that Tim knew better than he how to proceed.

'So what else do you need?'

'Money. I have to get to China with weapons and equipment and somehow find out where they're keeping her. That will cost money – money which I don't have.'

'OK, when the banks open in the morning I'll withdraw as much cash as I can lay my hands on. What currency?'

'U.S. Dollars are probably the best bet ... they're accepted almost anywhere.'

'OK, give me a couple of hours after the banks open to get the money and get back here.'

'I'll be back there at around 11.00 a.m. then.'

'OK ... and Tim ...'

'What?'

'Be careful.' As Roy uttered the words, he realised how utterly ridiculous they sounded in this context. *Be careful*, as if Tim were about to just cross a busy road or something.

'I will. See you at eleven.'

***

Once again, Tim felt the old familiar feeling which preceded a mission. Fear blended with excitement and anticipation, but this time there was something different: the gut-wrenching knowledge that it was not only his own life which was on the line, or those of his comrades, but of the one person in the world who meant the most to him. He gazed at the bed which he normally shared with Raquel. It was neatly made and undisturbed. He wondered whether they would ever share that bed again. He shook his head to dispel the chilling thought. *Focus ... it's a mission like any other ... don't let emotional involvement get in the way. You need to be operating at one hundred percent.*

He bent down and reached under the bed for the jemmy which he kept there. He moved to the corner of the room and pulled back the carpet before wriggling the edge of the jemmy into a gap between two floorboards. As he levered the tool backward, one of the floorboards lifted easily; it was not nailed down, for his was the second time that night that Tim had accessed this secret hiding place. He laid the floorboard aside and reached into the gap below, withdrawing a Heckler and Koch G36 assault rifle, laying it carefully on the carpet. He reached into the gap again, this time finding a biscuit tin containing several magazines of ammunition, which he laid down alongside the rifle. Finally, he took out a small explosives kit, designed for blowing any locks too sophisticated to succumb to his lock-picking tools.

He replaced the floorboard and carpet before standing up and gazing at the various items laid out before him. He didn't really know why he had taken the trouble to illegally purloin this rifle – or the SIG-Sauer pistol – when he left the SAS. He had intended to pursue a peaceful new career of some sort – not something requiring him to own firearms. And yet he had obtained them, and he had kept them. Maybe he had just been around guns for so long that he no longer felt secure without their comforting presence. Maybe he had somehow known that one day they would be needed. Well, that day had arrived.

He moved to the wardrobe and opened the door, rummaging within until he located a large black sports holdall which he laid on the bed. He gathered up the weapons and other items from the floor and placed them inside the holdall before picking up the SIG-Sauer handgun from where he had laid it on the dressing table and putting that in the bag too. He went out to the garage to locate the other things he needed: a coil of polyurethane rope and a small pair of bolt cutters. At the sight of the bolt cutters he felt a surge of anger as the image of the bloody tool at Wang Dong's house once again rushed into his mind. He struggled to suppress the unbidden emotion. He moved back into the house and up to the bedroom where he put the rope and bolt cutters in the holdall. He went over to the chest of drawers where he withdrew a small pair of binoculars, adding these to the other items in the holdall. Finally, he grabbed a couple of changes of clothing from the wardrobe and stuffed those into the bag on top of the weapons and equipment.

Satisfied that he had everything he needed, he zipped up the bag – now full to capacity – before hefting it onto his shoulder to test its weight. It was very heavy, but he had handled even heavier backpacks in the past; he would manage. He laid the bag on the floor alongside the bed and checked his watch: 4.03 a.m. Time to get some sleep: he had a tough day – maybe many tough days – ahead of him.

Chapter 28

Roy's morning had been frantic. At 8.00 a.m. he had begun the rounds of the automated cash dispensers, drawing as much cash as he could from every one of his credit cards and debit cards. At 9.00 a.m. he was the first customer in the bank where he held a current account. By 10.30 a.m. he had visited every bank and every building society in which he and Donna held accounts. It was now 10.45 a.m. and Roy was back at home. Up to this moment the morning had flashed by in a dizzying whirl, but now, as he waited anxiously for Tim to arrive, every minute which passed felt like an hour.

Finally, just before eleven, the doorbell rang. When Roy opened the door, he was immediately greeted by Sammy jumping up, scrabbling and licking at him, his tail wagging furiously. Roy bent down to ruffle the fur on the dog's head.

'Hi, little chap,' he said, allowing the animal to lick his hands and his neck until the initial rush of enthusiasm abated slightly.

Tim was wearing pretty much the same kind of clothes as he usually wore: blue denim jeans, trainers, and a grey polo shirt. What was Roy expecting? Black combat fatigues, a balaclava, a blackened face, and a grenade belt? In spite of the tense situation, he chuckled inwardly at the absurdity of the mental image he had conjured.

'Can you look after him while I'm gone?' said Tim

'Yes, of course. Come on in.'

Neither man smiled or wasted time on pleasantries as they moved through to the lounge. Sammy immediately jumped up onto his favourite chair by the window – Roy and Donna had long since given up trying to dissuade him from doing so, and had instead settled for permanently leaving a linen throw spread over what was now known as 'Sammy's chair'.

Roy picked up two packages from the coffee table. One was a plain brown envelope, the other a large, much bulkier, padded envelope

'There's £5,000 sterling in this one,' he said – Tim nodded as he took the envelope – 'and $31,000 US in this.'

'OK, thanks,' said Tim, 'but, I'm afraid this isn't actually going to be enough.'

Roy felt a sickening lurch in his stomach. 'It's ... well it's all I could lay hands on in cash at short notice. How much do you need then?'

Tim raised both his hands in front of him, palms forward, then lowered them slowly in a calming gesture. 'Look, this will probably be plenty in terms of ready cash for unforeseen expenses but the big issue is actually getting out to China. I can't just jump on a scheduled flight and check in a bagful of weapons and stuff. I've got to do it another way.'

'What other way?' asked Roy, puzzled.

'I have an old army buddy who's willing to help out; I called him late last night and spoke to him again this morning.'

'Go on.'

'He's now a pilot working for a charter airline company ... executive jets. You can hire a plane from his company and he'll fly it for me. As long as I can find a way to get onto the plane without going through the regular airport security checks there'll be no questions asked about what I'm carrying.'

Roy nodded, understanding now dawning. 'So it's chartering the plane that you need the money for ... and I imagine that isn't going to be cheap.'

Tim shook his head, grimacing. 'They only have one plane which can be made available at such short notice and it's bloody expensive.'

'How expensive?'

As Jeff – my army pal – is one of the company's own employees, they are prepared to discount the price, but it's still going to be almost three thousand pounds per hour.'

'Per *hour*?' He could hardly believe it.

'And,' said Tim, 'we have no way of knowing how long we'll need the plane. If we need to keep it for more than a few days the bill could run to hundreds of thousands.'

Roy nodded, slowly. 'But what choice do I have? ... I'll pay it.'

This would make a very big hole in the money which he had made as a result of the floatation of his company some years ago, but he was willing to spend his last penny if it might bring Raquel back to him safely. Thank God he actually had the means to pay this kind of money.

'Then we have a shot at doing this,' declared Tim, his voice resolute and firm.

'But wait' said Roy. 'Time is against us here – how long is it going to take to organise and pay for this charter?'

'Jeff has told his boss that he'll vouch for you. If you can pay a fifty thousand pound deposit by direct bank transfer today, they'll accept payment for the balance at the end of the charter.'

'OK, I'll make the transfer this morning. What happens now?'

'Well the plane is based at Farnborough, in Hampshire, but as time is so critical, I took the liberty of asking Jeff to fly it up to Birmingham this morning.' Tim glanced at his watch. 'He should be on his way right now.'

'OK, good,' said Roy. He exhaled heavily, massaging both his temples with his fingers. 'Now, once you get to China, how are you going to find where they're holding her? All we know is that it's somewhere in Shenzhen.'

'Chang will know,' said Tim.

'Yes he will,' said Roy, grimly.

'That's where I'll start,' continued Tim. 'Can you give me his home address and that of the factory?'

Roy grabbed his briefcase from where it was lying on the sofa and placed it on the coffee table, clicking open the catches and raising the lid. He withdrew some papers and copied down the relevant details.

'Do you have a photograph of Chang?'

'No, but I can get one.'

He fired up his laptop and connected to the internet. Within a couple of minutes he had accessed the Sotoyo Electronics website and found Chang's photograph. He printed it and handed it to Tim.

'You realise,' he said, as he passed the sheet of paper to Tim, 'that by now he may well have heard about your encounters with his henchmen over here. If so, he'll know that you're coming.'

Tim shook his head. 'I'm guessing that those two goons will be too scared to let him know that they spilled the beans. I can't imagine that Chang would take too kindly to *that* admission.'

Roy nodded slowly, his brow wrinkling as he digested this thought. 'Let's hope you're right. So, assuming you can actually get to Chang, what then?'

'Then,' said Tim, 'I'll have to play it by ear. There's no point in over-thinking this when I just don't know what I'll encounter.'

Roy felt helpless. Tim was just about to put himself in mortal danger in an effort to save his daughter, while Roy himself could do nothing but wait and hope.

'Look, Tim. I'm not sure there's much I can do to help, but *please* stay in touch won't you?' Tim nodded. 'And let me know if there's anything I *can* do from this end.'

'OK, I will. I have to go now.' He passed Roy a slip of paper. 'Here are the bank details for the money transfer.'

The two men shook hands and Roy grasped Tim's forearm. 'For Christ's sake, Tim, be careful.' *Why do I keep saying that stupid thing?*

Tim nodded. A few seconds later he was gone.

Roy inhaled deeply, holding the air in his lungs for a couple of seconds before puffing out his cheeks and exhaling through pursed lips as he tried to settle his nerves. *OK, what next?*

There was no way that Roy could go to work while this appalling crisis was unfolding; he called his PA. 'Hi Sophie, Roy here.'

'Oh, hello Roy,' she replied, brightly. 'I was wondering why you hadn't shown up for work this morning. Anything wrong?'

'Not exactly, but I … um, well … I have some unexpected domestic issues to deal with, and I'm afraid I am going to have to take a week's holiday at short notice.'

'A week?' she said, surprise evident in her voice. 'But you never said … I mean, well, er … nothing too serious I hope?'

Roy didn't respond to her question. 'Can you ask Kevin to stand in for me during the coming week? And perhaps you can try to clear my diary as far as is possible. Maybe Kevin can handle some of my appointments, but if there's anything that you think really needs my personal attention you'll have to postpone it until I'm back.'

'OK, Roy. I'll take care of it. Er … is there anything I can do to help?' She sounded genuinely concerned.

'Thanks, Sophie, but no … just make the arrangements we discussed.'

'OK, well … see you next week then.'

'Thanks. Bye.'

With that bit of housekeeping attended to, Roy's thoughts turned back to Tim's desperate mission in China. He was worried sick now for Tim's safety, as well as Raquel's. What if Tim's assessment was wrong and the Chinese he had brushed with in England had warned Chang that he was coming? Then they would be ready for him, which would render his chance of success much, much lower. Worse still, they might decide that this was reason enough to do more harm to Raquel … maybe even to kill her. He felt an icy shiver shimmy down his spine at the thought. Had he made the right decision in letting Tim go on this solo mission? Whether he had or had not, the decision was made, and if there was one thing he had learned during his many years in business, it was that however finely balanced a decision might be, once the decision was made, you stick with it come what may; changing course midway was almost always a recipe for disaster. Although this was a very different situation from anything Roy had ever faced in his business career, he felt that that principle still held true. There was no going back now.

He looked up at the clock on the wall: 12.17 p.m. He would just have time to set up the bank transfer before facing up to his most difficult task of the day: he was due to collect Donna from the airport in around two hours' time. So far he had told her nothing.

Chapter 29

Birmingham International Airport, West Midlands, England.

Tim crouched down by the perimeter fence and peered through his binoculars. As far as he could ascertain from what Jeff had told him, this was the part of the airport where the plane should be, but there was no sign of it. Nevertheless he had to be ready.

He laid down the binoculars, unzipped the holdall which lay on the grass alongside him and took out the bolt cutters. Although the tool was a small one, it made light work of the thin wire of the chain link fencing: in less than three minutes there was a gap large enough to crawl though. He returned the tool to the holdall and settled down to wait.

Interminable minutes passed, with still no sign of the plane. He checked his watch – 1.37 p.m. Jeff was thirty-seven minutes late now – what the hell had happened to him? Tim's heartbeat was quickening and a tight knot had formed inside him; he wiped away a rivulet of perspiration which had trickled down his temple. He withdrew his mobile from his pocket and called Jeff's number – no reply, just his voicemail. He left a message: Jeff, I'm in position; call me back.

Stay calm, he told himself. There could be any number of reasons why Jeff might be late. His take-off from Farnborough could easily have been delayed by Air Traffic Control, and similarly his landing at Birmingham. Surely if there was any real problem, Jeff would have been in contact, wouldn't he? But then again, why wasn't he answering his mobile? As the minutes ticked by, Tim's anxiety grew and grew like some monstrous tumour in his gut.

He checked his watch once more: 1.49 p.m. He decided to try calling Jeff again. But even as he began scrolling through the address book, the phone vibrated in his hand, trilling softly as it did so. Tim's heart leapt.

'Jeff? Thank God. What's happening?'

'Take-off was delayed; things were a bit busy at Farnborough. Anyway, listen – I've just been given clearance to take off by Air Traffic Control. I'm just about to taxi towards my take-off position; I'll be there in about five or six minutes. Start your run as soon as you see me begin to make the turn at the end of the runway. I won't be able to stop for long to let you aboard.'

'OK – got it. Let's hope no-one sees me.'

'Good Luck.'

He hung up.

Tim peeled back the flap of fencing which he had cut and pushed the holdall through the resulting gap. He tucked his head down and scrambled through after it. Now he crouched down, waiting, trying to make himself look as inconspicuous as possible, yet feeling that he must stand out in stark relief against the featureless grass background. He glanced up at the control tower, hoping that those inside would be glued to their computer screens rather than scanning their surroundings.

Then he saw it: a Gulfstream G550 executive jet in the distinctive navy and pale blue livery which Jeff had told him to look out for. The plane moved steadily along the taxi-lane parallel to the runway; Tim could hear the whine of the engines now. At last it slowed right down and began to make the one-hundred-and-eighty-degree turn which would bring it around to the end of the runway. This was it.

He scrambled to his feet, picked up the holdall, and set off at a crouching run towards the position where he judged the aircraft would come to a standstill, hoping against hope that he would not be spotted by anyone. Three hundred yards ... his heart was pounding ... two hundred yards ... his breathing was coming in heavy, laboured gasps ... he felt a pain beginning to burn in his side. The combination of running in this unnatural crouched position and having to carry the heavy holdall was taking its toll.

Shit! I wish I'd kept myself in better shape.

As the plane came to a complete stop, he still had about one hundred yards left to cover. As he kept running, he saw the cabin door swing open and a couple of seconds later the steps were lowered – thankfully they were on the blind side of the plane from the control tower.

Fifty yards... twenty ... ten ... finally he made it. With a superhuman effort, he hefted the heavy bag up the steps and into the open door, where Jeff grabbed it and swung it out of the way, before grasping Tim's hand and helping him aboard. Tim collapsed in a heap, panting heavily as Jeff retracted the steps and secured the door, before hurrying through to the flight deck and taking his seat.

Tim heard, and felt, the rapidly increasing whine of the engines as they revved up, the plane shuddering slightly as Jeff held it on the brakes.

'Hold on to something!' yelled Jeff.

Tim grabbed hold of the metalwork at the base of the front row of seats, bracing his feet against the flight deck bulkhead. The plane surged forward, accelerating at a pace which felt truly shocking to Tim, wedged awkwardly as he was on the floor. Just as the acceleration began to level off, affording him a moment's respite, the plane's nose swivelled skyward, tipping Tim backward and causing his head to smash painfully against the metal support below the seat. A myriad of multi-coloured stars exploded behind his eyes as he struggled to maintain consciousness. He hung on grimly as the plane climbed, maintaining the same crazy angle.

At length the aircraft began to level out sufficiently for Tim to scramble, unsteadily to his feet. He felt the warm sensation of blood trickling down his temple. He felt, gingerly for the cut, which was just below his hairline. He withdrew a handkerchief from his pocket and pressed it against the wound, using the other hand to steady himself as he staggered through to the flight deck and dropped into the co-pilot's seat alongside Jeff, who glanced across at him anxiously.

'Sorry about the rather abrupt take-off, but I couldn't hang about for too long at the end of the runway or Air Traffic Control would have given me hell.'

Tim gave a wry grin. 'I thought you'd at least have let me get strapped in first … and what about the safety demonstration from a lovely flight attendant?'

'I'm as lovely as you get on this flight – sorry, mate.'

Tim transferred the handkerchief to his left hand, pressing it once more against the cut on his head, before leaning across to shake Jeff's hand. 'Anyway, it's good to see you again, Jeff. I can't thank you enough for this.'

'No sweat,' replied Jeff. As he smiled, the skin at the corners of his startlingly intense blue eyes crinkled up, beneath his unruly mop of sandy-blonde hair. He was a ruggedly handsome man, but the deep lines around his mouth and eyes made him look older than his thirty-seven years. 'Look, there's a first aid kit in the locker just behind the door. Why don't you patch yourself up as best you can, and then you can tell me the whole story?'

***

Oh my God,' cried Donna, her face a mask of fear and disbelief. 'This just can't be happening.' She sank back into the sofa and placed her head in her hands, her breath catching in short, desperate gasps.

During the drive back from the airport, Roy had said nothing about Raquel's plight. Thankfully, Donna had spent practically the whole time talking about her trip to Boston: the funeral, the people she had met, and the hospitality she had received from Gabby and her family. But once they had arrived home he could put off the moment no longer, and the news had completely overwhelmed her.

He sat down alongside her, placing his arm around her shoulder, gently pulling her to him. She buried her head in his chest, sobbing, her shoulders heaving. When she looked up, her cheeks were lined with dark streaks of makeup and her eyes wore an expression which was desperate, pleading. She was struggling to speak.

When, finally, she was able to regain some level of control over her breathing, her tone was accusatory. 'Why didn't you call me?'

Roy placed both hands on her shoulders and looked her directly in the eyes. 'I wanted to be with you when I told you … I couldn't bear the thought of your having to deal with this alone.'

She nodded, but her eyes were not accepting. 'I can understand that, but … well, you had no right to send Tim off on this cloak-and-dagger mission without consulting me.'

'I didn't send him … he was the one who wanted to do it, but yes, I condoned it.'

Her eyes flashed with anger. 'For Christ's sake, Roy … she's my daughter too. Don't you think I should have a say in this?'

Roy felt a sickening sinking feeling deep in his gut. How could he have got it so wrong?

'I'm sorry. I … well … I did what I thought was best. I…'

She cut him off. 'So excluding me from the decision was what you thought was best?'

'No … I didn't mean that. If Tim was to have any chance of success it was going to be necessary to act fast. I just didn't think we had time to debate the issue, and … well, I didn't want to lay this on you while you were on your own in America.'

Donna had stopped sobbing now. 'I'd have thought that after all the years we've been married you would know that I'm stronger than that. You should have involved me.'

Roy felt empty, drained. 'Yes, I guess I should.' He felt the prickle of tears welling up in his eyes. He hung his head and they lapsed into silence for several seconds.

Donna placed a finger under his chin, gently raising his head until she was looking directly into his eyes. 'I'd have made the same decision.'

'What? You mean …'

'From everything you've told me, I think going to the police would be a mistake. I think you made the right decision.' She paused before adding, 'But you should have included me.'

His heart leapt. 'Oh, Donna, thank God.'

He hugged her to him. They were nowhere near any kind of resolution to this appalling situation, but it was an enormous comfort to know that Donna was with him.

Chapter 30

They were cruising at thirty-two thousand feet. Tim had just finished relating the whole horrific sequence of events surrounding Raquel's kidnapping.

Jeff whistled softly. 'That's quite a story. These sound like some seriously bad people that your girlfriend's dad has got mixed up with.'

Tim gave a grim, mirthless chuckle. 'That's for sure.'

'Look, I know you can take care of yourself, but are you sure you want to go in there alone? What if they know you're coming and they're waiting for you?'

'I'm sort of counting on the fact that they don't, but I'll be ready for anything.'

'Hmm, sounds bloody risky to me.'

'I know it's damned well risky, but what alternative do I have?'

Jeff didn't reply.

As they sat in silence, Tim began thinking about how he would plan his mission. The first thing he needed to know was the timeline within which he would need to work.

'How long will it take us to get there, Jeff?'

'Well, the plane has enough range, on the full tanks we started with, to make it to Shenzhen in one hop; that should see us landing around 2 a.m. tomorrow, UK time ... 9 a.m. Shenzhen time.'

Tim was anxious to get started on the hunt for Raquel as soon as possible, but he was already feeling tired – having had very little sleep the previous night – and he would be absolutely wrecked by the time they arrived in Shenzhen. He would be in no fit state to embark on his mission immediately; he knew that tiredness could get him – and Raquel – killed.

'I'm going to need to get some sleep before I go looking for Chang,' he said. 'I reckon our first priority is to hire a car and a satnav, and then get checked in to the nearest hotel. If we land at around nine we should be able to get into a hotel by, say, eleven. I could then catch four or five hours sleep before I go looking for Chang.'

'Sounds like a plan,' said Jeff. 'In any case, though, why don't you try and sleep for a while right now? You had hardly any sleep last night, and in any case I might need you awake a bit later.'

'Why?' said Tim.

'Well I didn't exactly have a great night's sleep myself. I might need to leave the plane on autopilot for an hour or two to catch a little sleep too. If so I'll need you fully awake to alert me if anything seems to be wrong.'

'OK ... and thanks for everything, Jeff.'

Tim pulled a blanket around his shoulders and tried to surrender to sleep.

***

'Hi Dad.' Roy immediately recognised the voice of his elder daughter, Beatrice.

'Oh, hello ... how are you doing?'

'Well I feel sick most of the time, and I have this ridiculous craving for marmalade and Marmite on toast.'

'What ... together?' For a second or two he was almost able to push from his mind Raquel's plight, as he listened to the cheerful tones of her sister's voice.

'Yes ... sounds gross, doesn't it?'

'Yes it does,' said Roy, chuckling.

'Anyway, the reason I'm calling is that I wanted to invite you and Mum round for lunch on Sunday ... and Raquel and Tim too.'

He felt a leaden boulder descend within him. 'Uh ... let me just see ...'

'The thing is I've been calling them and I can't get any answer ... Raquel's not answering her mobile either.'

'Just hold on for a moment.'

He covered the mouthpiece with his hand and turned to Donna. 'It's Bea ... I have to tell her.'

She nodded, her shoulders slumping.

Roy removed his hand from the phone, swallowing hard before continuing. 'Bea, I have some bad news.'

'Bad news ... what bad news?'

There was no way to soften the blow, so he came right out with it. 'I'm afraid Raquel has been kidnapped.'

Her gasp was clearly audible over the phone. 'Kidnapped? You have to be joking.'

'No joke, I'm afraid.'

'That's ... impossible. There must be some mistake.'

'There's no mistake. I'm afraid it's true.'

'But who ... why?'

'It's to do with my work. Our Chinese subcontractor has been infiltrated by some really bad people. They've kidnapped Raquel to force my hand on some business issues.'

'Oh my God ... this is unbelievable. Can't you do something ... I mean do something to get her back?'

'Look, I know this is a hell of a lot to take in all at once, but Tim's gone after her.'

'Gone after her ... where?'

'To China; that's where they've taken her.'

'China? Oh God, no ... this is madness. Can't you go to the police?'

'Oh, Bea ... I wish I could, but they are threatening to kill her if I do.'

'*Kill* her? I ... no ... this is ... this just can't ...' Her voice tailed off. Suddenly there was a loud clattering noise followed by a heavy thump. Roy felt a tight knot clench in his stomach.

'Bea, Bea ... are you OK?' came Rick's voice over the phone, faint but clearly distressed. 'Bea ... wake up ... oh my God ...' Roy heard the scrambled sounds of Rick picking up the phone from the floor. 'Roy ... you still there?'

'Yes. What's happened?

'She's collapsed ... she's unconscious. I have to call an ambulance.'

'OK ... call me back as soon as ...'

But Rick had already hung up before Roy could finish his sentence.

Chapter 31

Tim didn't know where he was. Everything was black, and his world was suffused with a subdued, but insistent, droning noise. Suddenly, he felt his stomach lurch as he became momentarily weightless before being jerked back upwards. He was instantly awake, grappling to understand what was happening.

'Sorry mate … a bit of turbulence.'

Tim rubbed his eyes and checked his watch; he had been asleep for about two hours. He felt awful.

'Feeling any better?' said Jeff.

'Not really, but I suppose a couple of hours is better than nothing.'

He reached for the bottle of mineral water between the seats and took a long swallow, relishing the feeling of the cool liquid flowing down his parched throat. He blinked and shook his head to dispel the last vestiges of sleep.

'Look,' said Jeff, 'while you've been asleep, I've been thinking …'

'Uh … what about?'

'Once we get to Shenzhen, I can't spend my time just hanging about waiting to fly you back if … I mean when you get Raquel out.'

Tim gave a grim smile. 'You're right to add the "if" – it's by no means certain that I can pull this off. Anyway, what were you going to say?'

'What I was going to say was ... well, why don't I come with you? I'm not intending to get involved in any shooting or that kind of stuff,' he added, 'but I could drive you to where you need to go and be ready to get you out in a hurry if needs be.'

Tim was deeply touched, but he couldn't ask Jeff – who was, after all, a pilot, not a combat soldier – to put his life on the line like this.

'That's a hell of an offer, Jeff, but this is not your fight.'

Jeff changed tack. 'Do you know your way around Shenzhen?'

'No, I've never been there before,' replied Tim, slightly thrown by this abrupt change of subject.

'Well I have. My dad – he's passed away now – used to take me there sometimes to visit my uncle, who lived there.

'Oh.'

'And I can speak basic Mandarin ... though apparently my accent is pretty terrible,' he added, with a chuckle. 'That might come in handy.'

'Christ Jeff, do you realise what you might be getting into? If you come with me, how can I guarantee that you won't get drawn into the thick of things?'

'Look, I know I haven't been in front-line combat like you, but I've had all the same weapons training and so on. I can take care of myself in a scrape.'

'I don't know ... it's ...'

'Look, mate ... my life is pretty tame since I left the SAS. I love flying, and I count myself lucky to be able to earn a living doing just that but ... well, sometimes I miss the buzz of the old days.'

Tim could see in his eyes that he really *wanted* to do this.

'And another thing,' continued Jeff, 'I just *hate* to see the bad guys win.'

'In that case,' said Tim, smiling ... 'you're on ... partner.'

With that pact made, the two men lapsed into silence once more. It was around twenty minutes later that Tim spoke again. 'So how'd you get into flying?' he said, turning to Jeff. 'I mean originally ... before you joined the army?'

Although the two men had worked together for some time in the SAS, they had never actually spent time sharing anything about themselves other than what was relevant to the missions they had undertaken. Tim had always liked Jeff on a personal level and with the long flight stretching ahead of them this was an opportunity to get to know him a little better.

'Well, as you know,' replied Jeff, 'I was born in Australia. My dad was a flyer ... crop spraying. As a kid I often used to go up with him, and I loved it. After a while he started letting me take the controls, and eventually he taught me how to handle take-off and landing. By the time I was fourteen I was a reasonably competent pilot.'

'Did you do all this without any formal lessons? Didn't you need some sort of qualification or certification?'

Jeff chuckled, his rugged features creasing up and his sapphire-blue eyes twinkling as he turned to Tim. 'Things were a bit more lax in Oz at that time. Most of the crop sprayers started out like me. Later on I got all the papers and so on but it was Dad who actually taught me to fly.'

'So what next?'

Jeff's upbeat expression evaporated and a sad shadow descended on his face. 'Dad died young ... cancer.'

Tim felt a twinge of sadness. 'I'm sorry,' he said.

'Oh, it's a long time ago now ...' Jeff seemed swiftly to shake off the melancholy mood which had briefly enveloped him. 'Anyway, Dad left the plane to me, so at the tender age of nineteen I became a crop sprayer, complete with my own plane.'

'So how come you ended up in England?'

Jeff smiled, deep crinkles forming around his sparkling blue eyes. It was a face that looked as though it had seen a lot of living. 'It was a girl ... her name was Jessica.'

'Ah,' said Tim, smiling, 'I should have guessed.'

'I met her while she was still at University – Oxford. She had decided to spend her second year vacation in Oz and when our paths crossed, I fell head-over-heels. She felt the same – at least I thought she did – and I decided to sell the old crate and follow her back to England to make a new life with her there.'

'So what happened?'

'Everything went fine for almost a year, but then she decided that one of the tutors at Oxford was a better long-term bet, and that was it ... she just dumped me.'

Tim winced. 'That must've hurt ... after upping sticks and moving halfway around the world.'

'Uh, huh,' murmured Jeff, his face clearly telegraphing that the memory was still painful, 'it did. Anyway, that was when I had to decide what to do next, and as there really wasn't anything waiting for me back in Oz, I decided to apply for British citizenship and make a life in England.'

'Was that when you joined the army?'

'Not immediately ... for quite a while I survived on the money left over from selling Dad's plane, supplemented by a number of casual jobs. That would only keep me going for a limited time, though, so when I saw that the British Army were advertising for trainee helicopter pilots, I jumped at the chance. With my previous flying experience they snapped me up and ... well I guess you know the rest.'

Tim nodded, without actually replying, and they lapsed into silence for a while.

A little later, Tim picked up the conversation again. 'So has there been anyone else since ... Jessica, was it?'

Jeff glanced sideways, his face breaking into a wry smile. 'No, and at my age, I guess there probably never will be.'

'Never say never,' said Tim. 'All the girls love a pilot.'

They both laughed, but, for Tim at least, it was a strained laugh, for his mind was focused on the task which lay ahead.

***

Donna had gone to join Rick at the hospital, but Roy felt he had to stay at home in case Tim called. He couldn't rely on his mobile having a good signal at the hospital and in any case, mobiles were supposed to be switched off inside the hospital – not that he would have had any qualms about flouting this rule, under the circumstances. Roy's stomach was knotted with tension, as he waited anxiously by the phone, occasionally getting up and pacing aimlessly back and forth across the room. Now *both* of his daughters were in danger, and he was finding it increasingly difficult to think straight … but think straight he must.

While Tim was out there on his own planning the rescue mission, Roy had been considering the aftermath, should Tim succeed in getting Raquel out. Given the lengths to which Chang had already gone to protect his crooked empire it was clear that he was part of some vicious criminal network. He suspected that Chang and his henchmen were Triad – Chinese Mafia – and from all he had heard about these shadowy organisations, he couldn't imagine that they would just let the matter lie. Unless he could figure out some way to gain some leverage over these people, he and his family would never be able to feel safe again. There had to be a way …

The phone rang; Roy's heart leapt; it was Donna.

'How is she … is she OK?'

'Oh, Roy …' Donna was sobbing softly. 'She's lost the baby.'

Chapter 32

Roy had not slept at all so far that night. He was consumed by a cauldron of varied emotions. The tension and anxiety for Raquel's safety were ever-present, and he was devastated that Beatrice had lost the baby which she had so desperately wanted, but now there was something else: an intense, raw sensation, growing and creeping, eating him up from inside. It was the desire for revenge. He had never before experienced such a powerful desire to do harm to another human being. God knows, he had had plenty of reasons to feel vengeful towards some of the unpleasant characters with whom he had crossed swords in his business career, but this was different: Chang had attacked his family, and Roy could not control the powerful feelings burgeoning within him. He wanted the bastard to *pay*. He tried to push these thoughts to the back of his mind. The first priority had to be to rescue Raquel, and that was what he had to focus on. Thinking about revenge against Chang Wei would not help him achieve that objective, and might even work against it by diverting his energies. He shook his head in an effort to dispel the unhelpful emotion.

He looked at the bedside clock: 3.32 a.m. It would be 10.32 a.m. in Shenzhen; this was as good a time as any to phone Tim. He levered himself out of bed, as gently as possible, trying not to wake Donna, but she stirred immediately; she was already awake.

'What are you doing?' she asked, the tension evident in the tone of her voice.

'I'm going to call Tim.'

She propped herself up on one elbow and nodded.

Tim picked up on the second ring. 'Roy? I was just about to call you.'

'What's happening?'

'We're in Shenzhen now ... we've hired a car and we're just on our way to a hotel to catch a few hours' sleep before we start the hunt. Jeff's offered to drive me wherever I need to go and be ready to get me out fast if necessary.'

'He has? I thought he was just going to fly the plane.'

'Well, that was the original deal, but he really wants to help, and right now I can use all the help I can get.'

'I guess so. OK ... well, what's the plan then?'

'I'm going to stake out the Sotoyo factory and try to identify Chang. I expect there'll be too many people around to try to grab him there so I plan to follow him to his home and then persuade him to tell me where they are keeping Raquel.'

'Why do you need to follow him? You have his address.'

'I want to see what his routine is, and also check out whether he has put in place any additional security, either at the factory, on the journey home, or at his home itself. I'm guessing that he doesn't know anyone's coming for him, but ... well you can't be too careful.'

Roy nodded, then realising that this gesture was lost on Tim – some five thousand miles away – he murmured, 'Uh, huh ... you're right, of course.'

'Listen,' said Roy. 'I'd like you to change your plan a bit.'

'What?' said Tim, sounding puzzled. 'Why?'

'You need to do a bit of shopping before you go to the factory.'

'Shopping? What on earth ...?'

***

It was just after 6.00 p.m. Tim crouched behind a bush just outside the perimeter fence of the Sotoyo factory, peering through his binoculars as workers poured out through the main entrance. They came mostly in groups of two or three or four, chatting happily as they were released from the shackles of their working day, making their way towards the main gate in the outer fence. As they passed through the main gate they all kept to the right-hand side of the central post onto which the two massive gates would later close. Another stream of people was passing on the other side of the post, moving in the opposite direction, entering the factory grounds. He swung his binoculars round to follow the progress of this second stream of people to where they entered the building via a second entrance at the side of the building. It was like a sort of one-way system, designed, Tim supposed, to allow free flow of workers to and from their respective shifts, minimising any downtime between shifts. The people entering the factory via the side entrance, Tim noted, looked much less cheerful than those leaving the building. They must be just about to start their shift.

As far as he could ascertain, the entire building was enclosed by a chain-link fence with only two gates. The one at the back of the building was locked, and overlooked by CCTV cameras; the other – the main gate, through which the workers were entering and leaving – was flanked by a security gatehouse. Tim swung the binoculars back to observe the gatehouse; a uniformed security guard strolled out, lighting a cigarette and inhaling deeply before blowing out a dense cloud of blue smoke. Tim noted, with some trepidation, the holstered handgun at his side.

Tim considered his options. He considered trying to blend in with the stream of workers trickling through the gate, but swiftly dismissed the idea: his six feet three inch frame and tanned skin – still bearing the remnants of the deep mahogany tone he had acquired in the Afghan desert – would stand out like a sore thumb among the mostly much shorter, yellow-skinned Chinese workers moving through the gate.

If he chose his moment, after the influx and egress of workers had subsided, he could overpower and incapacitate the guard; with the element of surprise, that should be simple. If he did this, however, it would not be long before his presence would be discovered and Chang Wei would be forewarned.

Finally, he could look for a suitable point to cut through the perimeter fence. There were plenty of CCTV cameras positioned around said perimeter, but he doubted that they were being monitored all that diligently. Certainly the security guard seemed to be paying scant attention to the TV monitor which Tim could just make out through the window of the gatehouse, glowing in the dim interior. This, he decided, was his best bet.

He swung his binoculars back to the main entrance to the building, alongside which were parked five cars: a dark grey Lexus; two BMWs, one black and one metallic blue; a bronze Range Rover; and a white Mercedes-Benz. Given the upmarket nature of these cars and the fact that they appeared to be the only ones allowed within the perimeter fence – the main car park was outside this fence – Tim supposed that they must belong to, or be allocated to, the senior managers.

A short, middle-aged man in a grey business suit emerged from the main entrance and moved towards the Range Rover, pointing his remote control. As the indicator lights flashed, Tim focused on his face; he was about the right age, and the features were similar, but the bald pate, flanked by wispy tufts of hair at the sides, was not right; Chang had a full head of black hair, with a distinctive sharply-pointed hairline. Tim settled back once more to wait.

Ten minutes later another figure emerged; he was much younger and his thin, angular face bore no resemblance to that portrayed in the photograph which lay on the grass alongside Tim. The man climbed into the black BMW and swung smoothly out of his parking space, moving towards the main gate.

A few moments later, two men emerged, stopping on the steps to engage in conversation. Tim scanned both of their faces and his heart jumped; he was almost sure that the one on the right was his quarry. He checked the photograph once more. There was no doubt: the crooked nose and widow's peak hairline were unmistakeable.

As the two men concluded their conversation, the one now identified as Chang Wei made for the white Mercedes. Tim gathered up his things and sprinted back to where Jeff was waiting in their grey Toyota hire car. He wrenched the door open, rudely jolting Jeff from his slumbers behind the wheel.

'White Mercedes,' barked Tim. 'It'll be through the main gate in a minute or two.'

Jeff shrugged off the clinging bonds of sleep, fastened his seat belt, and started the engine.

'Follow him home, and see whether there are any signs of special security. Get back here as soon as you can. Hopefully I'll already be out, and waiting right here.'

Jeff nodded. 'Good luck.'

'And you,' said Tim. 'Whatever you do, don't let him see that he's being followed ... I don't think he'll be expecting anything, but ... well, just be careful.'

Jeff smiled, those deep laughter lines creasing his leathery skin. 'Gotta go now mate, or I'll lose him.'

He pulled the door shut and pulled smoothly away, just as the white Mercedes rounded the first bend in the road and disappeared from view.

Tim made his way back to his previous observation point. He had chosen a point midway between two CCTV cameras, where he hoped he would be unobserved. The light was fading now; it was time to make his move. He withdrew the bolt cutters from his holdall and snipped enough links to peel back a section large enough to wriggle through. He crawled the first twenty yards on his belly, dragging the holdall with him, until he was satisfied that he was out of the field of view of the cameras, at which point he rose gingerly to his feet, and began walking the remaining two hundred yards or so to a small side entrance which he had observed from outside the fence.

He arrived at the door without incident, and was astonished to find that it was slightly ajar. It was a fire escape with a push-bar mechanism on the inside. Evidently someone had opened it from inside and neglected to close it properly.

This luck is almost too good to be true, he thought, with a wry smile. He stepped gingerly inside, into a long corridor which was in semi-darkness. It was deserted. *So far, so good.* He pulled the SIG from his waistband and released the safety catch. Then the search began.

As he worked his way along the corridor he heard, faintly at first, an indeterminate buzz of noise: an amalgamation of whirring and clattering, overlaid with the sound of piped music. He saw, at the end of the corridor, a faint glow of light leaking from somewhere off to the side. This, he supposed was where the main factory shop floor was located. He retraced his steps, passing the door through which he had just entered the building and moving down to where the corridor joined with another in a 'T' junction. He turned left to find a series of small individual offices; they didn't look like the offices of the senior management. He noticed that two of the offices ahead had lights on; maybe this was where the evening shift supervisors were located. He backed up to the 'T' junction and began working his way down the opposite corridor. This looked more promising: the offices were larger and had nameplates on the doors in both Chinese characters – which meant nothing to Tim – and English. The fifth door along the corridor bore the name he was looking for: Chang Wei – Plant Manager.

He tried the door handle; it turned easily and he swung the door open. There was a faint squeak from the hinges, causing Tim to freeze momentarily, turning his head to the left and the right, checking for any sign that he had been heard. Nothing. He stepped inside but the office was tiny, with just a single desk and none of the trappings of a plant manager. Then he saw another door, also signed 'Chang Wei – Plant Manager'. He realised that the outer office must be that of a secretary or personal assistant who guarded access to the inner sanctum. He moved over to the other door and tried the handle. Locked.

He set down his holdall and withdrew his lock-picking kit. The lock was only a standard door lock, nothing fancy. It took him less than twenty seconds to defeat it. He stepped into the room, and made straight for the large desk positioned in front of the window. He switched on the computer on the desk and waited while it went through its start-up routine. It went straight to the desktop screen, without requiring a password – sloppy. He reached into his holdall and withdrew the portable hard drive which he had purchased – with the aid of Jeff's more than passable grasp of Mandarin – that afternoon. He plugged it into the computer and began moving and clicking the mouse.

Then he heard it: the faint sound of footsteps, becoming gradually louder as the unknown person approached. He had not yet even begun to copy any data, so he quickly unplugged the hard drive and began shutting down the computer. The footsteps were very close now. The glow from the screen seemed like a floodlight in the otherwise totally dark office. *Hurry up and shut down!* The footsteps stopped. Finally the screen went blank, but the damage was already done – he could hear the sound of the outer door opening.

Chapter 33

Tim froze, his ears straining to catch every sound. The faint squeak from the unoiled door hinge was followed by the sound of tentative footsteps as someone entered the outer office. As quietly as possible, he gathered his things and thrust them into the holdall, grabbing it and swiftly ducking down behind the large button-backed armchair in the corner of the room. His heart was hammering furiously now.

The sound of several more cautious footsteps was followed by that of the second door opening. Tim decided to risk a tentative peek from behind the armchair. As the door opened, there was a faint click; a bright shaft of light sprang from the torch which the newcomer was carrying. Thankfully it was not pointing in his direction. Instinctively, he ducked back behind the armchair, blinking as he tried to get his eyes adjusted to the brighter light level in the room now. He could see the torch beam moving this way and that around the room. He froze as it was directed towards the armchair, holding his breath and willing his hammering heart to slow down – at that moment he almost believed it could be heard by the other person. He tensed, ready for action in case he had been spotted.

He hadn't; the torch beam swung away as swiftly as it had arrived. He heard a few more footsteps and risked another peek from behind the chair. The person who had entered the room was a uniformed security guard. The man moved around the desk and picked up something from it. *Shit!* It was the lock-picking kit. The guard untied the tapes and opened up the package, studying its contents carefully. He reached down and withdrew his gun from its holster, flicking off the safety catch. As silently as possible, Tim lifted his own weapon, checking that the silencer was properly in place and the safety catch was off.

The guard moved away from the desk and reached for the light switch.

In one swift movement, Tim leapt from behind the chair and toward the guard. The man turned to face the oncoming threat, raising his gun at the same time, but he was too slow. Tim swung the butt of his gun against the man's temple, and he sank to the floor with a groan, his own gun falling from his hand with a loud clatter.

Tim rushed through the door and into the outer office before gingerly approaching the outer door. He stuck his head out into the corridor, anxiously jerking it to right and left to see if there was anyone coming; there was no-one. He returned to the prone figure on the floor, who was not moving, or making any sound. There was a trickle of blood seeping from the gash in the man's temple. Tim felt for the pulse in his neck; it was strong and regular. He rummaged in his holdall and found the coil of polyurethane cord, which he used to bind the man's hands and feet. He picked up the still-illuminated torch and panned the beam around the room, looking for something with which to gag the man. He spotted another door off the office and opened it to reveal a small, private bathroom. He grabbed a towel and, using the Bowie knife which he had brought with him, cut a thin strip with which he gagged the man.

He picked up the guard's weapon from the floor; it was a Glock G22, 0.40 calibre. This might well come in handy, so he placed it, and the two spare ammunition magazines which the man was carrying, in his holdall. He dragged the man's limp body around behind the armchair where he had, just a few minutes ago, been hiding. Panting from the exertion, he returned to the desk and once again fired up the computer.

Once he had copied what he needed, he gathered up all his things, checking carefully that, this time, he had left no clues to his presence, and made for the door. He took one more careful look around the room to check that everything looked normal, switched off the torch, and left.

As he retraced his steps down the corridor, he began furiously reassessing his game plan. As soon as it was discovered that the security guard had been waylaid, any element of surprise which he had would be lost. Maybe the man had to report in somewhere at regular intervals; if so he might be discovered within hours or even less. At best his discovery would be no later than at the start of the working day tomorrow.

The time for careful and considered action was past; now it was a race against time.

Chapter 34

About forty-five minutes had passed since Tim had made his way out of Chang Wei's office. Now he sat, cross-legged, behind a large bush around ten yards back from the edge of the road, peering through a gap in the foliage, anxiously waiting for Jeff to return. Every second counted now, for once the bound and gagged security guard was discovered, surely Chang would be told and he would realise that someone was coming after him. *Dammit! Come on Jeff ... what's taking so long?*

It was completely dark now, and hard to distinguish the cars that lay behind the approaching headlights, but as one of them began to slow down, Tim could discern that it was the grey Toyota. *At last! Thank God.* He took a quick glance all around to check that he was not being observed, and then stepped out from behind the bush where he had been concealed. As Jeff swung the car up onto the grass verge, Tim rushed towards it, pulling open the back door before it had even come to a complete stop. He slung the holdall onto the back seat, slamming the door afterwards before opening the front passenger door and climbing inside.

'Everything OK?' enquired Jeff.

'Not exactly – I got what I wanted but I had to overpower and tie up a security guard. It's only a matter of time before someone finds him and alerts Chang. How did you get on?'

'OK ... Chang's place is a pretty impressive spread. It's in several of acres of ground, all fenced in and gated, with CCTV cameras everywhere.'

'Hmm ... any sign that he's expecting us?'

'Not that I could see, but how would I be able to tell anyway?'

'Good point, I suppose ... if he knows, he's hardly likely to advertise the fact, is he?'

Jeff did not respond directly to this rhetorical question, but simply said, 'Well, there's only one way to find out ...'

***

Roy sat on the sofa, idly ruffling the fur behind Sammy's ear. The dog yawned contentedly and shifted position slightly, laying his chin on Roy's thigh.

'We'll get her back, just you see,' said Roy, more to try to convince himself than for any other reason.

At the sound of Roy's voice, Sammy raised a bushy grey eyebrow in silent enquiry. Roy stroked the top of his head and he lowered his eyebrow, wriggling slightly to achieve a more comfortable position before closing his eyes. Roy gazed at the two phones on the table alongside him – his mobile and the main house phone – willing one of them to ring. *Why doesn't he call?*

Roy and Sammy were alone in the house; Donna had gone to see Beatrice in hospital. Roy desperately wanted to see her too, but decided that he just couldn't leave the house at this critical moment in case Tim tried to contact him.

Suddenly, Sammy's ears pricked up and he jerked his head upward. In a flash he was off of Roy's lap and bounding towards the front door. A moment later Roy heard the sound of a key turning in the lock. This would be Donna returning from the hospital. As Roy moved through to the hall, the front door opened and Donna stepped through. He could see immediately that she had been crying: her eyes were rimmed with red and her cheeks were lined with dark streaks of makeup. Sammy jumped up at Donna to deliver his usual enthusiastic greeting. Donna bent down and ruffled the fur on his head, forcing a small smile as she tried to settle him down.

'How is she?' enquired Roy.

'Oh, Roy, she's in a terrible state. She wanted this baby so badly ... and now...' Her voice tailed off as she began to sob once more.

'I know,' he whispered, taking Sammy's collar in his left hand and gently pulling him away, before taking Donna's hand in his right and leading her into the hall. 'Go and sit down while I get you a drink ... then you can tell me all about it.'

'Any news from Tim?' she asked, the anxiety clear in her eyes.

Roy shook his head. 'Not yet, I'm afraid.' Her shoulders slumped. 'Go and sit down while I get that drink.'

He moved through to the kitchen, opening the fridge and withdrawing a bottle of Pinot Grigio. *Thank goodness for screw caps,* he thought, as he poured two large glasses, the absurdly trivial thought bizarrely intruding on the desperate situation. At that moment, hunting for a corkscrew would have seemed just too much effort.

He took the two glasses through to the lounge where Donna was seated on the sofa with Sammy already curled up beside her. Roy shooed him off so that he could sit alongside her. Denied anyone to cuddle up to, Sammy decided to jump up onto his own chair and settle down there.

Roy passed one of the glasses to Donna, who took a deep swallow, exhaling heavily before setting it down on the coffee table alongside Roy's.

He paused for a few seconds before asking, 'I guessed she'd be distraught at losing the baby but is she OK otherwise ... I mean in a physical sense?'

'Well, yes ... I think so. They are talking about discharging her tomorrow unless any other problems show up.'

'Well, that's something at least ... but do they know what actually caused the miscarriage?'

She shook her head, catching her breath as she tried to compose herself. 'They can't identify any physical cause. They asked me if she had suffered any emotional trauma recently ... and of course I couldn't tell them.' She looked up at him, her expression pained. 'Oh Roy, maybe we shouldn't have told her. That was what triggered the whole thing. Maybe we should have ...'

'Shhh ...' He put his arms around her and hugged her to his chest. 'You mustn't think like that. Raquel's her sister; she had to know.'

'But ... well perhaps we should have waited until we knew whether ... I mean until we were sure that ....' She began to sob once more.

'Donna, what's done is done. It's no use agonising about what might have been.'

'Oh, I know, but I just can't help it ... and I'm worried sick about Raquel. Are you sure we shouldn't go to the police?'

'I'm sure,' said Roy, firmly. 'Tim is our best chance.'

Actually, Roy wasn't anywhere near as sure as he hoped he had sounded, but the decision had been made and Tim had already embarked on his quest to find Raquel. It was too late for second thoughts now.

'I hope you're right,' whispered Donna.

So do I, thought Roy.

Chapter 35

They had been crouching outside the fence of Chang's house for about fifteen minutes, having chosen a spot where they judged that they could not be overlooked by any of the security cameras. The night was quiet, with only the subdued, steady drone of distant traffic, and the intermittent hooting of an owl from the trees behind them intruding on the silence.

Tim scanned the building through his binoculars. Everything looked normal. The white Mercedes was parked on the gravel drive just in front of the garage. The curtains of the large window directly ahead were open and there were lights on. He had seen a single figure – presumably Chang – walk across the room once, before disappearing from sight. There was no sign that anyone else was in or around the house.

Tim turned to Jeff. 'OK, I'm going in now.'

He tucked the SIG into his waistband. 'I'll leave the rest of the stuff here with you,' he said, indicating the holdall which lay on the ground.

He stood up and took a grip on the iron railings, making ready to climb over, but then he hesitated. He let go of the railings and instead bent down and unzipped the holdall, delving inside and withdrawing the Glock handgun which he had taken from the security guard.

'Look, take this, just in case of any trouble,' he said handing the gun to Jeff.

In one swift, fluid movement he flipped out the ammunition magazine, checked it was full and slipped it back into the butt of the gun. He pulled back the slide to chamber a round.

Tim chuckled. 'Looks like you haven't forgotten your weapons training.'

'I already told you: I can take care of myself.'

'OK, I'm going in now. If you see any sign that things have gone wrong, get the hell out of here.'

Jeff did not respond to this instruction but merely said, 'Well get on with it then.'

Tim grasped the railings and shimmied up and over, landing heavily on the other side with an impact which expelled the breath from his lungs in a low grunt. He cursed himself for his lack of technique; he had lost his edge since the rigorous SAS training regime had ceased. Pausing for a few seconds to gather his breath, he set off towards the house in a crouching run. He didn't have time to worry about the CCTV cameras; hopefully there would be no-one monitoring them in real time. When he reached the house he flattened himself against the wall, panting. He remained like this for about a minute, until his breathing settled back to normal. There was no sign that he had been detected.

He moved to the front door and inspected the lock. It was a seven-lever security lock: too sophisticated for his lock-picking kit. He didn't want to risk using an explosive charge for the noise would surely alert Chang to his presence. He crept around to the back of the house where there was another door. He was dismayed to find this one similarly equipped. Clearly, Chang was a guy who took his security seriously. But then he spotted it: one of the windows to the kitchen was open a crack – *careless*. As he moved toward the window he could hear the faint sound of classical music emanating from within. Good, this would help mask any slight sounds he might make. He checked that the safety catch on his handgun was off before pulling the window fully open and reaching through to place

189

the gun on the worktop inside. He then stuck his head and shoulders through the window, grasping the edge of the worktop and pulling himself through.

He lowered himself, as silently as possible, onto the tiled floor, turning to pick up his weapon. His heart was hammering furiously now. He glanced around the huge kitchen. It was like something from a luxury show house: shining dark grey granite work surfaces, glossy white cupboards, and immaculately clean stainless steel appliances. Was this really the home of a man living alone? But was he alone? Maybe there was a Mrs. Chang. For some reason Tim had never previously even considered this possibility, and he did not relish the prospect, given what he might have to do to her husband to get the information he needed.

He waited, motionless, listening to the music – louder now – wafting through the open door. There was no other sound, no indication that he had been detected. He began moving forward, slowly, silently, his gun levelled. He entered the hallway; the music became a little louder still; he could smell cigar smoke. He could see the open door to what he assumed was the main living room; that was where the music was coming from. A soft light spilled though the doorway.

When he crept through the open door, there was an armchair facing away from him, its back directly in front of him. He could just see the top of a man's head: black hair combed back over a thinning crown. A tendril of blue smoke curled lazily upward. A hand appeared at the side of the chair, tapping a precariously balanced projection of ash from the cigar it was holding into the ashtray on the side table, before propping the cigar on the rim of the ashtray. The same hand closed around a crystal tumbler containing an inch of amber liquid – whisky, Tim guessed – and raised it slowly until it disappeared from sight in front of the armchair. He moved forward until he was right behind the armchair.

'Don't move a muscle,' he said, as he pressed the silencer of his gun against the side of the man's head. The man did as instructed, the whisky glass frozen in space midway between his mouth and the side table.

Tim moved around to the front of the armchair – all the time keeping his gun levelled – until he was facing the man directly. There was no doubt about his identity: the distinctive hairline and crooked nose were unmistakeable. Chang said nothing; he sat still, his expression impassive.

'Put the drink down,' ordered Tim.

Chang complied.

'Turn off the music.'

Chang reached slowly for the remote control on the side table and killed the music.

'Where is she?'

'And who would that be?' he said, his tone calm and untroubled. If Chang was scared, he certainly wasn't showing it.

'Listen, you arsehole,' snarled Tim, 'I'm in no mood to mess around here. You have five seconds to tell me where she is before I blow your right kneecap to smithereens.' He moved forward a couple of steps and lowered his gun to point directly at Chang's knee.

Chang raised his hand in what seemed an almost conciliatory manner. 'Please, there's no need for any unpleasantness. We haven't yet even been introduced.' He was almost smiling.

Why is the bastard looking so smug? Suddenly, Tim realised, but it was a fraction of a second too late. The impact to the back of his head was crushing. A mass of multi-coloured stars flashed in his sightless eyes. It was a split second later that he felt the pain: a searing, head-splitting bolt which flared through him. Then everything went black.

Chapter 36

The big, dark eyes gazed balefully at Roy from beneath the fluffy grey eyebrows.

'What is it, boy?' said Roy, bending down to ruffle the fur on Sammy's neck.

Sammy lifted his muzzle from where it had been resting on his paws and yawned. Unusually, he had spurned his favourite chair in favour of the doormat just inside the front door, as though expecting someone to arrive. He licked Roy's hand a few times but then laid his head back down. This was not the dog that Roy knew: the dog who would normally jump up excitedly at the first sign of attention, standing on his hind legs and scrabbling against you with his forelegs. If a dog could look miserable, then this was it. Sammy often spent a couple of days staying with Roy and Donna when Raquel and Tim went away for a weekend, but now it seemed that, somehow, he knew something was wrong.

Roy knelt down and looked directly into Sammy's eyes. 'Missing your mum and dad, eh?'

Sammy lifted his head and inclined it to one side, his overhanging eyebrows twitching alternately as he appeared to concentrate intently on what Roy was saying.

'Don't worry. They'll be back soon.' He wasn't sure who he was trying to convince: Sammy or himself.

Roy, sighed, ruffled the top of Sammy's head, and stood up. The dog resumed his previous position, with his head resting on outstretched paws.

Donna had gone out to do some food shopping. It seemed faintly ridiculous to be bothering about such a mundane task while Raquel and Tim were in mortal danger, but they still had to eat. In any case, Donna needed to do something to break the tension of long hours spent in the house waiting for any news from China.

Roy glanced over at the table where his mobile sat alongside the main phone. *Still no calls*. He picked up his mobile and checked for text messages: *nothing* – apart from junk texts that is.

Roy had tried repeatedly to get in contact with Tim, but had consistently failed. He began to think the worst: that Tim had failed in his mission, in which case … he dreaded to think. But then his rational side took over; even if everything was going according to plan, then whatever Tim was doing right now, he probably wouldn't have any time for progress reports or responding to calls. However, Roy had something important to tell him and he *needed* to get in touch. The best he could do was send a text message and hope to hell that Tim had time to read it before it was too late.

He began composing the message, cursing himself for the fact that his big, clumsy fingers seemed incapable of consistently hitting the correct keys on the touchscreen smartphone. How he longed for one of the old mobile phones with proper buttons which clicked reassuringly as you tapped them. He really didn't need to use his phone for Facebook or Twitter or watching movies or any of the other stuff that his daughters used theirs for. He just wanted to send a text message. Eventually, after much cursing, he succeeded in completing the message and hit 'send'. He hoped Tim would read it in time.

***

Tim could just about hear some sort of conversation in the darkness. He strained to discern the words, spoken with a strange, harsh intonation; it was impossible. He tried to blink but it felt as though his eyelids were clamped firmly shut. With a considerable effort he prized them apart to reveal a fuzzy grey image of a dimly-lit cavernous building with walls of bare brickwork and minimal furnishing: just a few grey metal shelving units and a couple of similarly-coloured metal cupboards. He tried to hoist himself into a more upright position, but found that he was tightly bound to the chair in which he was seated. He slumped back and concentrated once more upon the conversation which he could hear. It was, however, of no use as it seemed to be in Mandarin. He tried to swallow but his throat was as dry as sand. He tried to call out, but all that emerged from his parched lips was a strangled croak.

'Ah, you are awake at last,' said the voice behind him in perfect, though heavily accented, English.

Tim tried to swivel his head around but succeeded only in triggering off a searing bolt of pain though the back of his head. He gave up and continued to look straight ahead.

Eventually two figures moved around from the back of the chair. The first was a tall, thin Chinese man, holding the stock of an assault rifle under his arm, the barrel resting casually on his wrist. He smiled unpleasantly before stepping back a couple of paces and adopting a stationary posture, legs apart, rifle held at the ready. The second figure was Chang Wei. He looked appraisingly at Tim before taking a cigar from his pocket, clipping off the end and lighting it. He inhaled deeply before blowing a large cloud of smoke directly into Tim's face.

Tim spluttered and gagged as the choking cloud entered his lungs.

Chang moved unhurriedly to pull up a chair and place it a few feet in front of him, its back facing towards him. He sat down, his legs astride the backrest and his forearms resting atop it.

'Who are you? What are you doing here?'

Tim tried to speak but his parched throat and lips would not function. He succeeded only in emitting a guttural croaking sound.

Chang turned to his henchman and barked a brief instruction in Mandarin. The man bent down and opened a cupboard, from which he withdrew a plastic bottle of mineral water. He laid down his weapon while he unscrewed the lid. Picking up the rifle once more, he moved tentatively toward Tim, rifle held at the ready in his right hand and the bottle held in his outstretched left. He thrust the neck of the bottle in Tim's mouth and tipped it up. Tim gulped down the cooling liquid greedily, ignoring the copious quantities which escaped the corners of his mouth and spilled down the front of his body. When the man withdrew the bottle there was only an inch left in the bottom. He upturned the bottle over Tim's head disposing of the remaining liquid. Tim spluttered and gasped, blinking and shaking his head as he tried to clear the water from his eyes. Chang indicated, with a wave of his hand, that the other man should move back to his guarding position. He did so.

'Who are you?' repeated Chang.

Tim finally found his voice. 'Go to hell.'

Chang did not respond. He stood up, slowly, and walked towards the nearby wall, reaching for a light switch. As he flicked the switch, there was a random spluttering of buzzes and clicks as the ancient banks of fluorescent lights flickered into life. In the corner of the room was a sight which made Tim catch his breath. With a considerable effort he managed to avoid calling out or allowing his facial expression to change.

Raquel was sitting on the edge of an old iron-framed bed. Her hair was matted and unkempt, her clothes dirty. Her mutilated hand wore a makeshift dressing still stained with blood. Her other hand was handcuffed to the bedstead. She made no sound, as she was gagged, but it was clear that Chang had not missed the sudden widening of her eyes or the way that the fist of her good hand had clenched involuntarily. He nodded to his henchman and barked a brief instruction. The man roughly wrenched the gag down so that it hung loosely around her neck.

'Tim …' she gasped.

Tim shook his head, but it was too late.

Chang's lip twisted in an unpleasant smile. 'Ah, so you are the boyfriend.' He turned to a bench and picked up Tim's handgun, turning it slowly this way and that as he inspected it. 'I see you came here with serious intent. Did you think you'd be able to just walk in and rescue her?'

Tim said nothing.

'Did you think I'd be stupid enough to leave my window open and just sit in my house waiting to be surprised?'

'You … you knew I was coming?' said Tim.

'Of course I did,' retorted Chang, lazily levelling the gun at Tim.

'No … don't,' cried out Raquel, in alarm.

'Ha … see how much she cares about you,' sneered Chang. He walked up to within a few feet of Tim, pointing the gun directly at his face.

Tim did not flinch.

Chang started to squeeze the trigger, his eyes narrowed and his mouth set in a grim line.

'Noooo …' screamed Raquel.

He squeezed harder … *Click.* Tim's tightly clenched jaw abruptly relaxed, easing the pain which had beset his facial muscles. He struggled to maintain an outwardly impassive appearance.

'No ammunition you see,' chuckled Chang, pulling the magazine from his pocket and holding it aloft, before slotting it into the butt of the gun.

Raquel began sobbing, her breath coming in short, urgent gasps.

Chang continued. 'The guard you overpowered was discovered less than half an hour after you attacked him.' He laid down the gun and picked up the still-smouldering cigar, drawing on it deeply until the tip glowed brightly, before exhaling slowly, emitting a dense cloud of blue smoke, curling and billowing as it gradually dispersed. 'The idiot has now been suitably dealt with for his incompetence.'

Dealt with? Tim could imagine what that probably meant. He felt a pang of remorse for the guard, who was probably a perfectly innocent guy who thought he was fulfilling a legitimate security role for a legitimate company. These bastards were even more evil than he had given them credit for. Unless he could come up with some way out of the hole he was in, then he and Raquel could both end up dead. He began weighing up his very limited options.

'What were you looking for in my office?' continued Chang.

Tim stared at him but said nothing.

Chang took a last drag on his cigar and blew out another billowing cloud of smoke, before flicking the butt onto the floor and grinding it underfoot. 'I see you are determined to make this difficult for yourself.'

He picked up the handgun once more and resumed his previous sitting position, legs astride the back of the chair. He levelled the gun at Tim before motioning to the guard and uttering a few words which Tim could not understand. The man's face broke into a slow smile as he laid down his weapon and picked up something from the shadows by the wall. As the guard turned to face him, Tim could see what it was: a pair of garden branch loppers – the large, powerful type with long handles which require both hands to operate. The man advanced towards Tim before grasping the little finger of his left hand and prising it up from where Tim was trying to keep it clamped down onto the arm of the chair. He slipped one of the blades of the tool under Tim's finger and then stood back, grasping both handles of the tool. He looked enquiringly at Chang. Raquel was wailing inconsolably.

'Now,' continued Chang, 'I suggest you tell me what you were looking for in my office.' Tim said nothing; Chang sighed. 'Let me explain what's going to happen here. My friend here is going to take that finger whatever happens: it will provide some additional leverage with Mr Groves when he knows we have you as well as his daughter. Now, if you answer my questions, we can stop there. On the other hand … oh, sorry, no pun intended' – he laughed at his own unintended humour – 'if you continue to be uncooperative, we can continue to take the rest, one at a time, until you decide to talk.' He paused for a few seconds to let this information sink in before saying, 'So, one more time ... what were you looking for?'

Tim said nothing. He looked Chang directly in the eyes, his expression defiant. Chang sighed and nodded to his associate whose smile broadened as he began, very slowly, to close the handles.

Chapter 37

Chang was looking on, smiling as the blades began to close; Tim took a deep breath and clenched his teeth.

'Nooo ... please,' pleaded Raquel. Her eyes rolled back in their sockets and she passed out.

The next few seconds seemed to Tim to take place in slow motion as his brain went into overdrive.

The guard's face took on a startled expression as a neat, round hole appeared in the centre of his forehead. Tim registered the sound of the gunshot, and the sound of shattering glass a fraction of a second before a fountain of dark liquid spurted forth, spraying upwards as the man's head snapped backward with the impact of the bullet. There was a loud clattering sound as the garden tool slipped from the man's grasp and fell to the floor, the blade scraping a layer of skin from Tim's finger as it did so.

Chang looked up in astonishment, momentarily taking his eyes off Tim, who seized his opportunity. He gathered all his strength, tucked his head into his chest and lunged forward and downwards into a forward roll. The chair – to which he was still bound – was carried up and over him in an arc. Chang realised what was happening and levelled his gun, but he was a heartbeat too late. The leg of the chair struck his forehead just before he pulled the trigger. The shot went wide of its mark, but still gouged a shallow trough along the side of Tim's neck. He felt the searing pain a fraction of a second later.

Chang was knocked to the floor and the gun spun from his grasp. He muttered some unintelligible curse in his own language before getting onto his knees and reaching for the weapon. Tim was helpless, lying on his side, still bound to the chair.

'I wouldn't do that if I were you, mate,' said a voice from behind him. The faint Australian accent was reassuringly familiar.

Jeff stepped into Tim's field of view, his gun levelled at Chang's head and Tim's Bowie knife held in his other hand. Chang looked up into the muzzle of the gun and shrank back.

'Get up,' ordered Jeff.

Chang did so.

'Now sit there.' He motioned to a chair alongside the table, and Chang sank into it.

Jeff severed the ropes binding Tim's hands, while still keeping his gun trained on Chang. Once his hands were free, Tim took the knife and began cutting through the rest of his bonds.

'Am I glad to see you,' gasped Tim. 'Where the hell are we?'

'No time to talk: there are at least three more guards outside. We need to get out of here fast.'

Tim sprang to his feet and stepped over to Chang, holding out his hand. 'The key to the handcuffs,' he demanded.

Chang spat at him. 'Go to hell.'

'I don't have time for this,' hissed Tim.

He grabbed Chang's arm forcing him to lay his hand, palm downward on the table and plunged the Bowie knife into the back of his hand, pinning it to the table. The animal scream which escaped his lips was blood-curdling.

Tim withdrew the knife and pressed the point against the side of Chang's neck. 'The key,' he insisted.

'Alright, alright ... in that drawer,' he gasped, pointing at the top drawer of a metal filing cabinet.

Jeff continued to keep his weapon trained on Chang while Tim located the key.

'Keep the bastard covered,' he muttered. But Chang was too busy nursing his injured hand to pose much of a threat.

Raquel was just regaining consciousness as Tim released the handcuffs. She looked up at him through tired, groggy eyes and then flung her arms around him.

'Oh Tim, I thought I'd never see you again. They … Oh my God, look at your neck.' The wound was shallow, but the blood was flowing freely, soaking into his shirt.

'Shhh … no time; we have to go. Can you walk?'

She nodded.

Tim helped her to her feet before stepping over to the table and picking up his confiscated mobile phone, quickly checking it for missed calls and text messages. Amongst all the dross was one text message from Roy. He opened it and began to read.

Jeff's exasperation was clear in the tone of his voice. 'For Christ's sake Tim, we don't have time for …'

'Wait,' snapped Tim, far more sharply than he intended, considering that Jeff had just saved his finger, and probably his life. 'It's from her father … it's important.'

Jeff nodded, waiting while Tim read the message. When he had done so, he slipped the mobile into his pocket.

'What do we do with this bastard?' said Jeff, inclining his head towards Chang, who was clutching a handkerchief to his injured hand, whimpering softly.

Tim looked up, his face grim. 'We have to take him with us.'

'Why? What the …'

'I'll explain later,' said Tim.

Jeff shook his head in exasperation, but didn't argue the point. 'Get up,' he ordered, prodding the side of Chang's head with the muzzle of his gun.

Tim unlocked the handcuffs and detached them from the bed before handing them to Raquel. 'Cuff his hands together behind his back.'

Her eyes widened in fear as she looked across at her erstwhile captor.

'Raquel, do it *now*. Jeff's got him covered.'

'Hands behind your back,' ordered Jeff, emphasising his point by grinding the muzzle of his gun into Chang's temple. He complied.

Raquel stepped around beside him and snapped on the 'cuffs. Chang screamed in pain as they closed on his damaged hand. Raquel stepped back smartly.

'Ignore his whining,' said Tim. 'We have to leave right now.' He picked up the dead guard's assault rifle, checking that it was fully loaded and ready to fire.

Suddenly the door burst open and another guard rushed into the room, his rifle levelled. The split second he took to orient himself, glancing to left and right were enough for Tim to fire a short burst from the automatic weapon, cutting the guard down before he could get off a single shot himself. Raquel looked on aghast, struck dumb by the violent events unfolding before her eyes. Tim grabbed her hand and hustled her towards the open door.

'Which way?' he barked at Jeff.

'Straight ahead. See the main gate?'

Tim looked out and could see the gate; it was about three hundred yards away across open ground. The only cover consisted of two trucks parked about halfway across.

'Stay close behind me,' he said to Raquel, as he let go of her hand and shifted his weapon into a combat readiness position. 'Jeff, you bring Chang ... and if the bastard gives you any trouble, shoot him in the elbow. That won't stop him being able to run but it will hurt like hell, and he'll never use that arm again.'

'Understand?' said Jeff, using the muzzle of his gun to turn Chang's face towards his own. Chang nodded, his eyes haunted and fearful.

'OK, let's go,' said Tim

He lowered himself to a crouch and made ready to exit the door. As he did so, he heard the unmistakable metallic sound of a gun being cocked, just outside the door and to his right. He dropped to his knees and dived through the door, swivelling round to his right and firing off a burst of automatic fire, relying on instinct and training, rather than actual sight of his target, to direct his fire. A sharp spear of pain shot through his injured neck as he rolled over and jumped to his feet, ready to fire again. There was no need: the man was dead.

'OK, follow me,' he ordered, as he advanced in a slow, crouching run, Raquel close behind, followed by a reluctant Chang, with Jeff bringing up the rear.

They had almost reached the cover of the two trucks when Roy heard two gunshots close behind him. He spun round to see another guard spin to the ground about forty yards to their left flank.

'Keep going,' yelled Jeff as he swivelled round, smoke swirling from the muzzle of his gun.

They reached the cover of the trucks and flattened themselves against the side of one of them while they caught their breath and the two men checked their weapons.

''How many guards were there?' asked Tim, as he struggled to control his laboured breathing.

'I don't know ...' gasped Jeff, between ragged breaths, 'I clocked three, but there could be more.'

'OK wait,' said Tim.

He dropped down on to his stomach and looked underneath the trucks. Just to the other side he could see the black boots and lower legs of another guard. He levelled his rifle and fired a single shot at the man's leg, hitting mid-calf. There was a loud scream followed by the clatter of his weapon hitting the ground, before the man collapsed, clutching his injured leg.

Tim sprang to his feet and ran around the truck, still scanning the entire area in case there were other guards. The injured man was writhing on the ground, wailing loudly. Tim grabbed his rifle from the ground and ejected the magazine, slipping it into his pocket before flinging the weapon as far away as he could. The man glared at him, uttering a string of curses in his own language.

'You'll live,' said Tim, curtly.

He made his way back around the trucks to where the others were waiting.

'That's four down,' said Jeff. 'Surely there can't be any more.'

'Let's hope not,' said Tim, 'but don't count on it. OK, let's make for the gate. Is it unlocked?'

'Yes, I forced the lock. The car's parked directly opposite.'

'Right, go!' yelled Tim.

They made it without further incident, rushing through the gate and heading for the car parked across the road. The indicator lights flashed reassuringly when Jeff operated the remote control as they approached the car, still at a slow run.

Tim opened the front passenger door and shoved the assault rifle into the footwell before helping Raquel into the seat. Her breath came in ragged, sobbing gasps.

'Where are we?' asked Tim.

'Shekou Port ... warehouse area,' Jeff replied.

'How far to Chang's house?'

'About forty minutes I guess ... but surely you don't want to go back there?'

'I'll explain later. Do you know the way?'

'Well, yes ... but ...'

'Then you drive. Give me the gun ... I'll look after this bastard.' He glared at Chang, who looked fit to drop after the exertion of their dash towards the car.

Jeff handed the Glock to Tim, who bundled Chang into the back of the car and slipped into the seat alongside him. Jeff slammed both rear doors and ran around the car to get into the driving seat, pulling the driver's door shut behind him.

'OK,' said Tim, 'let's get going. We do need to go to Chang's house first; I'll explain later.'

Chang – who had said nothing since they left the warehouse – finally spoke, his voice trembling and weak. 'Why? What do you want at my house? What are you going to do with me?'

Tim turned to Chang and pressed the muzzle of the Glock to the underside of his chin. 'Shut up if you want to ...'

He was cut short abruptly by the sound of the door behind him being wrenched open.

As he swivelled his head around, he found he was looking straight down the barrel of an assault rifle.

Chapter 38

Tim shifted his point of focus from the tip of the muzzle to the face behind it. The large shaven head was set atop a short bull-like neck and massive shoulders. The oriental features were set in a menacing scowl.

It took only a second or so for Tim to assess his chances. There was no way he could turn around and bring his own gun to bear before the other man would be able to squeeze the trigger. He remained stock-still.

'You not move,' growled the big man behind the rifle. 'Or you,' he added, nodding briefly towards Jeff who had swivelled around in the driving seat, and was now glaring back at the intruder. 'Now, very slow, you give me gun,' he said, turning back to face Tim once more.

Tim turned the gun around so that he was holding it by the muzzle and very slowly turned to offer it, butt-first, to the guard. The man kept his rifle trained on Tim's face as he shifted it to a one-handed grip in order to take the pistol in his left hand.

In the front seat, Raquel was sobbing, struggling to breathe as the shock set in.

'Shut up, bitch,' yelled the guard, shoving the muzzle of the pistol right into her face.

A fraction of a second's distraction ... was it enough time for Tim to rush the guard? He tensed for action, but almost immediately dismissed the thought: a rash move now could easily cost Raquel her life. He would have to bide his time.

Raquel's eyelids began to flicker erratically, finally closing completely as she fell into a full faint, her head slumping sideways against the window of the car.

'Stupid bitch,' hissed the guard. He tucked the pistol into his belt before shifting his rifle back to a two-handed grip, all the time keeping it trained on Tim's face.

'You alright, sir?' said the big man to Chang.

'No, I am not,' snapped Chang. 'This bastard almost cut my hand off. But now he will pay.' He turned towards Tim and pushed his face forward until their noses were almost touching – his breath still smelling faintly of cigar smoke and whisky. 'You hear me, you shit? I'm going to make you *pay*.'

Tim did not flinch. He kept his expression impassive, but his brain was racing in overdrive as he tried to come up with some sort of plan to deal with the desperate situation in which they now found themselves.

Chang turned his attention back to the guard. 'Now, get me out of these damned handcuffs,' he barked.

The big man prodded Tim's chest with the muzzle of his weapon. 'Key ... now.'

Tim shifted position in the seat and began to reach into his pocket.

'Very slow,' warned the big man, leaning forward and bringing the muzzle of the rifle up under Tim's chin.

'OK, OK ...' said Tim. 'I'm just getting the key.'

Tim withdrew the key from his pocket and handed it over. The guard shifted the rifle to a single-handed grip and took the key in his left hand.

'Now you get out of car,' growled the guard. He took a pace backward to allow Tim room to step out of the car, all the time keeping the gun trained on his face. As the man stepped back and straightened up to his full height, Tim could see for the first time just how huge he was: about six feet four tall, Tim guessed, and built like a brick outhouse. 'Keep hands where I see them.'

Tim climbed slowly out of the car, all the time careful to keep his hands in full view. Once he had stepped out, he raised both hands above his head and turned to face the guard.

'Now you go there … by tree. Keep hands up.' Tim did as he was ordered.

With some difficulty, Chang swivelled around in his seat to turn his handcuffed hands towards the guard, who stepped forward to place the key in Chang's good hand, all the time keeping his weapon trained on Tim.

As Chang fumbled to unlock the handcuffs, the guard turned his attention to Jeff. 'Now you out, too … hands in air. Over there, next to him.'

Jeff did as he was ordered. By the time he had taken up a position next to Tim, Chang had succeeded in freeing himself. He scrambled out of the car and came around to stand next to the guard, facing the two men standing in front of the big tree, their hands aloft.

'So,' said Chang, his mouth curling in an unpleasant smile, 'the tables have turned now.' Tim noticed a brief expression of puzzlement flit across the guard's features – evidently his grasp of English did not run to interpreting such metaphors. It would almost have been comical if it were not for the gravity of their situation. 'You are going to wish that you never decided to poke your noses into my business.'

Tim was defiant. 'The moment you decided to kidnap my girlfriend, you made it *my* business.'

Chang took a few steps closer to Tim, looking him directly in the eyes. His face was twisted with hatred. 'You really don't know who you are dealing with, do you?'

'I know I'm dealing with scum.'

'Ha! Brave words … but ones you will soon regret.'

He turned away and started pacing up and down, stroking his chin as though considering what to do next.

'What you want me do with them?' enquired the big man.

'Shut up,' snapped Chang. 'I'm thinking.'

For several more seconds, Chang continued his restless pacing up and down, like some caged animal.

Eventually he stopped and turned to the guard. 'That one ...' he snarled, pointing at Jeff, 'you can kill. Shoot the other one in the knee ... I need him alive.'

The big man nodded, grunting his agreement, his face creasing into a slow smile. Slowly and deliberately, he raised his rifle.

Chapter 39

Tim's brain was racing. Could he rush the guard before he could squeeze the trigger? Unlikely: the man was standing some eight or ten paces away; he would probably have time to shoot both of them before Tim could reach him. But then they were probably both going to end up dead anyway eventually, whatever he did. It was now or never.

As Tim tensed to spring forward, the guards head snapped forward, his eyes rolled upwards in their sockets, and the rifle slipped from his grasp. Chang's eyes widened in shock and surprise, his attention now fully occupied by the sight of the guard collapsing alongside him.

Tim seized the moment. He rushed at Chang, who reacted surprisingly quickly, raising his hands into what looked like a very well-practiced Karate stance. In spite of his injured hand, Chang still looked dangerous. Tim was well-trained in unarmed combat himself and pulled up short rather than rush straight into a possibly-crippling blow. He decided to use one of the most effective and widely-used tactics of all. He adopted a martial arts stance of his own and feinted with his right hand. As Chang followed the move with his eyes, Tim shifted his balance and delivered a crushing kick to the man's testicles. Chang collapsed in a heap, doubled up with pain, his eyes bulging and his breath coming in short, laboured gasps.

With Chang temporarily incapacitated, Tim swivelled around to face any further threat from the guard, but Jeff was already there, straddling the prone figure, his fist drawn back ready to deliver a blow. It wasn't necessary, the man was out cold. Behind him stood the diminutive, bedraggled figure of Raquel, still holding the assault rifle by the muzzle with both hands. Blood dripped from the butt.

Tim rushed over and took the rifle from her, immediately shifting it to a single-handed grip. She sank to her knees, her breath coming in shallow gasps. Tim helped her up, hugging her to him with his free left hand and kissing her full on the lips. He stepped back and placed his hand on her shoulder, looking directly into her face. Her eyes were rimmed in red, staring out from a face covered in grime and smudged with the remnants of her makeup.

'Where the hell did you learn to swing a weapon like that?' said Tim, his voice a mixture of surprise and admiration.

'I don't know ... I ... well, I have no idea how to actually fire one of these things so I thought bashing him over the head with it was my best bet.'

'Well, you certainly did a job on him,' interjected Jeff, his fingers on the man's neck, checking for a pulse. 'He's dead.'

'I don't care,' said Raquel, her voice uncharacteristically hard and emotionless. 'These people are animals ... worse than animals.'

Tim was chilled by her apparently casual acceptance that she had just killed a man. Perhaps she had been through so much at the hands of these bastards that ... he didn't want to think about it.

He turned to look at Chang, still doubled up on the ground, wailing softly. He stepped over to the car and found the handcuffs, once more wrenching Chang's hands behind his back and securing them with the 'cuffs.

Once Chang was secured, Tim turned back to Raquel. 'I thought you were unconscious. How did you ...'

She was not listening to him; her eyes were fixed on the prone figure of Chang Wei, her expression uncharacteristically intense. She took a couple of steps toward him before drawing back her foot and kicking him, as hard as she could, in the stomach. As the breath was expelled from him, he let out a muffled groan. She drew back her foot again, ready to deliver another blow, but Tim grabbed her arm and pulled her away.

'Raquel, no ... he's no danger to us now.'

She shook her arm free, looking straight at Tim, her eyes burning with fury. 'You didn't have to go through what I went through. He ... they ... they...' She couldn't find the words.

'Shhh ...' He hugged her to him, pulling her head to his chest as she burst into an uncontrolled bout of sobbing. He felt an overwhelming urge to kick the downed man himself but, with a considerable effort, he suppressed it. 'He'll pay for what he's done soon enough but right now we need to get moving.'

She nodded, wiping away the tears with the back of her sleeve.

'Anyway, you didn't answer my question. Weren't you unconscious?'

Her dirty, tearstained face brightened a little. 'I figured that if they thought I had passed out they might not pay any attention to me, and then maybe I'd be able to do something to help.'

'You faked it?'

She nodded. 'Yes. It was obvious that if either you or your friend made a move, they'd shoot you before you could do anything. An unconscious girl on the other hand ...'

Tim smiled. 'You're quite something, you know.'

'Haven't I always tried to tell you that?' She managed a small smile herself now.

'Come on, we have to go now,' said Tim.

'Wait, your neck is still bleeding.'

Tim touched his hand to his neck. Sure enough the blood was still flowing freely and judging by the extent of the stain down the side of his shirt he was losing a lot of blood. There was precious little time to waste but the last thing he needed was to become weakened by blood loss.

'OK,' he said, 'there's a first aid kit in the holdall in the boot of the car. You can find something to dress the wound in there ... but hurry.'

Five minutes later Raquel had cleaned the wound with an antiseptic wound-wash fluid and applied a dressing of gauze secured firmly with medical tape. The gauze was already starting to show a small red patch in the centre but the flow of blood had been largely staunched.

'Thanks,' said Tim, giving Raquel a kiss on the cheek. 'Now we have to go.'

'What about my hand?' wailed Chang.

'You can bleed to death for all I care,' spat Raquel, with feeling.

Once again, Tim was shocked to hear his girlfriend speak with such venom; they must have put her through hell. He went over to Chang and unwound the blood-stained handkerchief from his injured hand, which had by now almost stopped bleeding.

'Raquel, give me the first aid kit,' he said. She didn't move. 'Please, Raquel, give it to me.'

Reluctantly she handed it over. Tim cleaned both the entry and exit wounds made by the knife and then applied a large Band-Aid plaster over each, before cutting a length of bandage from the roll in the kit and wrapping it several times around Chang's hand to ensure that the Band-Aids stayed in place.

'That will have to do for now,' he said, brusquely, knotting the bandage and passing the first aid kit back to Raquel.

He picked up the assault rifle and wiped the butt against his trouser leg to remove the worst of the blood, before once again propping it in the footwell of the front passenger seat of the car. He grabbed the Glock from the waistband of the dead guard, before dragging Chang to his feet and bundling him into the back of the car, the weapon pressed to the side of his head.

'OK, Jeff, you drive … Chang's house.'

Jeff shook his head in bewilderment, but did not argue the point.

They sped off, a shower of dirt flying into the air from the tortured rear tyres.

***

The four of them sat in the car, parked on the grass verge lining the road alongside Chang's house. The house was in darkness. There was no sign of life.

'Do you still have any guards here?' demanded Tim.

'How the fuck would I know?' replied Chang, evidently now recovering some of his old bravado, 'I've been with you for the last few hours.'

Tim pressed the muzzle of the Glock to Chang's neck. 'I would advise you not to adopt that tone,' he growled.

'OK, OK … but I really don't know. They obviously know that you kidnapped me from the warehouse, and I don't suppose they'd expect you to bring me back here … but I honestly don't know.'

Tim considered what Chang had said. He might just be telling the truth.

After a few seconds he turned to Jeff. 'OK, I'm going in with Chang. I want you to take Raquel to the airport and make everything ready for a quick departure.'

'No,' protested Raquel, 'you can't go in there … let's just get out of here, before more of them come for us.'

Tim's voice was firm. 'I have to. There's no time to explain everything right now but this is important.'

'No … you can't … it's too …'

'Raquel, no arguments … I'm going in.'

She let out a long, loud sigh and her shoulders slumped in resignation. She evidently realised that Tim would not be dissuaded.

He turned to Jeff, 'How long to get to the airport?'

'I'm not too sure … about forty minutes, I guess.'

'OK, if I'm not with you exactly two hours from now' – he looked at his watch – 'you go without me.'

'Oh, come on Tim … why don't we just wait here for you while you …'

'No,' said Tim, firmly. 'Two hours, right?'

Jeff sighed. 'OK … two hours.'

'Have the engines running and ready to take off … but if I'm not there when the two hours are up, you just go. Got it?'

Jeff nodded, his expression grim. 'OK, but how are you going to get there?'

'I'll figure something out.'

'Nooo,' protested Raquel once more, but Tim had already scrambled out of the car, leaving Chang still in the back seat.

'Cover him for a moment,' said Tim, handing the Glock to Jeff.

He went around to the boot of the car and pulled out the black holdall, briefly checking its contents.

'OK, I have my own weapons and everything else I need right here,' he said, withdrawing the SIG handgun and swiftly checking the magazine. 'You keep the Glock and the other rifle.'

Jeff took the Glock, shifting awkwardly in his seat as he tried to tuck it into his waistband while still seated. In the end he gave up and asked Raquel to hold it. She looked apprehensive but took the weapon, laying it on her lap and placing both hands on top of it.

'Get out of the car,' ordered Tim, levelling his pistol at Chang.

Chang, still handcuffed, levered himself awkwardly out of the car.

Tim slammed the rear door before moving up to the driver's door window to speak to Jeff. 'OK, now go … get out of here.'

Jeff nodded briefly before extending his hand through the open window. 'Good luck.'

Tim grasped his hand and shook it firmly. 'You too. Keep her safe.'

Jeff nodded once more before turning to face forward, engaging first gear, releasing the handbrake, and flooring the accelerator. The Toyota sped off up the road, leaving Tim and Chang Wei by the roadside.

Having satisfied himself, as best he could, that there were no more guards lurking in the vicinity, Tim made his way towards the double gates leading on to the main driveway, all the time keeping Chang just in front of him.

'Open them,' demanded Tim.

'My right-hand-side trouser pocket …' said Chang, 'there's a remote control.'

Tim set down the holdall on the grass and switched the SIG to his left hand, pressing it against the side of Chang's neck. 'Please don't think this is your opportunity to try anything stupid.' Chang shook his head.

Tim leaned forward and, from behind, slid his right hand into Chang's pocket. His fingers closed around a smooth, oval-shaped, plastic object which he withdrew. He took a step backward before taking his eyes off Chang for a moment to glance at the item in his hand: a grey plastic lozenge with two buttons. He pressed the right hand one; nothing happened. He pressed the left; there was a metallic-sounding click followed by a soft whirring sound as the gates began smoothly to swing open. He surveyed the long, straight, gravel drive leading to the front door. It was lined with a row of low-level lamps along either side, bathing it in a soft, yellowish light.

He pocketed the remote control before shifting the gun back into his right hand and picking up the holdall with his left. 'Let's go,' he said prodding Chang between the shoulder blades with the muzzle of the gun, 'but not straight up the drive … over the lawn … stay out of the light.'

They made their way slowly toward the house, Tim frequently glancing to left and right for any signs of danger. There were none that he could detect.

They made it to the house without incident and then, staying close to the wall of the house, shuffled across towards the front door.

Suddenly, Tim heard a faint click from just ahead of them and a split second later his eyes were assaulted by a dazzling white light. Instinctively, he ducked down, pulling Chang to him, prepared to use him as a human shield if necessary. His finger tensed on the trigger, but he was temporarily blinded; he couldn't see the target.

Chapter 40

Tim was blinking furiously as he tried to reset his dark-adapted eyes in readiness for the forthcoming attack. But nothing happened; there was no gunshot; no sudden rush of an unseen assailant; nothing.

Chang laughed. 'My, we are jumpy aren't we?'

Tim realised that the faint click had been nothing more than the sound of the relay which triggered a motion-sensitive security light.

'Shut up,' he barked, as he raised himself from the tensed, crouching posture which he had adopted.

He prodded Chang forward with the gun until they were right by the front door. 'Open it,' he ordered.

'I can't ... not with these handcuffs on.'

'Well give me the key then.'

'That, on its own, won't help you,' replied Chang. 'See that panel?' He inclined his head to indicate the unit to which he was referring.

'Well?' demanded Tim. 'What about it?'

'It's a fingerprint recognition unit; I have to place my finger on it. There's no way I can do that with my hands behind my back like this.'

Tim realised that this was true. The panel was mounted at roughly head-height: impossible to reach with your hands secured behind your back. For a moment he considered cutting the bastard's finger off and using it to operate the panel himself. After the

217

barbarism he had inflicted on Raquel it was surely justified. But he feared that, after what he had already done to Chang's hand the additional pain from such an action might cause him to pass out … and he needed Chang conscious.

'OK, I'm going to unlock one side of the 'cuffs. When I do, you pass your hands around in front of you and re-fix them. You try anything though, and I'll shoot you in in the kneecap. Got it?' Chang grunted and nodded.

Tim unlocked one side of the handcuffs and took a couple of paces back from Chang, keeping the gun levelled. Chang turned around to face Tim, glaring malevolently as he massaged the wrist which had been released.

'Relock them … now,' said Tim.

'I still need to get the key out of my pocket,' growled Chang.

'OK … slowly then.'

With his good hand, Chang reached into the top pocket of his shirt and withdrew the key.

'Put the key on the ground and relock the 'cuffs.'

Chang just stood there, glaring at Tim.

Tim lowered the gun to point at Chang's knee. He glowered, but took the point and did as he had been ordered.

'Step back a few paces.'

He did so; Tim stepped forward and picked up the key.

'Now open it.'

Chang reached up and pressed all four fingers of his right hand to the glass panel. *Hmm … guess I would have had to cut off his whole hand to unlock the door*, thought Tim, in a bizarre moment of black humour.

There was click followed by a subdued whirring sound. 'Now you can open it with the key,' said Chang.

Tim motioned with a sideways jerk of his gun for Chang to move away from the door. As he did so, Tim stepped forward and inserted the key in the lock, turning it before pushing the door open an inch or two.

'Welcome to my humble abode,' said Chang, his voice dripping with sarcasm.

'You first,' said Tim, stepping back to allow Chang to enter.

Tim followed him into the house, staying a couple of paces behind, his eyes flicking this way and that for any sign of trouble. But the house appeared to be deserted. They moved through to the lounge: the very same room where Tim had first come face to face with Chang, just hours earlier. He looked very different now from the smug, self-satisfied man that Tim had then encountered, lounging in his armchair, cigar in hand, and whisky tumbler at his side. He remained defiant, though.

'So now we're here. What the hell do you want?'

'Where's your computer?'

Chang's eyes narrowed. 'Why do you want ...?'

'Shut up. Where is it?'

'In my study ... through there.' He indicated a door off the lounge.

'You first,' said Tim.

Chang opened the door and moved through, with Tim close behind. Directly ahead was a large picture window, with a desk in front, facing into the room. Chang's computer was on the desk. Tim glanced around the room and ordered Chang to sit down in an armchair positioned in a corner opposite the window, facing towards the desk.

'You stay there, where I can see you, hands on your lap.'

'Where the hell else can I put them with these handcuffs on?' growled Chang.

Tim felt a fresh surge of anger flare within him. 'One more smart-arsed comment like that and I'll shoot you in the knee just for the hell of it,' he snapped.

Chang fell abruptly silent. Tim fixed him with a steely stare for a couple more seconds before moving around the desk and sitting down in front of the computer.

'I'm going to lay the gun down here, on the desk,' he said, 'but please don't try anything. I can pick it up and shoot before you get within half a dozen paces of me.'

Chang grunted, sullenly.

Tim laid down the gun and switched on the computer, waiting for a few moments until the welcome screen appeared. This time though, it required a password.

'Password?' he demanded.

Chang just stared at him, sullenly. Tim laid his hand back on the gun and closed his fingers around the butt, his eyes fixed on Chang's.

'I won't be asking a second time,' said Tim, his voice low and menacing.

'Hastings1066,' muttered Chang.

'What?' exclaimed Tim, incredulous.

Chang shrugged. 'I like to study English history.'

Tim shook his head in disbelief but, sure enough, when he entered the password Chang had given him, the computer sprang to life. He bent down to unzip the holdall and withdrew his portable hard drive, plugging it into one of the USB ports of the computer. He quickly checked how much data was contained on the machine's hard drive: three hundred and forty-seven gigabytes. This was good; his portable hard drive still had over five hundred gigabytes of spare capacity, even after copying the contents of Chang's work computer. He would be able to copy the entire contents of this computer too. He started the copying process. Estimated time to complete, twenty-seven minutes. *Damn. Why does it have to take so long?*

He laid his hand upon the butt of the gun, ready to pick it up quickly if necessary, and settled down to wait, keeping his eyes fixed on Chang. They sat there in silence for some ten minutes or so, each regarding the other.

Finally, Chang broke the silence. 'You won't get away with this, you know,' he said, his tone conversational.

'Shut up.'

'My people will be looking for me right now. If you want to stand any chance of getting out alive you'd best leave right away.'

'I said' – he picked up the gun and pointed it at Chang's knee – 'shut up.'

Chang shrugged and relapsed into silence once more.

Tim checked the screen: twelve minutes left. The little green blocks advanced across the progress bar with infuriating sloth.

Chang spoke up again. 'Do you actually realise what you have got yourself into by coming over here like some sort of amateur James Bond?'

'Listen, you bastard. You kidnapped my girlfriend and cut off her bloody *finger*. What the hell did you expect?'

Chang shrugged again. 'She was just an unfortunate casualty caught in the middle of something bigger. If you want to blame anyone, then blame her father: it was his stupidity in trying to defy us that caused all this.'

This was too much for Tim. He rose to his feet pointing the gun at Chang. 'One more word and I swear I'll blow your damned head off.'

Chang raised both of his handcuffed hands in a sort of defensive gesture, but at that precise moment, Tim saw the man's eyes flick momentarily to one side. He had seen something behind Tim. Instinctively, Tim dived to one side, just as he heard the sound of a gunshot and shattering glass. The bullet slammed into the opposite wall about one and a half metres to the right of Chang Wei's head. Tim whirled around and swiftly fired two shots at the shadowy figure just a few yards outside the shattered window. The man crumpled and fell without uttering a sound.

When Tim turned back he was faced with the sight of Chang clutching a handgun – awkwardly, given his handcuffed wrists – and levelling it at him. He leapt to the side once more, but this time he was too slow to avoid the bullet which ripped through the top part of his left arm. Before the pain of the impact had even registered with his brain, he had returned fire, striking Chang in the stomach. It wasn't where he had intended to hit him, but there had been no time to aim properly. Chang screamed in pain and the gun slipped from his grasp.

Tim walked over to where Chang was sitting, clutching both hands over the wound in his stomach which was already bleeding profusely. He used the toe of his shoe to nudge the gun on the floor away from Chang's possible reach.

Chang's face was screwed up in an expression of agony. 'You … you have to get me a doctor. I'll bleed to death here.'

Tim reached forward and eased Chang's hands away from the wound; the blood spurted forth freely. He had seen enough gunshot wounds to know that a stomach wound like this wasn't survivable without immediate expert medical attention, and even then, probably not.

'No you won't,' replied Tim, though gritted teeth.

He raised his weapon and squeezed the trigger, putting a bullet into the centre of Chang's forehead.

Chapter 41

Now Tim felt the pain acutely: a searing hot poker spearing its way through his flesh. He tucked the pistol into his waistband and examined the injury. He twisted forward, pulling his injured left arm forward with his right hand. The bullet had passed right though, leaving an ugly exit wound, which was bleeding profusely. If he continued to lose blood at that rate, he would soon be too weak to make the dash to the airport. He needed to stop the bleeding fast if he was to make it.

He took hold of his pistol once more – not that there was much likelihood of encountering another guard in the house, given the fact that the noise and disturbance of the last few minutes had not flushed one out – and set off to find the bathroom. He found it on the first floor.

There was a large, mirrored cabinet on the wall which, fortunately, contained a well-stocked first aid kit. He used the scissors he found in the kit to cut away his sleeve, just below the shoulder. He sprayed both exit and entry wounds with antiseptic wound wash, before making a tourniquet from a sturdy length of bandage. He winced as he struggled to pull it as tight as he could manage, awkwardly using one hand in conjunction with his teeth. After a few moments the blood flow slowed to just a trickle. Good, this would soon stop completely due to the natural coagulation of the blood. He completed his makeshift repair by wrapping a length of broad bandage around the whole wound site, securing it with some medical adhesive tape. There were no really strong painkillers – how he wished he could get a shot of morphine – but there was a bottle of regular codeine tablets. The label recommended that two tablets be taken at any one time. Tim took eight, in the hope that the increased dosage might just be enough to take the edge off the pain. Finally, he took a glass tumbler from the shelf in front of him and filled it with water, gulping it down quickly before refilling it and doing so again. This would help – in time – to replenish the blood he had already lost.

He looked at his watch; he had just fifty minutes left in which to make it to the airport. He needed to move right now.

He grabbed his gun, rushed down the stairs and over to the computer. The copying process was complete. He unplugged the hard drive and thrust it into his pocket. Glancing out of the window, he noted that Chang's white Mercedes was parked in the drive; he must have left it there while one of his henchmen drove him to the warehouse. This was his only hope of getting to the airport on time. But where were the keys?

He rushed over to where Chang's body was slumped in the chair. An ugly, dark pool of blood had formed on the floor beneath the chair, spreading rapidly and soaking the pale cream carpet. The dark, lifeless eyes stared at him, causing him momentarily to shudder. He shrugged off the feeling and stepped forward, trying to avoid standing in the blood while swiftly checking all the dead man's pockets; nothing. He noticed that the top drawer of the cabinet alongside Chang's chair was open. This was probably the place from which Chang had taken the gun. *Careless of me not to have checked it before I made him sit there in the first place*, thought Tim. He checked the contents of the drawer, but there were no car keys inside. He glanced desperately around the room, checking out every horizontal surface, but there were no keys to be seen. He rushed out into the hall and through to the kitchen. A quick glance around the room revealed no keys lying on any of the gleaming work surfaces. Where else to look? He stepped back into the hall, and there, directly ahead, just alongside the front door was a rack from which hung half a dozen sets of keys. Even from some twenty feet away, Tim could discern the distinctive Mercedes logo on one of the key fobs. The wave of relief which swept through him was overwhelming, but there was no time to waste now.

He returned to the study, tucked the pistol into his waistband and lifted the heavy holdall with his good hand. Moving back into the hall, he managed to lift his injured arm sufficiently to take the keys before opening the door and stepping out. He glanced all around for signs of trouble, but all looked quiet. He pressed a button on the key and the doors of the Mercedes unlocked with a reassuring clunk accompanied by a flash of the direction indicators. Pressing another button caused the boot lid to swing open. Tim heaved the holdall into the boot before unzipping it to withdraw the assault rifle. He opened the front passenger door and laid the weapon on the seat. He then returned to the holdall and rummaged around until he found the satnav which they had hired with the rental Toyota. *Thank God we thought to hire this little device!*

He slammed the boot shut and climbed into the driver's seat, laying his SIG on the passenger seat alongside the rifle. Fumbling awkwardly, one-handed, he fixed the satnav to the windscreen and plugged it in. He took a few deep breaths to steady his nerves, and his trembling fingers, before programming in his destination. As he waited for the route to be calculated he glanced at his watch; he had just thirty-six minutes left. The estimated journey time flashed up on the screen: forty-seven minutes. *Shit!* There was no plan B, though, so he would just have to drive like hell and hope for the best.

He noted, with relief, that the Mercedes was an automatic. He would be able to use his good right hand to steer without having to worry about gear changing. He started the car, slipped the selector into 'Drive' and set off, the rear wheels spraying a shower of gravel as the car roared up the drive. As he approached the gates he realised, with dismay, that the remote control to open them was still in his pocket. Should he just ram them and hope they would burst open without fatally damaging the car? No, those gates looked too damned solid to risk it. He slammed on the brakes, causing the car to slew sideways on the loose gravel, coming to an untidy halt facing some forty-five degrees off from its direction of travel. He twisted awkwardly in his seat, rummaging in his pocket with his good hand. *Damn! Not that pocket.* He shifted position once more and, gritting his teeth against the pain in his injured arm, forced his left hand into his other pocket. *There it was.* His fingers closed around the remote control and, with fumbling fingers, managed to operate it without even withdrawing it from his pocket.

He saw the gates give a slight shudder and even as they were just starting to open he shoved the selector lever into 'Drive' and floored the accelerator, fighting to control the car as one of the rear wheels slithered sideways onto the grass. After a few deft twirls of the steering wheel to left and right he succeeded in taming the wildly fishtailing vehicle, bringing it in line with the drive and accelerating hard towards the gates. They were only about half-open by the time he forced the Mercedes through, ripping off one of its door mirrors in the process.

The back of the car swung wide, the tortured rear tyres spewing smoke as he swung onto the road. He held the slide with a touch of opposite lock on the steering, and accelerated up the road, his foot pinned to the floor. Now the race was on.

He drove like a madman, ignoring every rule of the road, running red lights and charging across junctions regardless of 'Stop' signs. At one point he was forced to brake so sharply to avoid a truck crossing his path that both the weapons on the passenger seat shot forward, landing with a clatter in the footwell. It would be a miracle, he thought, if he made it to the airport without either having an accident or being stopped by the police. But he had no option; he pressed on regardless.

Finally, after what seemed like an eternity, the airport came into view. He didn't want to waste time being routed towards the main passenger terminal so he slowed down a little in order to steal a few glances at the satnav, desperately searching for a way to get onto the perimeter road which encircled the outer fence. *There it was!*

Ignoring, first, a 'No Entry' sign and then an 'Authorised Vehicles Only' sign he made it onto the perimeter road, speeding around it to a point near where he hoped the Gulfstream would be waiting.

But when he glanced at his watch he saw that it was too late: Jeff would already have taken off – around eight minutes ago.

Tim's heart sank as he eased his pace and began to consider his options. He still had most of Roy's money left. Maybe there was still a way out. He could perhaps seek medical attention for his injuries and then go to ground for a few days while he recovered his strength. If he abandoned his weapons he might be able to catch a regular scheduled flight back to the UK. However, with Chang and several of his men dead, Tim would now be a marked man; surely his chances of evading detection with such determined people looking for him were remote.

Maybe he could break into the airport and find a private pilot that he could forcibly coerce into flying him to his destination. There were problems with this approach too, though. In his current weakened state he would not be physically capable of climbing the perimeter fence. He doubted whether he would even have the strength in his injured arm to operate the bolt cutters and get through that way. Certainly he would not be able to hold his own in any sort of physical struggle. Things were not looking good.

His gloomy reflections were cut short abruptly and violently as the rear screen of the car shattered and simultaneously three holes appeared in the front screen, a network of cracks radiating outward from each of them. A split second later, Tim registered the distinctive rattle of automatic fire from somewhere behind him.

Chapter 42

As he floored the accelerator and the Mercedes surged forward, Tim glanced in the rear-view mirror. Through a large, jagged hole in the now-opaque glass, he could see a black saloon racing towards him, a figure hanging out of the passenger side window, gun in hand. As he yanked the steering abruptly to the right to follow the curve of the perimeter road, he saw a series of muzzle flashes, followed a moment later by the vicious chatter of automatic fire. This time the burst missed the Mercedes completely.

As he rounded the corner, the sight which came into his view was as unexpected as it was welcome. There, just turning at the end of the runway was the Gulfstream, engines whining lazily and navigation lights flashing, as it aligned itself with the runway. Clearly it was just about to take off.

Tim swung the car wide out to his left before bringing it back sharply to his right to face directly at the fence before flooring the accelerator. As the car ploughed into the chain-link fencing there was a screeching of tortured metal as several posts were torn from the ground. The Mercedes barely slowed its pace as it hurtled towards the plane, trailing a fifteen-yard length of fencing and several uprooted posts. He began frantically flashing his headlights and blasting his horn – spears of pain shooting through his injured arm – in a desperate attempt to attract Jeff's attention. Behind him, the black saloon came careering through the gap in the fence, its back end sliding wide as the driver fought to maintain control.

Ahead, the Gulfstream had stopped at the end of the runway. Had Jeff seen him? Tim was barely thirty yards from the plane now. He stamped on the brakes, bringing the car slithering to a halt, before reaching down to pick up the assault rifle from where it had fallen into the footwell. He twisted around in his seat and rested the weapon on the seat back, struggling to hold it steady, one-handed as he took aim. He squeezed the trigger and panned the sights to left and right, shredding both front tyres of the pursuing car. It slewed sideways before the front corner dug into the grass, causing the vehicle to roll right over onto its roof and then over once more, finally coming to rest right-way-up amid a shower of flying mud and grass.

He turned back to look at the plane. The door was open and the steps were being lowered. A couple of seconds later, Jeff appeared in the doorway, frantically beckoning him. Tim flung the car door open and scrambled out, abandoning the rifle as he made a headlong dash for the plane. His heart was pounding furiously and with each thud of his foot onto the ground, a bolt of pain seared through his injured arm. *Only ten yards now ... five ... I can make it!*

As he reached the aircraft, Jeff leant down and grasped his good hand, helping him scramble up into the aircraft. The pain from his arm was excruciating.

'You're late,' admonished Jeff, as he retracted the steps and slammed the door.

'I got held up,' replied Tim in-between laboured gasps of breath.

'Let's get out of here,' said Jeff, scrambling back into the pilot's seat.

Tim flung himself into a front-row seat in the main cabin, not wanting any repeat of his previous experience of living through a take-off while sprawled on the floor. He looked anxiously through the cabin window. As the noise of the engines built, Tim could see a dazed-looking figure emerge, unsteadily, from the black car. He was still holding his assault rifle.

'Hurry,' urged Tim, 'they haven't given up yet.'

As the brakes were released, the plane surged forward, rapidly gathering pace.

The figure by the car raised his weapon; a few seconds later, the rapid, angry spitting of muzzle flashes could be seen once again. But the figure holding the gun was swaying unsteadily and his fire went wide. He steadied himself, legs apart and feet firmly planted, before letting loose another burst, but by now the plane was out of effective range.

Jeff pulled back on the stick and the plane lifted smoothly from the ground.

***

When Roy's mobile bleeped twice, he pounced on it like a starving man on food. It was a text message from Tim.

> Roy,
> Raquel is safe. We are in the air and on the way home. Long story. Speak soon – Tim.

He felt his knees begin to buckle beneath him, and he sank back into the sofa, overcome with relief. He reread that brief message several times, almost unwilling to believe that it was actually for real.

Donna had been in the kitchen making them some coffee. As she came through the door carrying two steaming cups Roy looked up from his mobile and gazed into her eyes.

'What? … What is it?' she said, her hands beginning to tremble and causing coffee to slop over the rims of the cups. 'Have you heard something?'

'They're safe, Donna.'

The emotion was too much. She dropped both the cups, which hit the soft carpet without breaking. The steaming liquid splashed far and wide, rapidly sinking into the pile, creating a large, unsightly dark stain. She didn't even seem to notice.

'They're safe? Are you sure?'

He nodded. 'Tim's just sent a text. They're already in the air.'

'Thank God,' she breathed, rushing over and flinging her arms around his neck.

'What happened? Is everyone OK? When will they get here? How ....?'

'Whoa there ... I don't know any more ... look.' He showed her the message.

'Well, call him back. Find out what's going on.'

Roy nodded. He located Tim's number and tried to call, but couldn't get through.

'He must have sent that text just after they had taken off. They're probably too high by now for his mobile to work.' She clutched her fists into tight balls in frustration. 'At least they're safe though.'

'Oh, Roy,' gasped Donna, tears welling up in the corners of her eyes, 'I thought we might never see her again.'

The tears of relief and happiness began to flow freely, as Roy hugged her to him, sharing those same emotions.

He knew it wasn't over yet, though.

Chapter 43

As Raquel was busy applying a fresh dressing to his wounded arm, using the first aid supplies kept on the plane, Tim related the events of the last few hours.

'It's a bloody miracle you made it out of there alive mate,' opined Jeff.

Tim smiled, grimly. 'To be honest, I didn't think I was going to.'

'It's incredible,' said Raquel, tying off the final knot of the bandage, 'that these people would go to such despicable lengths. When my dad decided to bring back the manufacturing operation to the UK he couldn't possibly have imagined what it would lead to.'

'How could he?' said Tim. 'Although he knew that Chang wasn't playing by the rules, he thought it was just a case of dishonest business practices. He had no way of knowing that a criminal network was running the show.'

'So what happens now?' said Raquel.

'What … you mean in terms of the business?'

She nodded.

'I guess that's down to your dad. I've done my bit,' said Tim.

'Yes you have …' she said, putting her arms around his neck and pulling him to her for a kiss, 'and I love you even more now.'

Tim coloured up.

'Hey you lovebirds,' said Jeff, 'you can save all that stuff until we get back to England.'

She giggled and released Tim from the hug.

After a few moments' silence Tim turned to Jeff. 'We'd never have pulled this off without you, you know.'

'Glad to have helped,' he replied, grinning.

'Getting involved in the thick of the action wasn't part of the deal ... why'd you do it?'

'Oh, like I said earlier, my life's been a bit dull recently ... and I hate to see the bad guys win.'

Tim smiled. 'And what about our agreement that you'd go without me if I wasn't there within two hours?'

'Well, when the two hours had passed and you still hadn't arrived, I decided to employ some delaying tactics with air traffic control ... I told them I had a slight technical glitch with the plane. I couldn't have spun that out much longer, though, or they'd have ordered me back to the terminal and I'd have missed my slot completely.'

'But why did you wait for me, anyway?'

'Three reasons. Firstly, your girlfriend here was giving me so much grief for contemplating going without you that I didn't think I could stand it.'

Raquel laughed.

'Secondly, like I said before, I hate to see the bad guys win.'

'Well, thank heavens for that,' said Tim. 'So what's the third reason?'

'Oh, I don't know ... I guess I kinda like you.'

Now all three of them laughed.

'Well,' said Tim, more serious now, 'I'm more grateful to you than I can ever express ... I don't know how we can ever repay you.'

'I have a feeling you'd do the same for me if the situation arose ... which, I hasten to add, I sincerely hope it never will.'

They lapsed into silence for a while and, before long, Raquel had fallen into a deep sleep. Tim began to yawn too; he was absolutely exhausted.

Jeff glanced across at the two of them. 'Yeah, I'm feeling pretty bushed, too. We're all desperately short of sleep, but we have a long journey ahead of us. I'm putting the plane on autopilot but I don't really want us to all be asleep at the same time. Why don't you get your head down now and I'll wake you in a couple of hours so that I can get some sleep too.'

Tim nodded. He settled back in his seat and within seconds, sleep overtook him.

***

Sammy was snoozing on his armchair. All of a sudden his ears pricked up; a second later he raised his head, inclining it to one side; his tail stiffened, curling forward in an arc until it almost touched the centre of his back. He leapt from the chair and charged toward the front door, yelping and scrabbling at it. As Roy and Donna got up from the sofa, the doorbell rang.

When Roy opened the door the three of them standing there made a sorry sight, their filthy, dishevelled clothing making them look like refugees from a warzone – which actually wasn't so very far from the truth. Sammy went absolutely crazy, launching himself bodily at Raquel, who caught him in her arms, gathering him up to her face and allowing him to smother her in licks.

'Come on in,' said Roy, standing aside to allow them to do so.

Raquel lowered Sammy to the floor; he began jumping up and scrabbling at Tim, who bent down and, with his good hand, ruffled the fur around the animal's neck. Sammy squeaked and snuffled contentedly.

Donna stepped forward and enfolded Raquel in her arms. 'Thank God ... thank God you're safe.' They clung together for several seconds as though both of their lives depended on it. When they finally eased apart from one another, Donna registered the dressing on Raquel's hand. 'Oh, your poor finger ... Does it hurt terribly?'

'It did,' said Raquel, 'but not now.' Donna took the bandaged hand in both of hers, stroking it as if to try to soothe it.

Raquel eased herself away and turned towards Roy. 'Hi Dad ... can't tell you how glad I am to be back home.'

Tears sprang from the corners of Roy's eyes. 'Come here ... I ...'

She rushed toward him and buried her head in his chest while he hugged her to him.

Raquel was sobbing now. 'I thought ... well, I thought I'd never see you ... see any of you again. I thought ...'

'Shhh ... you're safe now.'

Eventually, they eased apart from each other. Roy turned towards Tim, eyeing the extensive bloodstains on his clothing and the dressings on his neck and arm. 'You look as if you've had a pretty tough time.'

'You could say that,' replied Tim, with a small smile. 'We have quite a story to tell.'

'I'll bet,' said Roy, 'but there'll be time enough for that later. First, though, we need to get you two to hospital to have those wounds properly attended to.'

Tim nodded, stepping aside and gesturing towards Jeff. 'This is Jeff. We owe him our lives.'

Jeff's tanned countenance flushed red. 'Aw c'mon Tim ... don't exaggerate.'

'I'm not,' said Tim. 'We could never have done this without his help.'

Roy stepped forward and shook Jeff's hand. 'I don't know how we can ever thank you enough for what you have done.'

'Glad to have helped,' he said, clearly uncomfortable with the effusive thanks.

'We can talk later, but first let me take Tim and Raquel to the hospital,' said Roy, releasing his grip on Jeff's hand.

'Before we go,' said Tim, 'I have to make a phone call.'

'Well while you do that,' said Raquel I just *have* to shower and change ... look at my clothes and my hair ... I'm absolutely *gross*.'

'I'll find you some clothes,' offered Donna. 'I'm still not *that* much fatter than you.'

Roy chuckled; Donna's trim figure had hardly changed at all since the day they were married. She was, indeed, more or less the same size as her daughter.

As soon as the two women had left the room, Roy became more serious. 'OK, so what's going on? Who do you have to call?'

'As soon as they see that I have gunshot wounds,' replied Tim, 'they'll be obliged to report it to the police.'

'Hmm … and we really don't want the police crawling all over this.'

'No we don't. Look, I've probably called in all the favours I'm due, but I have to try and stop this turning into a full-blown investigation. If that happens, who knows where it will lead.'

Roy nodded. 'OK … make the call.'

Tim took out his mobile phone and tapped a few keys.

'Hello, Steve? It's Tim.'

Tim fell silent for around ten seconds, evidently listening to the person on the other end of the line.

'I know … yes … I overstepped the mark … I'm sorry.'

Tim fell silent once more for a few seconds.

'I know I've caused you … yes I know we're even now … but …'

Tim took the phone away from his ear and clamped it against his chest. 'Is there somewhere I could talk privately?' he whispered.

'In the study,' said Roy, pointing towards the door through the hallway. Tim moved through and closed the door behind him.

Roy could still hear snatches of the conversation emanating from the study, but it wasn't until Tim raised his voice to a much higher volume, his tone insistent and commanding, that he could fully discern what he was saying.

'OK, here's the deal. We're going to the main hospital in Shane Street. I'm going to be in deep shit here if you guys start digging into this, so I'm asking you as a friend and ex comrade-in-arms … just

drop it will you? You know that if the situation was reversed I'd ...'
Silence.

Tim walked slowly back into the lounge, his shoulders slumped forward.

'What happened?' said Roy.

'He hung up on me.'

Chapter 44

'How did this happen?' asked the nurse, as she examined the stump of Raquel's severed finger.

'I was chopping a joint of meat with a meat cleaver. I guess I got … well, careless.'

Before the nurse could comment, Tim withdrew from his bag an insulated plastic box, full of ice. 'I have the finger here. Is there any chance … well, of saving it?'

The nurse's expression was grim. 'This wound looks … well, it doesn't look very recent. Look, I'm not sure … I'll have to get the consultant to take a look.'

She rushed off, returning a few minutes later with a white-coated man who introduced himself as a Mr. Pritchard, Senior Consultant on duty.

'OK, I'll take a look at the young lady's finger. Nurse, perhaps you can take the gentleman into the treatment room next door and examine his arm?'

Tim was duly ushered into the adjoining room.

'Is this a gunshot wound?' said the nurse, after peeling off the dressing on Tim's arm.

Tim nodded. 'It was an accident … shot myself at the gun club while going to reload. I didn't realise there was still a round in the chamber.'

Her face creased in a frown as she turned her attention to the graze along the side of his neck. 'And this one?'

'The shock of the bullet going through my arm made me stagger backwards and I caught the side of my neck on a sharp piece of metal sticking out of the fence.'

Her expression betrayed her scepticism, but she said nothing to challenge or contradict what Tim had said. She proceeded to clean and redress the wounds before announcing, 'I'm afraid that all gunshot wounds have to be reported to the police.' Tim nodded, disconsolately. 'Please wait here while I speak to the doctor.'

A few minutes later, the doctor appeared at the door of the treatment room, followed by Raquel, with a fresh dressing on her hand.

'I'm afraid there is no chance of reattaching the finger,' said the doctor. 'If we had been able to attend to it within an hour or two of the injury, perhaps, but now ... well, it's far too late.'

Tim looked into Raquel's eyes. 'Oh, Raquel, I'm so sorry.'

'It's OK,' she replied, her expression neutral, accepting. 'We didn't really think there was much chance, did we?'

'No, I guess not,' said Tim, quietly.

Nurse Watkins tells me that the wound to your arm should heal well, given time and rest. Fortunately the bullet passed right through without hitting the bone.

'Look,' said Tim, 'I know you're supposed to report gunshot wounds to the police, but what you don't understand is that ...'

The doctor raised his hand and waved it, palm-forward, from side to side, gently cutting Tim off. 'There's no need to explain. I've already had a call from a Detective Inspector Stephen Salt.' He tapped his finger against the side of his nose. 'He has explained to me that he is fully aware of the circumstances of your injuries and that these are related to a matter of national security.'

Tim felt a massive wave of relief wash over him. *Thanks Steve. Now I owe you ... big time.* He looked up at the doctor and nodded, trying to look as secretive and significant as possible, while not actually saying anything.

'I believe,' continued the doctor, 'that Nurse Watkins has already treated your wounds but I'd like to take another look at them anyway ... and we'd like to keep both of you in overnight for observation.'

Tim nodded, saying nothing more.

'You know,' said the doctor, leaning forward and lowering his voice to a conspiratorial whisper as he panned his gaze from Tim to Raquel in turn, 'we all owe a lot to the unsung heroes like yourselves who keep the rest of us safe.'

Tim gave a slight shake of his head and cast his eyes downwards, declining to comment. Just what the hell *had* Steve told this guy?

'Now then,' continued the doctor, 'let's take a look at that arm ...'

***

While Tim and Raquel stayed overnight in the hospital, Roy and Donna invited Jeff to stay the night with them, an offer which he gratefully accepted. After a shower and a change of clothes – borrowed from Roy, and a little on the large side – Jeff related, over a hot meal, the whole story of everything that had happened in China.

'Incredible,' said Roy. 'It's a miracle that you all made it home alive.'

Jeff's face broke into a broad grin, the skin crinkling at the sides of those sparkling blue eyes. 'Gotta admit,' he said, 'that when I offered to help, I wasn't expecting things to get *quite* as hairy.'

'No,' said Roy, 'I don't suppose you were.'

'Anyway,' said Donna, 'thank heavens you're all home safe now.'

Jeff drained the last of his red wine, stifling a yawn as he set the glass down. 'Oh, sorry,' he said, 'kinda long day, I guess. Mind if I turn in now?'

'No, of course not,' said Donna, smiling. 'You must be absolutely exhausted.'

'Goodnight then,' said Jeff, pushing his chair back and standing up.

Roy stood up too. 'Goodnight Jeff … and thanks for everything.' It seemed a wholly inadequate thing to say considering all that Jeff had done.

Jeff shrugged. 'Glad to have been able to help.' The two men shook hands.

'Come on,' said Donna, 'I'll show you to your room.'

***

The next day, Raquel and Tim were both discharged, Tim with his arm in a sling, and Raquel with a bulky dressing on her left hand. Roy picked them up from the hospital.

When they walked through the door, Donna came rushing up to hug Raquel, and then Tim too, before stepping back and looking appraisingly at their dressings. 'How are the injuries?'

'Under the circumstances,' said Tim, 'pretty good. Miraculously, neither of us have contracted any infection and we should both heal OK.' He hesitated for a moment. 'Raquel's poor finger couldn't be saved though. Although Roy had kept it in the freezer, there was no hope of reattaching it after all this time.'

'Come here,' whispered Donna, her voice cracking as she gathered Raquel to her breast.

After several long seconds she stepped back. Jeff's told us about everything that happened. It must have been … well, just terrible. I can't imagine what you have been going through.'

A dark shadow flitted across Raquel's eyes. 'It was awful, Mum. Those people … they're *animals*. They …'

'Shhh' – she hugged her once more – 'at least you're home and safe now.'

Raquel wiped away a tear from the corner of her eye. 'Oh, Mum, Tim was *so* brave … and Jeff too. I thought I was going to die out there until they turned up.'

'Hey, come on,' said Tim, 'it's over now.'

Roy only wished it was, but he feared otherwise. This was not the moment, though, to raise the subject.

'Why don't the three of you stay and have dinner with us tonight?' he said. 'We can invite Bea and Rick round as well. They're dying to see you.'

Raquel nodded, seemingly shaking off the dark cloud which had briefly enveloped her.

Donna spoke. 'I think it'll have to be a takeaway, though. With everything that's been going on I really don't have much food in the house.'

'A takeaway's fine,' said Tim. 'Just one thing though …'

'What's that?' said Donna, looking quizzical.

'Not Chinese.' His tone was deadpan.

There was a brief silence – no more than a second – as the joke sunk in, before everyone laughed out loud, Jeff's baritone boom the loudest of all.

They settled for pizza. For Raquel and Tim, both of whom only had the effective use of one hand, it was easiest to eat, taking slices in their hands without having to use a knife and fork.

Inevitably, much of the conversation revolved around telling and retelling the incredible story of what had taken place in China, but the mood was upbeat now. The danger was in the past and they were safe now, at least in everyone's mind apart from Roy's.

Finally, as they were drinking coffee at the end of the meal, Roy decided it was time to air his concerns.

'Look, I'm sorry to be the one to put a damper on things, but I'm afraid that this whole thing may not yet be over.'

The room fell suddenly silent.

'What do you mean?' said Raquel, her face now a mask of concern.

'When I discovered what was going on at Sotoyo, I thought this was just a case of corrupt business practices. I thought I could just pull our business out of there and that would be the end of it. It was always going to be a complex and costly project to do so, and bound to be somewhat acrimonious too, but nothing like this.'

'Of course,' agreed Tim. 'How could you have known otherwise?'

Roy nodded in acknowledgement of Tim's comment before continuing. 'I had no idea that the place was effectively being run by a Triad, and certainly no idea of the lengths to which these despicable people would go in order to protect their racket.' He could see Raquel's one good hand clenching into a tight ball atop the table. 'Anyway, the point is that we have now crossed swords with one of the most vicious criminal organisations in the world, and caused it considerable trouble, not to mention a fair few casualties.'

'I know where you're going with this,' said Jeff, his tone devoid of emotion. 'What's to say they won't come after us again?'

Chapter 45

Jeff's alarming assessment of their situation caused an anxious silence to descend, broken a few seconds later by Roy. 'Jeff's right: we will only be able to feel totally safe once we have found a way to ward these people off once and for all.'

'So what are you suggesting?' said Tim.

'You and Jeff ... and you Raquel' – he turned his head towards her and placed a hand over hers on the table top – 'did a fine job of beating them at their own game in China, but to some extent that relied on the fact that they just weren't expecting such ferocious opposition. If they come after any of us again, they'll know what to expect, and we can't hope to beat them long term.'

'I wouldn't disagree,' said Tim. 'So what's the answer?'

'We have to attack this problem in business terms. We have to make it financially and politically unattractive to pursue any of us ever again. I have a plan, but I have to go back to work to see if it will fly. It may take me several days to work things out. In the meantime we have to consider that we are all potentially at risk.'

He paused for a few seconds to let this assessment sink in before continuing. 'For the next few days we all need to be extra vigilant and I'd suggest that no-one should be alone, even for an hour.'

'Well, I can stay with Raquel,' said Tim. 'She won't be going back to work for a few days at least.'

'And I can take a little time off work to stay with Bea,' said Rick, 'but I'm not sure how much use I'd be in a fight. I've never even handled a gun, let alone fired one.'

'I know,' said Roy, 'and someone needs to stay with Donna while I'm at work, so what I'd suggest is that the two of you stay here with Donna and that Jeff stays too. He's already proven his effectiveness in a fight. In any case I think it's highly unlikely that they'd risk provoking a firefight here in the UK.'

Jeff nodded. 'Sounds like a plan. There's one problem though ... if we *should* need to defend ourselves, we don't have any weapons. We had to leave the guns behind in China.'

'I anticipated that you might have to do that,' said Roy.

He stood up and moved over to the sideboard, opening a drawer and withdrawing a bulky bundle wrapped up in a grey cloth. He laid it on the table and unwrapped it. Inside were two handguns and six ammunition magazines.

Donna's eyes widened in surprise. 'Where did you get those?' she gasped.

'It doesn't matter,' said Roy. 'In any case, they probably won't be needed. I'm just trying to cover every eventuality.'

'I can't believe what I'm seeing,' said Donna. 'Guns in our own home?' She shook her head in disbelief.

'Donna, I'm just trying to ...'

She cut him off. 'No ... this just isn't right. We've got Raquel back now, so why don't we just go to the police for protection?'

Tim spoke up. 'I really don't think we want to involve the police at this stage. It would just raise all sorts of questions about how we got into this situation in the first place. I've already pulled in all the favours I can from my contacts in the police ... and more. I really don't want to have to explain what Jeff and I were doing taking illegally-owned weapons to China and killing those people there.'

She looked at him, and then at Roy, her eyes confused, uncertain.

'Donna,' said Roy, gently, 'Tim's right, you know … and there's another aspect to consider.'

She looked at him with enquiring eyes, her head tilted slightly to one side.

'These people have very long memories. Even if we do go to the police for protection, how long do you think they'll keep it up? A week? A month? A year?'

Her head tilted forward and she shook it slightly from side to side. 'I don't know,' she admitted, a tear escaping from the corner of her eye.

Roy continued. 'My guess is that they'll give us about one month, at most. If, after that, nothing has happened, they'll gradually lose interest.' Now her eyes looked desperate, hunted. 'Unless we can put a permanent end to this thing we will never be able to walk down the street again without looking over our shoulders.'

Her shoulders slumped in defeat and she began to sob. Roy hated having to hammer home so brutally the harsh facts of the matter, but Donna had to understand, had to give him her support.

She wiped her eyes with the back of her sleeve and looked him in the eyes. 'Go ahead then. Do what you think is best.'

He hugged her to him. 'Don't worry, we'll get through this.' He didn't feel as confident as he hoped he sounded.

Tim broke the tense mood. 'Let's give Roy the few days he wants to try to warn these people off. We're in too deep to back off now.'

Donna nodded in acquiescence.

Tim picked up one of the guns and examined it. 'Glock G25, 0.38 calibre. Not what I'm used to, but it'll do just fine.' He slipped the weapon into the pocket of his jacket, which was hanging over the back of his chair and slid the second gun across the table to Jeff.

Donna turned to Roy, her eyes suddenly uncertain once more. 'I hope you know what you're doing.'

So do I, he thought.

The first thing that Roy did when he returned to work the next day was to convene a board meeting to explain to his senior team just what had been happening over the past few days. They listened, open-mouthed, as Roy gave a blow-by-blow account of the incredible sequence of events which had unfolded. They all knew that something was very wrong at Sotoyo Electronics, but none of them had imagined that this company was in the grip of organised crime, or the lengths to which Chang would go to protect his fiefdom.

When, at last, Roy had finished, Len Douglas summed it up. 'It was obvious that bastard Chang was up t' no good, but I never thought he'd do 'owt this low. Anyway, I guess he got his just desserts in the end.'

Mick McNulty added his thoughts. 'Yous all know what this means don't yous?' No-one actually answered but the enquiring looks on the faces of everyone present clearly invited Mick to continue. 'It's a pound ta a pinch o' shit that Chang was responsible for Chuck's death.'

'You're probably right,' said Roy, his expression grim, 'though I doubt we could ever prove it.'

'D' ya think we should tell Chuck's widow about our suspicions?' said Mick.

'Hmm ... that's a tough one,' said Roy stroking his chin. 'Whilst we'd all like to see justice served, I think the chances of that being achieved now are close to zero; any evidence of what happened will have been well and truly disposed of by now.'

'I agree,' said Kevin. 'The chances are that the police and other local authorities were complicit in a cover-up. We'd never be able to flush out the truth now.'

'And,' said Roy, 'although we all suspect that Chuck's death was arranged, we don't have any actual proof. Furthermore, there are other ... well, other aspects to this which we need to consider.'

'What other aspects?' said Mick.

'Look, for now, can you all just leave this one with me? I'd like to think it over a lot more before we make any hasty decisions.' His dilemma was Gabby: how would she be affected if she was told that her husband might have been murdered? 'For now, let's concentrate on the business matters ... we have a lot of issues to consider which won't have gone away just because Chang Wei is dead.'

'OK,' said Kevin, 'so what happens now? Do you still want to go ahead with pulling the whole manufacturing operation back to the UK?'

'Yes, I do,' said Roy, 'but only if I can ensure the safety of my family' – he paused for a few moments – 'and all of yours. There's no guarantee that these people will stop with just me and mine ... we are *all* potentially at risk.'

Everyone fell silent for several long seconds as Roy's statement sank in.

'What do you have in mind?' asked Kevin.

'OK,' said Roy, 'here's what we're going to do ...'

***

By the time the board meeting was finished and Roy had returned to his office it was almost lunchtime, but Roy wasn't hungry. He decided to check the online version of the *China Daily* to see whether the events of the last few days had made national news. He trawled through every page of the last three issues. There was no news of Chang Wei's death, nor anything about the trail of other casualties left by Tim and Jeff in their bid to rescue Raquel. It was clear that the people he was dealing with had covered everything up most effectively.

One thing they had been unable to suppress, however, was news of the incident at the airport. The headline and article took a prominent position on the third page of the newspaper.

GANGLAND SHOOTOUT AT SHENZHEN INTERNATIONAL AIRPORT

In a bizarre incident at Shenzhen Bao'an International Airport last night, two bullet-ridden cars were found abandoned near the west runway. A large section of the perimeter fence had been breached where, it appears, the cars crashed through. Both cars were extensively damaged and there was evidence of a fierce firefight. However the people involved in this incident had evidently fled before the authorities arrived on the scene. There was no evidence of any casualties having been incurred.

The police investigation is still underway, but in an initial statement they have said that they believe this incident to be related to a dispute between rival criminal gangs. Both of the vehicles involved had been reported as stolen. The fact that the cars crashed through the airport perimeter fence is believed to be an unintended consequence of a battle which was raging, initially, outside the airport. There is no evidence of any terrorist activity or any attempt to cause damage to aircraft or passengers.

As Roy read through the rest of the article it became increasingly clear that the details of the incident had been massaged to conceal the real story. Further evidence, Roy thought, that Chang's people had the police – at least the local police – in their pockets.

He scoured all the headlines from the last few days once more, but could find nothing else relating to Tim's escapade in China. He decided to check his emails, to see whether there was anything from either Sotoyo Electronics, or from the sinister forces which had taken control of the company.

'You have 357 unread emails' read the header; Roy's heart sank as he contemplated the tedious task of sorting the wheat from the chaff.

After two hours, Roy had deleted two hundred and seventy-four emails without even reading them. As he set about systematically working his way through the remaining messages, he finally found one which piqued his interest.

To: All Sotoyo Electronics customers
From: Wang Hu, Group Chief Executive, Sotoyo Manufacturing Group
Subject: Chang Wei – Sotoyo Electronics

It is with great sadness that I have to inform you that Chang Wei, Plant Manager of Sotoyo Electronics, has suffered a massive, unexpected heart attack which has led, tragically, to his untimely death. I am sure you will all join me in sending condolences to his family and friends at this difficult time.

The business, however, has to go on, and as of today Chang Wei is replaced by Yang Long, a very experienced general manager from elsewhere within the Sotoyo group. He will, over the course of the next few weeks, be contacting all customers individually to introduce himself and discuss the individual requirements of each company. In the meantime, there should be no interruption to normal business with any of our customers.

Regards,
Wang Hu

So they had decided to cover up the details of Chang's death too. The question in Roy's mind was whether this Wang Hu – with whom he had never had any contact in the past – was a legitimate businessman who had no knowledge of what was going on in one of his companies, or of how Chang had really died. It was perfectly possible that the Triad which had infiltrated Sotoyo Electronics had done so without the knowledge of the group's chief executive; he could have been kept completely in the dark. On the other hand he too could be part of the Triad – Roy just had no way of knowing. Should he contact Wang Hu to try to find out more?

After considering this question for some minutes, he decided not to. This email was just a general circular letter to all Sotoyo Electronics customers. Better to wait until someone contacted him directly regarding the recent events in China and his proposal to pull back his manufacturing business to the UK.

He returned to the task of wading through the remaining emails. Fifty minutes later he had skimmed them all; there was nothing else relating to China. He would just have to wait; he just *knew* the email or phone call would be coming soon.

***

Several hours later, Roy was preparing to go home. He had spent the rest of the day catching up on matters relating to the day-to-day operations of the business and had tried to put to the back of his mind the forthcoming confrontation which he knew was inevitable.

He had shut down his computer, and was busy tidying his papers when there was a soft tapping on his office door. The door was open – Roy always kept it so unless engaged in a confidential conversation – and when he looked up he saw Chris Williams, Head of IT, standing in the doorway, clutching a slim A4-sized folder.

Roy smiled and stopped what he was doing. 'Hi Chris ... come in.'

Chris hesitated. 'Oh, you look as though you were just about to go home.'

'I was, but come and sit down anyway.'

He came over and sat down opposite Roy. 'You won't want to go until you've seen *this*,' he said, sliding the folder across the desk towards Roy.

Roy pulled the papers out of the folder and began to examine them. After scanning just the first few lines of the first page his heart jumped in his chest; *this was it*. He looked up at Chris who was leaning forward, hands pressed on the desk, fingers splayed. His face wore a wide-eyed smile.

'Is this what you were looking for?' he said, a little breathlessly.

'Yes, I believe it is,' said Roy, almost unable to believe it himself. 'How did you get to it so quickly?'

'Well,' said Chris, 'It wasn't too difficult to narrow down the contents of the hard drive to a number of files which might, potentially, contain the information you were looking for, but as expected, most of them were password-protected.'

Roy nodded. 'But, as you explained to me earlier, you intended to use some sort of password-cracking program to get into them. But I thought you said that could take many days ...'

'Yes,' said Chris. 'My program basically just works its way through the billions of possible combinations of letters – both upper-case and lower-case – numbers, and symbols. Depending on how well the password has been constructed it can take hours, days, weeks, or even more to crack it. There may even be some that it will never unlock.'

'So how ...'

Chris held up a hand to indicate that he hadn't yet finished his explanation.

'I found five files whose titles suggested they might hold the information we were looking for. One of them wasn't password-protected at all, but it turned out to be of no interest, so that left four to work on. I decided, before using the password cracker program, to try a bit of human intuition based on what you told me about Chang. Using this approach I managed to get into two of the four files and this' – he rose to his feet and jabbed the papers in front of Roy, smiling triumphantly – 'was one of them.'

Roy was completely perplexed. 'But there's nothing that I told you which would give you any clue as to ...'

'Ah, but there was,' interjected Chris. 'Remember what you told me about Chang's main logon password?'

'Er ... yes .... It was "Hastings1066".'

'Exactly!' exclaimed Chris jabbing the air with a forefinger. 'That gave me an idea about how he might come up with other passwords.'

'You mean,' said Roy, understanding now dawning, 'historical events?'

Chris nodded vigorously. 'More specifically, *English* historical events.'

Roy shook his head in disbelief. 'So what was the password?'

'Bosworth1485,' declared Chris.

Roy's jaw dropped. Chang had protected this most sensitive of information using a password based on the Battle of Bosworth Field: the defining battle of the Wars of the Roses and a turning point in English history. *Incredible.*

Chapter 46

'So,' said Roy, 'what do you think?'

As they lay in bed, Donna's head was cradled in the nook between Roy's head and his shoulder; his arm enfolded her warmly. Neither of them felt particularly sleepy, so Roy had chosen this moment to seek Donna's opinion on the thorny question of whether to make Gabby aware of his suspicions regarding Chuck's death. Her instincts on delicate personal matters such as this were invariably, unerringly accurate, and after all, she now knew Gabby far better than he did.

'As it happens,' she said, 'I've been mulling over the very same question myself.'

'You have?' said Roy, surprised, 'But I never said anything before now about any suspicions surrounding Chuck's death.'

'Oh, Roy … I'm not stupid. As soon as I saw what lengths Chang Wei would go to in attacking our own family, I realised that he might well have been behind Chuck's death.'

Roy exhaled heavily. 'Yes … of course you did. I should have guessed that you would.'

She tutted. 'Yes you should. Anyway that's not the issue – the question is: should we tell her?'

'Alright … so what do you think then?'

Donna sighed heavily. 'Right now Gabby believes that Chuck died of a heart attack. She's buried him and made her peace … as best she can; she's achieved some sort of closure and is rebuilding her life back in America. Can you imagine what it would do to her if we raised the possibility – and don't forget that you have no actual proof – that her husband was murdered?'

Roy didn't reply.

'And what if that suspicion was never, ever properly proved or disproved?'

Roy still didn't reply.

'And think about our own family too. You said yourself that we are not out of danger yet. If you start talking to Gabby about your suspicions regarding Chuck's death, you'll end up having to tell her the whole story about Raquel's abduction and Tim and Jeff's rescue mission. The more people who know about that, the more we are in danger of further reprisals.' She paused for several seconds as Roy digested what she had said before continuing. 'So in this case, I'd say there's little to be gained by raking over Chuck's death ... and possibly much to lose. If you want my opinion, let it be, and concentrate your efforts on safeguarding our own family.'

Roy was once again – as he had been so many times in the past – stunned by Donna's ability to see through a complex situation like this and point clearly at the answer. He took only a few seconds to respond.

'I think ... no, I know ... that you're right. Although I hate to see the bastards get away with Chuck's murder, I have to agree that stirring things up at this stage will probably do more harm than good.' He tilted his head and kissed her ear. 'And by the way ...'

'What?'

'Thanks for helping me unscramble the tangled mess which passes for my brain right now.'

'Go to sleep,' she said, sliding her hand across his chest, ruffling her fingers through his chest hair.

***

The following day, Roy was in the office early, feeling much better for having aired some of his problems with Donna, and now energised to pick up the reins once more. He had, in effect, been out of commission for a whole week, but the day-to-day work of running the business had not put itself on hold because he had had a domestic crisis to deal with. Now he had a ton of work to catch up on.

He contemplated the towering, unstable stack of paper in his in-tray, threatening to topple over and spill onto the floor. With a sigh, he set about sorting through it.

Two hours later he had created three piles: 'Priority', 'Do by tomorrow', and 'Do by end of week'. Actually there was also a fourth pile, but that had already been consigned to the metal waste bin alongside his desk. He took the first item from the 'Priority' file and was just about to start work on it when his phone rang.

The interruption – before he had even dealt with the first item – really wasn't welcome. 'Yes?' he answered, rather abruptly.

'Am I speaking to Mr. Roy Groves?' said the high-pitched sing-song voice. The accent was unmistakeably Chinese.

Roy's throat was instantly dry as sand; his buttocks clenched involuntarily. 'Yes,' he replied, as calmly as he could manage, 'and who is this?'

'My name is not important. I am calling in relation to discussions which you had previously conducted with my colleague, Chang Wei ... now, of course, unfortunately deceased.'

The high-pitched voice had an inexplicably chilling, menacing quality in spite of its almost effeminate timbre.

'So what did you want to discuss?' said Roy, struggling to keep his voice calm and level.

'Firstly, I should advise you that there is no point in your trying to trace this call ... if indeed you have set up the necessary facilities with which to do so.'

Roy was mentally kicking himself. Why *hadn't* he thought to set up equipment capable of tracing incoming calls? The unknown caller, however, quickly made it clear that this would, in any case, have been a waste of time.

'This call is being routed through a complex series of links which would take hours to penetrate, even with the most sophisticated tracing equipment. I suggest, therefore that you forget about any such notions and listen to what I have to say.'

'I'm listening.'

'You have caused us considerable inconvenience, Mr. Groves. Chang Wei was an experienced and senior member of our organisation.'

'He was an animal. He kidnapped my daughter ... he cut off her *finger* for God's sake.'

'Ah, well, had you not been so stubborn regarding certain business, issues that would not have been necessary.'

'Stubborn? The bastard was ...'

The unknown caller cut Roy off with a shrill admonition. 'Shut up and listen!' Roy did so. 'As well as Chang Wei, you have also eliminated several of our operatives. I am extremely unhappy about this ... these men take many months, and a great deal of money, to train. You cannot possibly have expected that there would not be consequences.'

'So what exactly do you want?' said Roy.

'Firstly, I expect you to abandon your proposal to withdraw your business from Sotoyo Electronics.' He paused, evidently waiting for a response.

'And what else?'

'I require some financial compensation for the problems caused to us by the deaths of Chang Wei and our other ... employees.'

'How much?'

'Fifteen million dollars U.S.'

'Fifteen million?' spluttered Roy. 'We don't have that sort of money lying around spare ... it would bankrupt my company.'

'Oh, come, come ... please don't be melodramatic. I have studied your company's finances and it's clear to me that you can comfortably afford this sum.' He paused for a few seconds. 'I'll tell you what: as I am a reasonable man, I will allow you to spread this payment over five quarterly instalments of three million each. Now,

I could hardly be fairer than that, could I?' He paused again for a few moments before adding, his tone conversational, 'Of course, should you refuse to cooperate I cannot guarantee the continued safety of your family.'

Roy's throat was now so dry that he couldn't actually form the words to reply. He picked up the plastic cup, full of water, which was on his desk and took a deep swallow.

'Mr. Groves?' came the lilting, sing-song voice. 'Are you still there?'

'Yes, I'm still here,' said Roy, finding his voice at last.

'Then I assume you find my proposal acceptable?'

Roy steeled himself: this was it. He gathered all his resolve before replying. 'Actually, no ... I don't find your proposal at all acceptable.'

There was a slight pause before the caller replied. 'I would strongly advise you to take a little time to consider your response. It would be extremely unwise to jump to an ill-considered reaction.'

'I don't need any time to consider my response. Now *you* listen to *me*. I've heard your proposal ... well, here's mine. I will continue with plans to withdraw all of our manufacturing business from Sotoyo Electronics. You will ensure that my staff are afforded complete cooperation during the transfer, and the costs of the transfer will be borne in full by Sotoyo. I will not pay you one penny in so-called "compensation". Furthermore you will, for ever, keep your thugs away from me, my family, the rest of my management team, and all of their families too.' He paused for some reaction.

'Brave words, Mr. Groves, but I'm afraid you are in no position to try to bargain with me.'

'Oh, but I think I am. I am in possession of a complete list of every company in the whole of China – and indeed in several neighbouring countries – in which your organisation has a controlling interest.'

The phone went silent for a moment before the reply came back, 'You're bluffing.'

Roy flipped open the folder which he had kept on his desk continuously, in readiness for this phone conversation, ever since Chris Williams had brought it to him. 'Zheng Insurance Company, Golden Sun Foods, Cheng and Liang Manufacturing Company ... do I need to continue?'

The high-pitched voice rose another couple of semitones. 'Where did you get this information?' it demanded.

'When my representative was visiting Sotoyo electronics on a fact-finding mission he copied certain files from Chang Wei's computer; that was how we found out about the various ways in which Sotoyo had been defrauding my company. While analysing the data we had copied, we found a reference to a list of other companies involved in similar practices, but the relevant file was not among those which we had copied. We eventually deduced that it must be either elsewhere on Chang Wei's work computer or possibly on his home computer. My ... associate, who came to Shenzhen to rescue my daughter, copied the entire contents of the hard discs on both. After a bit of digging, we found that the list had been on his home computer.' He paused for a few moments before concluding, 'So now I have the list.'

'This was all completely unethical,' spluttered the caller.

'Unethical?' said Roy, incredulous. 'You are seriously accusing *me* of unethical behaviour? That comment does not even merit a response.

'Now shut up and listen. I have made three hard copies of the list and distributed them, via a third party, to three different lawyers for safekeeping. None of these lawyers knows the identity of the others, and even I do not know the identities of all three. If anything untoward happens to me, to any of my family, to Tim Steele, to Jeff Patterson, to any of my work colleagues, or any of their families, these lawyers have instructions to pass the information to the Chinese national authorities.' Roy paused for a response, but as none was forthcoming, he continued, 'I expect you have the means to control the local police and God knows who else, but I doubt that you would risk the national authorities launching a full-blown investigation into your activities.'

The phone went silent for several seconds before the voice – which had now dropped considerably in pitch – said, 'You are a very resourceful man, Mr. Groves; completely wasted in your current position. I don't suppose you would consider coming to work for me? I am always in need of good people in the UK and in mainland Europe.'

Roy could not believe what he was hearing. 'Now, you really *do* have to be joking.'

'No joke. I can pay you ten times what you are currently earning.'

Roy felt a surge of anger. 'Go to hell,' he hissed.

The phone went silent for a few moments. When the caller spoke again his voice had somehow taken on an even more menacing quality. 'If that is your position, then, reluctantly, I accept your proposal' – Roy's heart jumped – 'but with a warning: if I stick to my side of the bargain, but the information which you are holding *does* come to light, then the deal is off, and you will have made a very dangerous enemy. I will relentlessly pursue you, your family, and your wretched company.'

These words chilled Roy to the bone, but he tried to sound calm and confident when he replied. 'I will not renege on our deal.'

'Then I guess we have nothing more to discuss. I hope for all our sakes that we never have occasion to speak again. Goodbye, Mr. Groves.'

The phone went dead.

Perspiration was streaming down Roy's temples, over his cheeks and soaking his shirt collar. His heart was thumping at a furious rate. He loosened his tie, sank back in his chair and drained the rest of the cup of water on his desk. He had done it.

Chapter 47

It was 11 a.m. Friday morning. Donna had just finished the ironing. She eyed, with satisfaction, the numerous stacks of neatly folded clothes adorning the sofa. Just one hour ago they had been nothing more than a mountainous tangle of clean laundry. She hated ironing with a vengeance, yet always felt a warm glow of contentment once the job was done. She decided to treat herself to a coffee and a ten-minute break before taking the freshly-ironed clothes upstairs and putting them away.

Once she had made the coffee, she set it down on the low table before picking up the local newspaper and sinking back into the armchair with a satisfied sigh. The main headline on the front page read 'Community centre to close – residents furious'. She didn't even know that there *was* a local community centre; if that was front page news, it didn't bode well for there being much of interest in the rest of the paper. She began reading the article – somewhat disinterestedly – but, before long, her attention drifted away from the words on the page in front of her and back to the events of the last few months.

It was now two months since Tim and Raquel had returned from China. Their physical injuries had healed well, and Raquel had thrown herself fully back into her teaching career. She did, however, still seem prone to occasional melancholy moods – due, Donna guessed, to her dwelling on her experiences in China.

Tim had a job now, too. He had always had a bit of a flair for technology and computers, and although not formally qualified, he could, in practice, knock spots off many qualified professionals when it came to IT issues. Now he had landed a position as a senior IT support engineer at Unicorn Private Equity – a large and well-respected venture capital company. He was really enjoying the work, and the pay was pretty good.

But most important of all, there had been no sign that anyone from China was coming after any of them. It seemed that the uneasy deal which Roy had struck with Chang's boss was holding.

The phone rang; it was Raquel.

'Hi Mum.'

'Oh, hello … nice to hear your voice, but how come you're calling at this time? I thought you'd be right in the middle of your double English lesson with the dreaded 9C class.'

'Well I should be, but … well I've pulled a sickie.'

'Oh,' said Donna, concerned now, 'what's wrong?'

'There's nothing wrong … well I mean I'm not actually sick, but … well I need to talk to you.'

'Well, yes, of course. What is it?'

'Can I come over?'

'What, now?'

'Yes … if that's alright.' Her voice was starting to crack.

'Of course,' said Donna. 'Come right over.'

Donna had never, ever known Raquel to fake illness in order to take time off work. Something was very wrong here.

***

'I'm pregnant, Mum.' Raquel blurted it out as soon as she stepped through the front door.

'Are you sure?'

Raquel nodded, 'I've missed two periods and I've tested myself three times … each time positive.'

'OK, come and sit down,' said Donna placing her arm around Raquel's shoulders and guiding her through into the lounge.

She pushed all of the neat piles of ironing up to one end of the sofa – in the process, undoing much of her own good work – so that she could sit next to her daughter.

'I don't know what to do, Mum.' Raquel's voice was faltering and tears began to well from the corners of her eyes.

'Hey there ... why so unhappy? I always imagined you and Tim would have children eventually.'

'Well, yes,' replied Raquel, but ...' her voice tailed off.

'Is it the fact that you're not married? That doesn't matter much these days, and neither your dad nor I would ...'

'No,' she interjected, 'it's not that ... it's ...' She burst into an uncontrollable bout of sobbing.

'Shhh ... don't cry.' Donna hugged her daughter to her until her sobbing eased. 'I'm assuming from the fact that you're so upset, that this wasn't planned?'

Raquel pulled away from Donna, then looked her directly in the eyes. 'I don't think it's Tim's.'

At last Donna understood. 'You mean it's from ... it's because of what happened in China?'

Raquel nodded, miserably.

'Are you sure?'

'As sure as I can be. Tim and I were always very careful to take precautions, but when I was in China ... well I couldn't ... it wasn't possible ...' She began to cry once more.

'Shhh ... it wasn't your fault.'

Raquel wiped her eyes – in the process smearing her cheeks with black streaks. 'The baby's father is most likely to be either one of those obnoxious Chinese guards or ... or even Chang Wei himself.'

'Oh, my poor baby,' said Donna, hugging Raquel to her breast.

They clung together like that, saying nothing, for a full minute.

Eventually, Raquel eased herself away from Donna, sniffing and wiping her eyes with her sleeve. 'What should I do, Mum? Should I ... should I get rid of it?'

Donna took several seconds to reply. 'Only you can decide that.'

'I don't know. I don't really believe in abortion ... it's almost like ... *murder,* but then, what's Tim going to think?'

'Haven't you told him?'

She shook her head, starting to sob again.

Donna placed a finger under Raquel's chin, gently lifting her head so that she could make eye contact. 'Look, it's your decision. No-one can make that decision for you, but I think you should talk to Tim about it before you decide.'

'But ... will he still love me?' The tears were now flowing freely once more.

'After what he went through to get you out of China? Do you seriously doubt how much he loves you?'

'I know ... but ...'

'Talk to him. See how he feels about the baby, and then make your decision. Whatever you decide, I'm certain he'll be right behind you.'

Raquel nodded, looking uncertain, but managing a small smile as she wiped away the tears from her face with her sleeve. 'I will. Thanks for listening, Mum.'

Half an hour later, after Raquel had left, Donna was sorting through the piles of clothing which had been hurriedly swept aside earlier. As she went through the motions, mechanically, of rearranging the clothes into organised piles, she was struck by the bitter irony of the way things had turned out.

Beatrice had been desperate to have a baby, and had been so delighted when she finally fell pregnant, yet her joy had been cruelly snatched away when she miscarried as a result of the shock of learning of Raquel's kidnapping. Raquel, on the other hand, had had no plans for a baby just yet, but now found herself carrying the child of some Chinese criminal. It was all so damned *unfair.*

Would Beatrice be able to conceive again? Could Tim accept the idea of Raquel giving birth to a half-Chinese child sired by a Triad thug?

She didn't know the answer to either question.

Chapter 48

Ten months later

As Roy walked down the aisle to the strains of the 'Wedding March' with Raquel on his arm, he was bursting with pride. He glanced sideways at his daughter; she looked beautiful in her ivory-coloured wedding gown and translucent veil. She caught sight of his glance and turned her head, responding with a small, sweet smile. As they made their way towards the front of the church, guests in the pews in front of them stole brief glances over their shoulders, smiling as they caught sight of the bride.

Tim waited at the front of the Church. He looked splendid in his formal suit. Roy couldn't remember ever previously seeing Tim in a suit, but today he wore it with confidence, his posture upright and proud. As he turned to look at Raquel walking towards him, his smile said it all: he was clearly overwhelmed with happiness at the sight of his beautiful bride.

Roy passed Raquel over to Tim before stepping back and taking his place alongside Donna in the front row of pews. As he did so, he caught sight of Beatrice, Raquel's Maid of Honour, arranging the train of Raquel's dress behind her. Beatrice was four months pregnant now, and the closely tailored cut of her bridesmaid's dress did nothing to conceal her growing bump. Not that she wanted to disguise her condition; she was happy and proud to display the evidence of the forthcoming arrival.

As the minister began to recite the well-rehearsed lines of the wedding ceremony, Roy began to drift off to another place. The events of the past year had drained him, mentally and physically, but he felt that he had to resolve the situation which had arisen, on his watch, before he could do what his heart – and, increasingly, Donna too – was telling him he should do. And now he had finally done it.

The transfer of the manufacturing operation back to England was now more or less complete and he had announced his decision to retire, handing over the reins to Kevin Brethan, previously Technical Director. There had been no comeback from his adversaries in China, so he assumed that the uneasy deal he had struck with the unknown Chinese man with the high-pitched voice was holding, and would continue to hold. But what now? After years of high-pressure roles in business, what would he do with his time?

Maybe he should take on some consultancy work; after all, he had a wealth of business experience which surely could be useful to others. Perhaps he could find one or more non-executive directorships. Then there was the apartment in Spain which he and Donna had bought some years ago, but had hardly had any time to use and enjoy. They would definitely make more use of that now. Maybe he should take up golf: there were several top-class golf courses on the Costa del Sol very near to the apartment.

Roy was pulled back to the here and now by the sound of a baby crying. He turned to Donna, who was rocking little Bethany – just three months old – back and forth to try to calm her. As she settled down and her cries subsided to subdued gurgles, he regarded her perfect little face, topped with an improbably dense covering of silky black hair. Her almond-shaped eyes, squat nose, and yellowish skin tone meant that people would always assume that Tim was not the father, but both Raquel and Tim loved her anyway.

Roy's reflections were interrupted by the sound of the Minister asking for the ring. Jeff – who Tim had chosen as Best Man – stepped forward and handed it over. Like Tim, Jeff looked smart and confident in his formal suit, and for this occasion, his unruly mop of sandy-blonde hair had been neatly trimmed and slicked down with gel.

As Tim slipped the ring on to Raquel's finger, Roy eyes locked, unbidden, onto the mutilated stump of Raquel's missing little finger. He felt a new surge of furious anger, not just for the physical abuse but for the mental scars which he knew she still bore. But he knew such anger was pointless. He had done everything possible to safeguard his family for the future and any attempt to wreak revenge on the perpetrators of this outrage would surely open up a Pandora's Box which was best left closed.

No, this was a time to draw a line under the past and look forward. Raquel was embarking on married life with Tim and Bethany, Beatrice was looking forward to the arrival of her new baby, and he and Donna ... well, he didn't really know what they would do next. He felt terribly confused and conflicted. He would undoubtedly miss the buzz and the continual challenges of running a business in a competitive market but, in all honesty, he wasn't sorry to be leaving. After years of dealing with corporate politics – with all the attendant lies, double-dealing, and deception – he had brushed with one of the most feared criminal organisations in the entire world. By the skin of his teeth he, and his family, had managed to escape its clutches, not unscathed, but at least alive and reasonably intact.

Now, he had had enough ... it was time for a change.

Epilogue

Marbella, Spain – one year later

The sun was slowly sinking behind the mountain ridge, the sky taking on a beautiful orange glow, causing the few sparse fingers of dark cloud to stand out in stark relief. After a scorching hot day, the temperature was finally starting to drop to a more agreeable level. Roy drained his coffee cup and eased himself down to a more comfortable position in his chair.

'That was a wonderful meal, Marion,' said Donna. 'You must give me the recipe for that fantastic dessert.'

'I'd be glad to,' she replied. 'I'll get you a copy right now.'

While Marion went off to get a copy of the recipe, her husband, Neil, gestured toward Roy and Donna's empty wine glasses. 'A spot more wine?'

'Not for me, thanks,' said Donna.

'Nor me,' added Roy.

'Well, perhaps a liqueur then?' insisted Neil.

'Well, if you're twisting my arm, a small brandy would go down well,' said Roy, chuckling.

'Good idea; I think I'll have the same. What about you Donna?'

'Do you have a Tia Maria?'

'Of course,' said Neil. 'I know it's your favourite.'

Roy and Donna were sitting on the terrace of their next door neighbours' apartment. Now that Roy had retired, they had far more time available to enjoy the apartment in Spain that they had bought some years ago. In fact they were now spending perhaps fifty per cent of their time in Spain, and had become close friends with their neighbours there. Neil and Marion were both English – like many of the residents in the apartment complex – but they now lived permanently in Spain. Neil was a retired lawyer, while Marion had worked part-time in a bank before retiring. Neil was in his mid-sixties, his bald pate framed by a narrow strip of grey hair which ran from just above his ears around the back of his head. He still kept himself in good shape, playing golf regularly and running several times a week. Marion was a little younger, a little plumper, and, unlike Neil, not a big fan of exercise, though she, too, played a little golf. They were both lovely people, and great company.

Neil and Marion both reappeared on the terrace at the same time, Neil bearing a small tray of drinks, and Marion the recipe.

'Here's to another lovely summer evening in sunny Spain,' said Neil, raising his glass.

Everyone leaned forward and clinked their glasses together.

The conversation fell silent for a short while as everyone took a moment to sit back and appreciate the beautiful sunset.

Eventually Neil spoke. 'When do you have to go back to England?'

'A week on Sunday,' replied Donna.

'Ah, will you be coming to the EGM next Friday then?'

'EGM?' asked Roy. 'What's that all about?'

'There's an Extraordinary General Meeting of the Community of Owners.'

'The Community of Owners? Oh, you mean the residents' committee thing?'

'Yes … it's the framework which allows all of us who live here to decide how the money we pay in maintenance charges gets spent, and what rules we want to apply in the Community.'

'To be honest,' said Roy, 'We haven't paid much attention to any of that stuff. We just pay our fees and assume they are being well spent.'

'Hmm,' said Neil, taking a sip of his brandy before setting down his glass and placing his elbows on the table, making a bridge with his fingers upon which to rest his chin, 'well there are a few things you might like to know ...'

'Go on.'

'Have you noticed that the communal gardens are getting rather untidy lately?'

Donna interjected, 'Yes ... now you come to mention it I *had* noticed that they weren't quite up to their usual standard. So why is that then?'

'The gardening company who we contract to maintain the gardens haven't been paid for more than four months. They are refusing to do any more work now until they have been paid right up to date.'

'But why haven't they been paid?' said Roy.

'I'll come to that in a moment, but listen, there's more. Our own staff – the cleaners, the maintenance guy, and the two security guards – haven't been paid for two months either. Sam – the guard who speaks good English – was bending my ear about it the other day.'

'So are you saying we're broke?' said Roy. 'That's hard to believe given the hefty charges we all pay.'

'Well, you and I pay, but I know that there are quite a few owners who haven't paid for months, or even years ... and it just seems that no one is doing anything about it.'

'So is this what the EGM is all about?'

'Yes,' replied Neil. 'I have been talking to a number of other concerned owners and we have sort of forced the President of the Community to hold a meeting where all this stuff can be aired and we can find out what's going on.'

'Well,' said Roy, 'given what you have just told us' – he looked at Donna – 'I think we should come along.' Donna nodded her agreement.

'The thing is,' said Neil, 'we're not at all confident that the current President really has any idea how to dig us out of the hole we're in. We think we are going to need a new President with the management and financial skills to figure out what's going on and sort things out.'

'Oh ... wait a minute,' said Roy, as it finally dawned on him where this conversation was going. 'If you're suggesting that *I* should do it ...'

'Just come along to the meeting and see what you think. We can talk about it afterwards.'

'Oh Neil, I hardly speak any Spanish and I'm only here on a part-time basis.'

'But you *have* run a successful multi-million pound business.'

'Well yes, but ...'

'How difficult could it be for someone with your background to sort out an organisation with an annual budget of only half a million euros?'

'Well ...'

Donna rescued him. 'OK, Neil, we'll come along to the meeting and see what transpires. There's no need for any hasty decisions just now is there?'

'Of course not,' said Neil, smiling. 'Anyway, enough of that subject for now. Another brandy, Roy ... and a Tia Maria, Donna?' They both nodded.

As Neil went inside to get the drinks, Donna and Marion began chatting over the recipe which Marion had brought out earlier.

Roy thought about what Neil had said. On the face of it, sorting out the Community's financial and management problems should be relatively easy compared to the challenges he had faced in his business career. And at least he wouldn't be facing the corruption, double-dealing, and criminal activities which he had previously encountered. Furthermore, if he was honest, he did have enough time on his hands to take this on. Donna was right: they should just go along to the meeting and see what unfolded. If he *did* decide to take on the Presidency − not that he had any idea of the mechanism for changing Presidents − it really couldn't be *that* difficult, could it?

Made in the USA
Charleston, SC
23 August 2015